GRIM VOWS

An Aisling Grimlock Mystery Book 9

AMANDA M. LEE

WinchesterShaw Publications

Prologue

"You're supposed to say 'I do,' not 'I guess so.' Are you trying to make me cry?"

Jeremiah "Jerry" Collins planted his hands on his hips as he regarded his best friend (and pretend bride) with a dubious look. Dressed in a tuxedo — no, really — he had spent hours organizing the library of the Grimlock house so it would look perfect for his pretend wedding. The fact that his bride refused to play along correctly was simply unacceptable. "You're ruining all my hard work!"

Aisling Grimlock was used to her best friend melting down, so she barely blinked when he exploded. Instead, she remained standing in the center of the room — flowers pilfered from her mother's garden held in one hand — and openly glared at Jerry. "Why are we even playing this game? It's stupid."

Jerry's eyes flashed. "You're stupid."

"You're the biggest stupid ... guy ... in the world," Aisling fired back.

"Oh, well, that's great." Jerry threw his hands into the air in exasperation. "I can't believe you're ruining my wedding!"

The noise from the library was so fierce it drew looky-loos. The first was Cormack Grimlock. Aisling's father thought he should have been surprised to find his only daughter dressed in a white gown and pretending to marry a boy. But because it was Jerry — a boy he was genuinely fond of — Cormack was more curious than annoyed.

"What are you two doing?"

Jerry jolted at the sound of Cormack's voice, his face instantly flushing with color. "Hello, sir. We were just ... playing."

"Uh-huh." Cormack wasn't convinced as he folded his arms over his chest and flicked his eyes to Aisling. She was a tiny terror, one he spoiled rotten even though he denied it at every turn. She was the only girl amongst four brothers. She was also the youngest. In Cormack's mind, that meant she deserved to be spoiled ... and overprotected to the point no boy would want to marry her. "This isn't your usual type of game."

"It was Jerry's idea." Aisling's annoyance was on full display as she gripped her flowers tighter. "He said he was sick of me picking all the games and wanted a shot at deciding what we should do."

Cormack smirked. Aisling was, as always, a bossy little thing. She liked to take charge and make the rules when it came to playing games. She preferred the same games her brothers played — zombies, cowboys, Space Invaders, Jedi knights — but Jerry was another story. He preferred quieter games. Lily, Aisling's mother and Cormack's wife, insisted Aisling compromise when Jerry came to spend the night. That meant playing games she hated.

"I guess I'm confused." Cormack pushed himself away from the wall and walked into the library, pursing his lips when he took in the folding chairs and flower petals. "Where did you get the chairs?"

"They were in the attic closet," Aisling replied. "Jerry said we need chairs for our guests even though they're invisible. Apparently it's rude if people don't have a place to sit."

"Ah." Cormack's lips curved. "And the flowers?"

Aisling's expression shifted. "Oh, well ... ." She trailed off without answering. "You should play with us." She was good at changing topics, an ability that was fully on display now. "We need someone to walk Jerry down the aisle."

Cormack tilted his head as he regarded his youngest child. "You want me to walk Jerry down the aisle?"

Aisling nodded without hesitation.

"Aren't you the bride?" Cormack challenged. "The bride is the one usually walked down the aisle."

Aisling shrugged. "I think it's more important to Jerry."

"Really?" Cormack shifted his eyes to his daughter's best friend. They'd been inseparable since kindergarten. Even though Jerry wasn't yet ten, Cormack had a feeling he understood exactly how Jerry's life was going to play out. It was good he had Aisling to fight with and for him. It was also good Aisling had him to smooth her rough edges, because growing up with four brothers made Aisling the sort of girl who would need help with her edges.

"She doesn't play right," Jerry lamented as he sank into one of the chairs. He looked tired, which wasn't difficult to understand given the number of chairs in the room. "I don't understand why she doesn't want to be the bride."

"I don't want to be the bride because I'm never getting married," Aisling said. "Being a bride is stupid."

Cormack lowered his massive frame into a chair and fixed his daughter with a questioning look. "Why don't you want to get married?"

"Because boys are stupid."

"That's a good answer." Cormack grinned at her. "In fact, that's a very good answer, kid. Boys are stupid. I want you to remember that when you're fourteen ... and sixteen ... and twenty ... and don't forget it when you're thirty either."

"Mom says I will change my mind and like boys at some point," Aisling supplied. "I think she's lying. I think that's like when she said I would eventually like asparagus. That's never going to happen ... and neither is the liking boys thing."

She was so serious Cormack couldn't stop himself from chuckling. "Oh, Aisling, you make me laugh."

"I'm not trying to be funny."

"That only makes it funnier." He patted the chair next to him and watched as Aisling climbed into it. "I would like to believe that you'll stick to your guns and hate boys forever."

"I will."

"I doubt karma will be that good to me," Cormack countered. "At some point, I'll have to pay for spoiling you."

"That's how the universe wanted things to be. Spoiling me was a good idea."

Cormack's chuckle was quick and throaty. "Somehow I knew you would say that. But it's not true. I'm going to pay for spoiling you. I don't know how or when, but it's coming."

"And you think it's going to happen with boys?" Aisling didn't look convinced. "Why?"

"There will come a time when you go boy crazy," Cormack replied without hesitation. "I can already see the beginning signs, like when you watch that show with the vampire with the soul. You get all moony when you see him."

Aisling balked. "I don't get moony." She looked to Jerry for confirmation. "Tell him I don't get moony."

"I don't know what to tell you, Bug." Jerry was blasé as he stretched his legs out in front of him. "You do get quiet when *Angel* is on television. I don't blame you. He's great."

Cormack slid Jerry a sidelong look. "You like him, too?"

Jerry held his palms out. "I don't know. I guess I'm supposed to like Fred or Cordelia because they're girls, right?"

Cormack stilled. This was a sticky situation. He wouldn't change Jerry for anything — the boy had a giving heart and put up with Aisling, which meant he was practically a saint — but he didn't want to insert himself in a conversation that he figured was best shared with Jerry's overprotective mother. "Wait ... Fred is a girl?"

"Winifred," Aisling automatically answered.

"Okay." Cormack cleared his throat. "I think you two are allowed to like whoever you want when it comes to *Angel*. There are no rules."

"Well, I don't like Angel because he's a boy," Aisling clarified. "I like him because he's an awesome fighter and he kills bad guys. That's what I want to do when I get older ... kill bad guys. Screw all this wedding stuff."

Cormack was reminded of why he stopped to interrupt the game in the first place. "Watch your language. Look, you might change your mind, Aisling. There's a very good chance you'll decide that you want a fancy wedding like Jerry has set up here."

"I don't think so." Aisling was adamant as she swung her legs. "This dress itches, the flowers make my eyes water, Jerry kept trying to get me to wear a tiara — which is so not going to happen — and I don't like the idea of anyone giving me away."

Cormack arched an amused eyebrow. "You don't?"

"Mom says I'm not property and to remember that when I'm older," Aisling replied. "She says I'm my own person and no matter what other boys say I don't need permission from anyone to do what I want."

"I believe your mother threw in a caveat there," Cormack noted. "You need permission from her or me to do what you want until you turn eighteen."

"I was hoping you would forget that part," Aisling added ruefully, causing her father to smile.

"I can guarantee you're not going to get that lucky, kid." Cormack patted her knee. "As for the marriage stuff, I would like to believe you'll wait until you're thirty and let me pick your husband when it's time."

"No way!" Aisling made a face. "You'll pick Jerry. We're friends, not ... you know."

Cormack bit back a chuckle. While he had no doubt Jerry would forever be in Aisling's life — he was the best friend any father could've asked for his daughter — he held no illusions that Jerry and Aisling's friendship would turn into romance. Jerry had a different path in front of him, and it wouldn't always be easy. In some ways, that made the bond Jerry and Aisling shared much stronger.

"I won't pick Jerry," Cormack assured her. "He's too good for you."

Jerry beamed. "Ha!"

Aisling rolled her eyes. "Then you'll pick someone boring," she argued. "You'll pick a guy who works in a library or something."

"And what's wrong with working in a library?"

"I want to marry someone exciting, like an FBI agent."

"You want to marry Fox Mulder," Cormack said. "You've got a crush on him, too."

5

"I do not!" Aisling's voice turned screechy, one of her tells when lying. "I don't like boys. They're stupid."

"Fine." Cormack held up his hand in a placating manner. "You don't like boys. I get it."

"It took you long enough," Aisling grumbled.

"I still think you'll change your mind," Cormack persisted. "It'll happen in a few years, and then you'll bring your first boyfriend home. Don't get attached to him, by the way. I know how teenagers think. That first boy you bring home will be a walking hormone and I'll have to bury him in the backyard for being handsy."

Aisling giggled. "Can I help bury him?"

"Absolutely." Cormack nodded. "That's a lot of work for me to do on my own. You know how my back acts up when it comes to manual labor."

"Okay."

"I'll probably hate the second and third boys you bring home, too," Cormack explained. "You might slip a boy in that I do like, but he won't last because the second you figure out I don't hate him he'll become odious to you."

Aisling furrowed her small brow. "What's odious? Does that mean stinky?"

"Not quite, but close enough."

"So, you're saying that you'll never like any boy I bring home but Jerry," Aisling surmised. "Is that right?"

Cormack smiled as he smoothed Aisling's flyaway hair. It looked to him that, at some point, Jerry had tried to put a veil on his daughter and she'd fought the process. Ah, well, she never liked being constrained. "I probably won't like any of the boys you bring home," he agreed. "That's the way of the world when it comes to fathers and daughters."

"So ... you really don't want me to get married," Aisling noted. "If you hate all the boys I'm going to bring home, you agree that I'm never going to get married."

"No, that's not what I said," Cormack countered. "I said I will hate most of the boys you bring home and that you will end up hating the ones I like. That's only up until a point, though. Eventually, you'll stop bringing home the wrong boys and bring home the right one. Then I'll definitely be unhappy."

Aisling face was pinched as she absorbed her father's words. "Who is the right one?"

"Yeah," Jerry echoed. "Who is the right one?"

"The one we both like," Cormack responded. "Oh, I'm sure I'll be disagreeable and try to hate him, but I have no doubt you'll eventually find a guy who fits and then I'll be sad for a different reason."

Aisling stared into his eyes. "Why will you be sad?"

"Because then you won't be my little girl any longer. You'll be his ... big girl."

Instead of reacting with sadness — or even a muttered curse, as Cormack expected — Aisling merely shook her head. "I'll always be your girl."

"You will?"

"Yeah. You get me omelet bars. You give me licorice when Mom's not looking. Oh, and you play zombies with us."

"I do all those things. You're right."

"You're also going to walk Jerry down the aisle so we can stop playing this stupid game," Aisling added, hopping to her feet. "You won't do it because you want to. You'll do it because we want you to."

"Really?" Cormack thought about arguing on principle but the look on Jerry's face told him that wasn't an option. "You're right." He was smiling when he got to his feet. "I will gladly walk Jerry down the aisle. You're going to need flower petals to throw at him to finish off the ceremony."

"I was thinking popcorn," Aisling countered. "It's more fun and then we can eat it."

"I like the way your mind works."

"Everyone does," Aisling agreed, grabbing her bouquet from the chair before lifting her chin to snag Cormack's steady gaze. "I don't think you have to worry about me finding the right guy. You and my brothers will scare him away long before it gets to that point. I'll always be here with you, so ... don't be sad."

She was rarely sweet, so Cormack instinctively reached out and clasped her hand. "If you choose the right guy, nothing that ever happens with this family could scare him away. I know it sounds impossible now, but something tells me you'll find him."

Aisling shook her head. "I don't like boys. I keep telling you that, but you won't listen. It's just going to be Jerry and me forever."

"That would be nice." Cormack straightened Aisling's dress. "As I said, though, karma always comes back to bite you when it's least expected. That will happen to me because it happens to everyone."

"Well, it's not going to happen today." Aisling gestured toward Cormack. "I need to start the music. You should get in your position."

Cormack mock saluted. "Yes, ma'am." He grinned as he moved to Jerry. "Are you ready to walk down the aisle?"

Jerry nodded, his lips curving. "Yeah. She's wrong, you know. She'll find the perfect boy."

"How do you know that?"

"I've seen him."

The simple statement threw Cormack for a loop. "You've seen who."

"The man she'll end up with."

"How have you seen him?"

"Mrs. Grimlock showed me in a dream, but she said I had to be quiet about it because Aisling would fight it if she didn't think everything was her idea."

"That's very wise." Cormack stared into Jerry's solemn eyes for a long moment. "How often do you have this dream?"

"I don't know. Not often. It's like I'm not supposed to remember after I dream it, but I do."

"And you dreamed about Aisling's wedding?"

"No, I dreamed about all of us in the future," Jerry explained. "I saw us ... and we were all together. The new guy, too. And a few girls I'm sure belong with Cillian, Braden and Redmond."

"I'm sure they'll go through a few girls," Cormack agreed readily. "What did Aisling's boyfriend look like?"

"I don't know. I didn't see his face. I just saw him when he saved her."

"Saved her from what?"

"The bad thing."

"What bad thing?"

"The bad thing that's to come." Jerry was rapidly losing interest in the conversation. "I can't really remember. It was a dream."

Instinctively, Cormack knew that getting worked up over Jerry's dream was a bad idea. He couldn't shake how matter-of-fact the boy was. It set his teeth on edge. "Are you ready for this?"

"I was born ready." Jerry puffed out his chest. "Bug, make sure you have the popcorn ready. I want my big moment to be awesome."

Aisling rolled her eyes. "Yeah, yeah, yeah. I've got it. Stop being a pain."

"I'm not a pain. I'm a star."

"Those two words sound the same in my head."

"They're not the same at all."

"Stop the squabbling," Cormack ordered. "This is a big event. You should be happy."

"I'll be happy when it's over," Aisling said. "We have cake for when it's over. I'm looking forward to that."

"Cake?" Cormack grinned. "Now I'm looking forward to that, too."

"That's the best part of a wedding," Aisling agreed.

"Definitely. Bring on the cake."

Jerry slapped his hand to his forehead. "I'm going to have to take over Aisling's wedding to make sure it's not a disaster. I just know it."

"I think that's a plan," Cormack hooked his arm through Jerry's and smiled. "Shall we?"

"Yup. The future awaits."

One

"Listen, demon, I'm not going and there's no way you can make me."

Dorothy Sprite – I was of the opinion her last name should be Spite – was defiant as she watched me prowl around her living room. She stood behind the couch, close to where her body tumbled when a heart attack claimed her, and glared as I looked over the photos she had arranged on her shelves.

"How many kids do you have?"

"What?" Dorothy furrowed her brow and followed my gaze to the framed photographs. "What does it matter to you?"

"I'm just curious." That was true. I, Aisling Grimlock, am always curious. It was something my father said he loved when I was a kid ... although it often gave him headaches as I aged. "You have a lot of photos of kids around here, although you're hardly young enough to be taking care of dependents."

Dorothy, who had pristine blond hair despite the fact that she was in her nineties, turned haughty as she folded her arms over her chest. "Excuse me? Are you saying I'm old?"

"You're ninety-one," I replied without hesitation. "I saw it in your chart. That's why I assumed you'd be an easy charge. I traded with my brother Cillian for you."

"You traded for me?" Even though Dorothy wasn't really there — she was dead on the floor, after all — the eyebrows on her ethereal figure (which were drawn on) migrated higher on her forehead. "I don't even know what that means."

"I'm a reaper." I saw no reason to lie. Dorothy wasn't going to be able to share my secret with the world and she was my last charge of the day. "I collect souls and ferry them to the other side."

"Souls?" Dorothy's discomfort was obvious. "Are you saying that I'm dead?"

"You're standing by your body."

"Yes, but ... I thought that was a trick." Dorothy kept her cool eyes on me as I moved to look at the photos on a different shelf. "Don't get too close. I know Brazilian jiu-jitsu and I'm not afraid to use it."

"What's the difference between Brazilian jiu-jitsu and other types of jiu-jitsu?" I wasn't really interested in the conversation, but wasting a few minutes talking to a tortured soul was a kindness I could easily provide. Er, well, at least I told myself that. In truth, I was really wasting time. Dorothy didn't need to know that, though.

"Brazilian jiu-jitsu focuses on grappling and ground strength."

Hmm. "You're ninety-one," I reminded her. "How are you getting up and down from the floor to wrestle with people without breaking a hip?"

"I'm spry for my age."

"That sounds fun." It didn't sound fun, but I had no idea what else to say. I focused on the photos instead. "You look young here. You have five kids?" I counted just to be sure. "Yeah. Five of them. Four boys and a girl." I grew up in a family with the exact same count, so I couldn't help being intrigued. "How did that work out for you?"

"How do you think it worked out?" Dorothy's agitation was on full display. "I had five kids within eight years. It was a nightmare."

"My parents had five kids in five years."

"That's impossible."

"No, they were really busy. Plus, Aidan and I are twins. So, they had five kids but only four pregnancies. Essentially, every ten months my mother would get knocked up. After Aidan and me they started using birth control."

Dorothy rolled her yes. "Birth control is wrong in the eyes of the Lord."

"Catholic, huh?"

Dorothy balked. "How did you know?"

"I saw it in your file."

"What file?"

"The one they sent to us when you showed up on our list," I replied. "We get daily lists of the souls we have to gather. My brother Cillian initially snagged you, but I'm getting married — and soon — so my father ordered my brothers to trade with me whenever I ask it of them so I can focus on the wedding. He's spoiling me ... he's always spoiled me."

Usually the prospect of my father doting on me was enough to earn a smile. My mind was too busy for that. "You had five kids," I barreled forward without waiting for Dorothy to respond. "Did you ever feel overwhelmed?"

"Of course." Dorothy's expression was hard to read as she focused on me. "In my day, the husband went out to earn a living and the wife stayed home to raise the children. That meant I was stuck with kids for years on end."

"Your husband didn't help?"

"Did your father help?"

I nodded without hesitation. "Yeah. He spent a lot of time with us. He played ball with my brothers and he read me stories every night. He took us camping once, but that didn't end well. He rode bikes with us ... and sometimes he just sat and listened when we had something to say ... even if it was an inane conversation."

"Then your mother was lucky," Dorothy supplied. "My husband did none of those things. He went to work, came home, ate dinner and then yelled at me to keep the kids quiet."

"My father yelled at us to be quiet a lot, but he didn't really mean it."

"He sounds like a nice man."

"He is."

"And your mother?"

The fact that Dorothy was trying to elicit family information from someone she didn't know rather than focus on her own situation wasn't lost on me. "She died when I was a teenager."

"Oh, I'm sorry." Dorothy looked legitimately sympathetic. "That must have been hard on you. Cancer?"

"Fire."

"Oh, that's awful."

"Yeah, it sucked," I agreed, shaking my head to dislodge the heavy thoughts that had been weighing me down for weeks. "She came back, though. A little over a year ago, she came back. I guess, technically, she was back before then, but she let us know she was still alive a year ago."

"Wait ... your mother faked her death?" Dorothy finally emerged from behind the couch. "That's like soap opera stuff. Why would she fake her death?"

"She didn't. Another reaper family took her."

"Took her?"

"It's a long story."

"I'm dead. I have nowhere to go."

That was true. I wasn't really interested in dwelling on the story, though. I'd gone over it so many times in my head I knew it by heart. The story of my mother's fate was sad ... but it was complete. It was what happened after she escaped her captors that intrigued me, and I had no way of filling in those gaps.

"The people who took her were crazy," I explained. "She was weak for a long time. Then she got better and escaped. Then she did stuff for years, although I have no idea what that stuff entailed. She came back to us a year ago."

"Why aren't you happy about that?"

"Because I think she's evil."

"She's your mother."

"That doesn't mean she's not evil."

"It means she's owed respect." Dorothy was firm as she squared her shoulders. "That woman gave birth to you. It sounds as if she's had a hard time. You should be thrilled that she's back and shower her with love."

"I don't think that's the way the real world works." And that was my biggest problem with this entire scenario. "In a movie, it would've ended with her return. It would've been a triumphant scene and moviegoers would've assumed everyone lived happily ever after. There is no such thing as a happily ever after. You have to work to keep a family together, and sometimes even then it's impossible."

"Well, aren't you just a Debbie Downer." Dorothy made a derisive sound before shaking her head. "You have your mother back after she died. Do you know how many people would kill for something like that? That's something most people only dream of, a loved one returning from the dead. It's not reality for anyone but you, girl, and yet you don't appreciate it."

Was that true? Did I not appreciate my situation? Oh, that was just crap. "I tried to accept her, but I don't think it's going to work. She's been hiding things, working against us. A few weeks ago she hid the fact that she was helping people create magical storms that ended up killing people. She doesn't know that I'm aware of what she did, but I know."

"Wait ... magical storms?" Dorothy's forehead wrinkled as she absorbed my story. "I heard about that. It was all over the news. The newscasters said it was some sort of mental thing – combustion in the brain or something – and there's a scientific explanation for everything that happened."

"Yeah, tainted water," I said. "I heard that, too. It's not the real story." I used the arm of my hoodie to dust off one of the frames. "Did you have a favorite kid?"

My shift obviously confused Dorothy because she could do nothing but blankly stare.

"I'm serious," I pressed. "Did you have a favorite kid? I know you're not supposed to — mothers love all their children equally, yada, yada — but I have a theory that all parents have a favorite kid, even if they don't admit it."

"I did not have a favorite. That's a horrible thing to ask."

"Really?"

"Of course not."

I heaved out a sigh. There went that theory. "Well, great."

"I did, however, have a special bond with my son Donnie," Dorothy admitted, causing me to snap my head in her direction. "I didn't love him more, but we talked more."

"Do you think he'll be hurt most by your death?"

Dorothy's expression turned unbelievably sad. "He died five years ago."

"Oh. That sucks."

"They're all gone," Dorothy intoned, her expression mournful as she focused on the photographs. "I outlived all my children."

"That's the worst thing that can happen, right?" My heart went out to her despite the fact that I was supposed to be numb to my charges at this point. "No parent wants to outlive their child, do they?"

"That is the worst thing that can happen," Dorothy agreed. "All of my children are gone now. I have grandchildren, of course, and they'll have a funeral for me. I'm sure a few will cry and be genuinely upset at my passing. But it's not the same."

"No, I can see that."

"A parent should always go first." Dorothy's smile was fleeting. "It didn't go that way for me, but I get it now."

"Then why were you arguing with me when I told you I had to absorb your soul?" I challenged, referring to the woman's belligerent reaction to my announcement that it was time to move on. "You said you weren't going with me."

"You took me by surprise," Dorothy admitted, hovering closer. "Death is jarring ... even when it seems as if you've been waiting for it for a long time."

"Have you been waiting for it?"

"Sometimes it feels as if I'm the woman that time forgot," Dorothy admitted. "When my first child, Gordon, died, it was difficult. He died in a car accident. That wasn't natural, if you know what I mean. But I had my other children."

"Right. It was a fluke. It was terrible, but those things happen."

"Exactly." Dorothy bobbed her head. "When Michael followed four years later, I was devastated. He died of a heart attack and the doctor who informed us of his death in the waiting room at the hospital told us it wasn't unheard of for people his age. That's when I realized things were going to be different for me."

"My father is like you." I offered her a rueful smile. "He would sacrifice himself for my brothers and me without a second's thought. In fact, as I've grown older, I realize that he always sacrificed for us. Sure, he's rich so he doesn't go without, but when our mother died ... he was a rock. He took care of us."

"He sounds like a good father."

"He is."

"So, what's the problem?" Dorothy took a long moment to look me up and down. "You're still relatively young. You should have decades left with your father."

"I hope so." I meant it. "It's my mother I'm worried about. She could do a lot of damage in one year, let alone a few decades."

"I think I'm missing part of the story." Dorothy was rightfully confused. "Is there something about your mother I don't understand?"

"She eats people to stay alive."

"Like cannibalism?"

"Kind of. She eats souls, not bodies. The cannibalism would almost be better."

"I don't think there's any situation where cannibalism is a better option," Dorothy countered. "I mean ... ."

"What she's doing is worse."

"What is she doing?"

"Playing us."

Dorothy stilled. "I don't understand."

She couldn't possibly understand. It was too convoluted and painful to absorb. I rationalized that was why I was having so much trouble right now. Watching my mother toss a magical talisman into a fire when she thought no one was looking — a talisman that signified she was working with bad people from the start, not the fanciful lies she told to cover her tracks — had been like a punch in the gut.

"It doesn't matter." I forced myself to break from my melancholy and shook my head. "You can't help without all the facts, and I don't have time to explain."

"Where do you have to be that's more important than this?"

"I'm getting married." I forced a smile. "I'm getting married, and my fiancé's family is arriving at the airport in an hour. I'm supposed to head there so I can help facilitate their trip to a hotel."

"You're getting married, huh?" Dorothy looked amused rather than annoyed. "Are you sure you want to risk that after the conversation we just had? If you get married you'll end up having children. If you have children, you have to take care of them. Are you ready for that?"

Was I ready for children? That was a terrifying thought. "I'm ready to get married," I answered after a beat. It was true, which was mildly amusing given the terror I'd felt during the wedding planning. "I love Griffin. He's a good man."

"Of course he's a good man. You're not the type to marry a lazy loser. Just make sure he's not the type to repeat movie lines back to you. My husband was a good man, but he constantly repeated movie lines to me, especially in comedies, as if I was too stupid to hear the lines myself."

I pressed my lips together to keep from laughing at her down-trodden expression. "Oh, well, that's ... very annoying."

"You have no idea. We were married for forty years. He repeated lines for decades, and I never said a word about it."

"That means you never fought about it?"

"Yes, but it wasn't honesty," Dorothy countered. "Honesty is always better."

"I don't have to worry about that," I supplied. "I drop honesty bombs on Griffin all the time. He's used to it."

"That's good."

"He doesn't repeat lines in movies either," I added. "My brother Braden does that. It's beyond irritating. I know exactly what you're talking about."

"Whoever marries your brother Braden is in for a sad life."

I barked out a laugh at Dorothy's hangdog expression. I couldn't help myself. "I should probably get going. That means I need to absorb your soul."

Dorothy nodded, thoughtful. "What happens after? I mean ... where will I go?"

"You're going to Heaven." I'd checked her file long enough to confirm that. Where souls landed in death depended on how they'd lived their lives. Even though she was a bit crotchety, Dorothy was a good woman who had a happy afterlife in her future. "I'm going to guess you have a lot of people waiting there for you."

"Do you think so?" Dorothy brightened considerably. "Do you think my husband and kids are there?"

There was no way I could know that, but I wasn't above voicing a hunch. "I have a good feeling, if that counts for anything."

"It counts for a lot." Dorothy smiled as she straightened. "I'm ready. Take me to my husband."

"Okay." I dug into my pocket for my scepter. "Do you think he'll be excited to see you?"

"I think he'll have fifteen years of dialogue saved up to repeat back to me," Dorothy replied, her excitement obvious. "You know, now that I think about it, the movie thing isn't that annoying. He offered a lot, besides that, I mean."

"I'm sure he did." I extended the scepter. "I hope they all have dinner ready when you get there."

"Dinner?"

"My family enjoys rowdy meals several times a week," I explained. "They're ridiculously over the top and yet ... ."

"They're your favorite part of the week," Dorothy finished. "I get it."

"I guess that's my version of repeating lines during movies, huh?"

Dorothy turned pragmatic. "In the end, the only thing that matters is the truth ... and what's in your heart. If you follow your heart, you'll always do the right thing."

I wished I could believe that. Life was more difficult than she made it sound "Have a good trip." I waved because I didn't know what else to do as the scepter started doing its magic.

"I will. Have a good life." Dorothy half waved as she disappeared.

"That's the plan," I muttered as I shoved the scepter in my pocket.

"All I have to do is figure out what to do with the cannibal in the family and then it's smooth sailing."

I was running out of time. I had to figure out my mother's master plan before she stole something from the Grimlock family that we could never get back.

Two

I delivered my souls to Grimlock Manor, the huge mansion where my father and three of my brothers resided. Dad was in his office when I swung by, and he smiled at my early arrival.

"All finished?"

I nodded. "It was an easy day."

"That's the plan. You're getting married in a few days. Bruises don't make for good wedding photos."

"I haven't been bruised in several weeks," I reminded him. "Things have been quiet."

Dad was a commanding man, his black hair (which all of my siblings and I shared with him) gleamed under the soft lights. Gray touched his temples, but he was still handsome and distinguished. "You shouldn't jinx us by saying things like that."

"You don't believe in jinxes."

"I'd rather be safe than sorry."

"Right." I nodded as I sank into one of the chairs across from his desk. They were oversized, leather, and reminded me of my childhood. I spent hours in his office when I was a kid, listening to him describe the work I would one day be responsible for while he slipped me pieces of licorice. "You don't have to keep giving me the easy assignments. You know that, right? That doesn't seem fair to everyone else."

"You're the one who traded with Cillian today," Dad pointed out. "You wanted an easy assignment."

That was true. "Just for today. I have to head to the airport. Griffin's family is coming in."

"Are you nervous about that?"

I shrugged. "I don't know. I've met his mother. She didn't like me at first, but it turned out okay. I figure she was my biggest obstacle."

"Probably," Dad agreed. "I'm looking forward to seeing Katherine. Have you talked to her since she left? That was a lot for her to absorb."

I knew what he was really asking. Katherine Taylor witnessed several things while visiting that most "normal" people wouldn't be able to swallow, including a mirror monster that tried to kill me. Much like her son, she turned out to be open to the possibility of paranormal experiences. I was grateful for that. Of course, that didn't change the fact that she was aware of the family secret and we could be in real trouble if she decided to spread it around.

"She understands the need for secrecy," I offered. "She won't squeal."

"I never suggested she would." Dad steepled his fingers as he regarded me. "I think you can trust Griffin's mother, just as you trust Griffin."

"You didn't feel that way when I first brought him home."

"Yes, well, even I make mistakes." Dad winked, but his smile faded when I didn't perk up. "What's wrong with you, kid? Are you having second thoughts about the wedding?"

"No." I immediately started shaking my head. "I want to marry Griffin. It feels ... right. The wedding itself is a little bigger than what I'd envisioned, but that's what happens when you give Jerry free rein to do whatever he wants."

"Jerry isn't the only one who wants you to have the perfect wedding," Dad pointed out. "Your mother and I want it for you, too."

There it was: the monster in the room. My mother, Lily Grimlock, was back from the dead and helping plan my wedding as if nothing had happened. As if she hadn't died, come back, and started eating people to stay alive. It was jarring.

I'd yet to tell my father about what I saw the day at the cemetery, that odds were good my mother helped our enemies after all. He'd been happy that day, relieved that my mother stepped in at the right moment to help. Trust was an issue in the Grimlock family — but only where my mother was concerned — and my father was on edge whenever she deigned to visit. Constant vigilance made him weary, and the last thing I wanted was for him to feel worn down.

So I kept that tidbit to myself. Okay, not entirely to myself. I told Griffin, and he was equally suspicious, but he agreed to keep the secret until we knew more. He didn't say it, but I knew it was a gift for me. If he'd had his druthers, he would've dragged my brothers and father together for a family meeting and my mother would either be dead or locked up. The fact that he managed to refrain from freaking out was a testament to his love for me, and I didn't take it for granted.

"I'm not sure a perfect wedding is possible," I said, choosing my words carefully. "Something is bound to go wrong. All we can do is roll with it. I'm sure it will be fine."

"I'm sure it will be, too," Dad agreed. "That doesn't change the fact that you're in a sour mood, and not your usual mood where you're spoiling for a fight. You're quiet today. I don't like it."

That was enough to elicit a real smile. "Would you prefer I was fighting with a brother and screaming loud enough to put the entire household staff on edge?"

"Actually, yes."

"I'll keep it in mind for later. As for my mood, I guess my last charge made me sad. She had five kids, four boys and a girl. She outlived all of them."

Dad made a clucking sound with his tongue. "That is sad. Did she put up a fight?"

"Not really."

"If you'd absorb and run without talking to the souls none of them would put up a fight."

Of course he would bring that up now. It was something he couldn't let go. "And, on that note ... ." I pushed myself to a standing position. "I have to get going. Griffin is probably already at the airport. He's excited for his family to visit. He's especially excited that you agreed to host dinner tonight, because his relatives are excited to see the castle Katherine told them about."

"It's my pleasure." Dad stood and shuffled to me, taking us both by surprise when he pulled me in for a hug. We aren't an emotionally demonstrative family, so hugs weren't handed out as readily as candy. "I love you, kid. I know you're probably nervous, but everything will be fine. You're more charming than you give yourself credit for."

That was a damnable lie and we both knew it. I enjoyed the effort all the same. "I'll see you in a few hours." I patted his back. "Make sure Braden is on his best behavior. If he's a jerk, I'm going to take him down, and I'm sure that will mean bruises for both of us."

"Duly noted." Dad kissed my forehead. "Hurry back. I'm arranging an ice cream bar for dessert tonight."

He always knew exactly how to brighten my spirits. "Gummy bears or sharks?"

"Both ... and worms."

"Yay!" I clapped my hands. "The day is looking up."

"Everything will work out, Aisling. I promise."

GRIFFIN WAS WAITING NEAR baggage claim when I arrived at the airport. I could read the agitation on his handsome face as he scanned the crowd, but his expression softened when he snagged my gaze.

"I was starting to worry you wouldn't make it." He gave me a hug and kiss before releasing me. "How was your day?"

My job was often a sore spot between us. Griffin knew what I did when we hooked up — which caused a few days of strife before he decided he could tolerate dating a paranormally-blessed woman with mother, father and brother issues. Once he committed, that was it. He never looked back. I understood what a rare thing that was.

"It was good," I replied, running my hand over his brown hair to smooth it. "It was an easy day. My father is combing through our charges himself to make sure I have an easy time of it, although I did trade with Cillian today to make sure I was done early."

"I'm glad he's doing that." Griffin slung an arm over my shoulder as he shifted his eyes to the arrival board. "The plane is here, but the passengers haven't disembarked. I don't think they're at the gate yet."

"It won't take long." I leaned my head against his chest. "Are you nervous about them coming?"

"No."

Griffin's answer was a little too quick to be believable. "I'd understand if you were nervous," I offered. "My family is an acquired taste."

"Like a fine delicacy," Griffin teased.

"Something like that." I briefly pressed my eyes shut and inhaled Griffin's masculine scent. He'd splashed on aftershave this morning, I could still smell it, and he was wearing a dress shirt with his well-worn Levi's. "The last soul I collected today was ninety-one. She had five children, four boys and a girl."

"Wow." Griffin slid his eyes to me. "That's quite the coincidence. Were all her kids pains, too?"

"What makes you think I talked to her long enough to find that out?"

"Because I know you and how curious you are."

"You do know me," I agreed. "As for being curious, it was more sad than funny. She outlived all her children."

"That sucks."

"Yeah. She told me to beware men who repeat movie lines."

"I don't repeat movie lines."

"I told her that."

"Sometimes you repeat movie lines," Griffin said. "Especially if we're watching *Lord of the Rings* ... or one of the Harry Potter flicks ... or *Star Wars* ... or *The Goonies*."

"I only want to make sure you catch the important stuff."

"I think I know what's important." Griffin kissed my cheek as he playfully turned me to face him. His smile didn't last. "Why are you so sad? You're really worrying me."

I forced myself to toss off the doldrums. Griffin worrying about my mental state wasn't going to help anything. "I'm not sad. I'm just ...

tired. Jerry has been keeping me up late with seating charts and stuff for the wedding."

"That's not it." Griffin slipped a strand of hair behind my ear. I'd considered dying it before the wedding to cover the white streaks that had become something of my trademark but ultimately decided against it. I liked the streaks — as did Griffin — and I thought they'd look great with my dress. "You're worried about your mother, aren't you?"

I fought the urge to scowl ... and lost. "I'm trying to put it behind me like you said, but I can't forget what she did. She had that talisman on her the entire time, Griffin. That means she knew about the storms and did nothing to stop them even after you almost lost it."

Now it was Griffin's turn to frown. "I did lose it. Don't gloss it over. I could've hurt you."

The storms were meant to subvert people's ability to control their tempers, so that was a true statement. "You didn't hurt me," I reminded him. "In fact, in the end, you overcame the storm and protected me."

"Yes, well, I almost hurt you all the same." Griffin couldn't quite get over the situation. I couldn't blame him. "It's over now. Maybe your mother had the talisman because she was secretly working against them from the start and she simply didn't tell us because she thought it was the safest way to go."

That seemed unlikely. "She knew how worried I was about you. She saw how upset I was when you refused to talk to me." My temper grew with each word. "She wasn't trying to protect you."

"Okay. Calm down, tiger." Griffin's eyes widened as he stroked his hands up and down my arms. "I didn't mean to start another argument. I'm with you whatever you decide about your mother."

"That's just it. I don't know what to do. If I tell my father, he'll side with me and then it will be over. He'll kick her out of the house and start a war."

"That might not necessarily be a bad thing."

"No, but it's something we don't need," I said. "If Dad kicks Mom out then Braden will melt down and he won't refrain from doing it in front of your family."

"My family fights as much as the next family. I think they can take it."

"They shouldn't have to. I mean … a Grimlock family explosion right now would be more than anyone can bear. I just want to get married. Is that too much to ask?"

Griffin's smile was sweet. "No, baby, it's not. I'm glad to hear that you still want to get married, though. I was starting to get worried."

"Never worry about that." I gripped his hand tightly. "I want to marry you. I won't lie about the wedding making me nervous — I just know I'm going to spill something on my dress and be forced to walk around the reception with an obvious stain the entire night — but I'm looking forward to being married."

Griffin's expression softened. "Me, too." He gave me a soft kiss. "I can't wait to see you in your dress."

"Oh, you're getting schmaltzy."

"I don't care. We're getting married. If a man can't get schmaltzy with the woman who is going to be his wife then there's something wrong with this world."

"Fine. Be schmaltzy." I kissed the tip of his nose before stepping away. "I need to run to the bathroom before your family gets here. Once they're all staring at me I'll have a nervous bladder. I want to get ahead of it."

"The only reason they'll be staring is because you're the prettiest woman in the world."

"Oh, so schmaltzy." I lobbed him an amused look before starting toward the bathroom. "I'll be back in a second. Do you want anything while I'm close to the shops?"

"Nope. Just you."

I couldn't meet his gaze because my cheeks were burning. "You're really on a roll today."

"I'm getting married. I can't seem to stop myself."

"Yeah, yeah, yeah."

I RELIEVED MY BLADDER, checked my makeup and sprayed some of the scented body spray I carried in my purse on my neck before leaving the bathroom. I knew I had plenty of time because it would take forever for Griffin's relatives to claim their luggage, so I pointed myself toward the Starbucks rather than heading directly back to Griffin.

Thankfully the airport wasn't overly busy at this time of day, and there were only two people ahead of me in line. I had my order within five minutes and was meandering back to the baggage claim carousels when I caught sight of a familiar figure. I did the world's biggest double take, but confusing Zake Zezo for someone else was impossible.

The shaman stood in the small hallway that separated the bathrooms, his gaze focused directly on me. The hair on the back of my neck rose even though I had no reason to believe the man was a threat — I'd faced off with him before, after all, and the only thing to fear was his ridiculous speech pattern — and I came to a complete stop as I held his gaze.

A normal person would've stalked over and demanded answers. I hadn't seen Zake Zezo in weeks, not since we were mired in the storm catastrophe and he offered very little help. I certainly didn't want to see him now, so I remained rooted to my spot.

Zake was the first to break and he motioned for me to approach him. When I continued to stare, he became more insistent with his movements. He was too far away for me to hear him, so finally he dug into his pocket and returned with a phone. I wasn't surprised when my phone started ringing in my pocket as he pressed his device to his ear.

"What?" I hissed.

"I have something I need to tell you," Zake said. "I don't think it should be yelled across an airport."

"Yes, well, I suggest sending it in an email."

He furrowed his brow. "I'm trying to help you."

"You didn't try to help me a few weeks ago," I reminded him. "Then you wanted to play games. I'm not in the mood to play games. In fact ... how did you even know I was here? It's not as if I put it on Facebook or anything."

"I'm not on Facebook," Zake said dryly. "Why would you possibly think I'm on Facebook?"

"Because Facebook is full of a lot of scammers," I answered honestly. "You have no idea how many dick pics I'm sent in any given week by people who want me to send them money. I mean ... it's not all Nigerian princes anymore."

"Ugh." Zake heaved out a sigh as I sipped my coffee. "You are very annoying."

"Right back at you."

"That doesn't change the fact that I have something to tell you," Zake persisted. "That's why I'm here. I have to warn you of ... trouble."

I narrowed my eyes. I didn't trust him. I had no reason to feel otherwise. Still, if he went out of his way to follow me to the airport there had to be a reason. "Fine, but if you try something perverted we're going to have issues."

"Fair enough." Zake disconnected and waited for me to cross toward him. He was completely focused on me, apparently to the detriment of everything else.

I heard a whizzing sound before I saw anything, jerking my head to the right as I felt something fly past my face. I was confused when I found nothing there, although certain that I hadn't imagined the phenomenon even though there was no visual proof to the contrary. I didn't get much time to consider my predicament, because the next thing I heard was a scream.

When I snapped my head in its direction, I found a woman standing about ten feet away from Zake, who had tumbled while I wasn't looking and was prone on the floor. She kept screaming and pointing. Zake didn't move.

"Oh, man." My stomach twisted as I searched the sea of faces for one that might give me a hint as to what had happened. I came up empty. "Son of a ... !"

Three

I wasn't sure what to do.

Zake was on the ground, his face pitched into the tile. He didn't move a muscle.

Perhaps reading my indecision from across the way — or picking up on my fear — Griffin ignored the people screaming and strode directly toward me. He was on top of me before I could even register what was happening.

"What is it?"

I shifted my eyes to him, dumbfounded. "I ... don't know."

"What do you mean?" Griffin looked in the direction of the fallen man. "Do you know him?"

I swallowed hard and nodded. "The shaman, the one I told you about during the storms. That's him."

"Why was he here? Does he work out of the building?"

"I don't think so."

"So ... why was he here?"

"He wanted to talk to me." I lifted my phone for proof. "He called me, although I'm not sure how he got my number. He wanted to talk about something. He said it was important."

"What did you say?" Griffin's expression was hard to read. He stood next to me, a protective force practically daring anyone to approach. Airport emergency medical personnel were at Zake's side, working on him, but I had a feeling they were too late.

"I agreed to talk to him." Lying would do me no good. Griffin was liable to be angry, but there was nothing I could do about that. "I never made it over there."

"What stopped you?"

"I ... heard something?"

"What?"

His relentless questioning was starting to grate. "I don't know. It was a whizzing sound. I can't explain it. The next thing I knew, he dropped like a stone and a woman was screaming. Then you were here and ... I don't know what happened."

"Okay." Griffin wrapped his arms around me and held tight. "It's okay." He kissed my temple as he watched the paramedics work on the man. "Do you think he wanted to hurt you?"

I tilted my head, considering the question. "No." That didn't feel right.

"He said he had something important to tell you."

My temper flared. "If I knew what, I wouldn't have needed to talk to him."

"Okay." Griffin gave me a hard look. "Don't raise your voice and draw attention. That's the last thing we need."

I wanted to argue, but he wasn't wrong. "Fine."

"Good." He went back to rubbing his hands over my back as he stared at the prone shaman. "Can you tell me ... do you see his soul?"

Hmm. I hadn't even considered that. I scanned the area, taking time to look over each face. Finally, I shook my head. "I don't think he's dead."

"Well, that's good. Maybe he had a heart incident or something."

"I don't think it was that."

"It doesn't matter. You can't go over there. What are you going to say if they start questioning you? How are you going to explain what he does?"

"I don't know. If he dies and they decide to investigate, though, his phone records will show he called me."

"We'll deal with it then." Griffin gently tugged me back toward the baggage carousels. "You have to let it go for now. There's nothing more you can do."

Silently, I agreed with him ... but I wasn't happy about it.

GRIFFIN'S FAMILY CONSISTED of his mother, several cousins, a grandfather and myriad aunts and uncles. We didn't have enough room in our vehicles to transport all of them, but my father sent a limousine that could hold the entire crowd ... which meant Griffin and I were forced to drive back to Grimlock Manor alone. The limo arrived well before us. I meandered to the point I was the last to arrive. I was surprised to find Griffin waiting for me.

"What's wrong?"

Griffin, hands in his pockets, smirked. "Can't a guy wait for his fiancée without getting the third degree?"

"I guess." I stopped directly in front of him. "I'm sorry about being snippy with you at the airport." We didn't have the chance to talk once his family arrived. It was a flurry of hugs and kisses ... and rather jarring back slaps ... after that, to the point I was fairly certain I would have to take some Motrin and get out the heating pad if I expected to sleep without aches and pains.

"It's okay." Griffin ran his hand over my hair. "You were surprised by what happened. I was, too. There's no reason to fight."

"Still ... I was short with you. That's not exactly how we're supposed to be spending the run-up to our wedding."

"How are we supposed to be spending it?"

"Naked ... with a lot of food deliveries. I know that kind of defeats the purpose of being naked if all you do is eat, but it sounds heavenly."

Griffin laughed as he pulled me against his chest. "How about we get my family settled in the east wing, have dinner, and then do the naked thing when we get home? We don't have to order takeout. We'll just take whatever dessert your father plans to serve."

That was an intriguing suggestion. "He's having an ice cream bar."

"We can figure a way to make it work."

"You're on." I gave him a hard kiss and a genuine smile as he grabbed my hand and led me toward the front door. "I wonder what we've missed. I hope my family hasn't locked your family in the dungeon already."

"I think you'll be surprised." Griffin held the door open for me. "My family is just as tough as yours."

"That's bold talk."

"Just wait."

IT TURNED OUT THAT GRIFFIN'S family was fairly tough. Other than gawking at the size of the house — and the number of house employees my father had running around — they seemed to fit right in.

Griffin's grandfather, Clint Taylor, was a bull of a man who immediately bonded with my father. They were drinking bourbon and smoking cigars when Griffin and I strolled into the second parlor, which happened to be the first parlor when it came to entertaining.

"Where have you been?" Dad asked, puffing a ring of smoke in my face. "I was starting to think you got lost."

I waved my hand to fan away the smoke and grabbed the cigar before he could pull it out of my reach. Griffin widened his eyes when I inhaled, smirking when I coughed a bit before handing the stogie back. "Cuban. Those are illegal."

"I didn't see a thing," Griffin teased.

"I got them out because it's a special occasion," Dad said. "There's no harm in having a little fun."

"Did I say anything?"

"No. You're late. I was getting worried."

I opted not to tell him about Zake Zezo. There was nothing he could do and if I pulled him away for a private tête-à-tête when Griffin's family was on the premises it would be rather obvious that something had gone terribly wrong. "I wish you would've told me you were sending a limo. I wouldn't have needed my car if I'd known."

"I didn't think about it until you'd already left," Dad replied. "I thought multiple cabs and vehicles was a waste. And why not bring Griffin's family to the house in style?"

Why not indeed? "Well, I still wish I'd known." I flopped onto one of the couches and frowned as I scanned the room. "Where is everybody else?"

"Getting the grand tour," Dad replied. "They like the house. When they heard there was a game room and full library, they had to check it out."

"Who is conducting the tour?"

"Cillian and Maya."

Cillian was my calmest brother. My mother used to jokingly say he had the heart of a poet, and she wasn't far off. He was the most intellectual of my siblings, happy to spend long hours reading ancient tomes in the library. In addition to being Cillian's girlfriend, Maya was Griffin's younger sister. She came into our family thanks to her ties with Griffin, and even though he wasn't keen to see her dating one of my brothers at the start, he'd warmed up to the idea.

"I'm kind of glad we missed the tour." I nodded in thanks to Griffin when he delivered a drink to me. "What's this?"

"Whiskey sour."

"Good choice."

"I figured you needed something strong." He sat next to me, resting his hand on my leg, and met his grandfather's steely stare without blinking. "What's wrong with you?"

Griffin's grandfather was in his seventies and clearly set in his ways because he merely made a huffing sound while shaking his head.

"Was that an answer?" I asked, legitimately curious.

"There's nothing wrong with me," Clint finally answered. "I was simply taking it all in."

"Taking what in?" Griffin asked.

"You and her ... in this place. This huge, huge place."

"I grew up in this place," I offered. "I barely notice the size anymore. When you procreate like my parents did, you need a big house to cut down on the noise."

"Thank you, Aisling." Dad shot me a warning look. "Even though I would've phrased it differently, she's correct. This house has more than twenty bedrooms, but it feels smaller whenever my children are locked inside due to unforeseen circumstances."

Clint made a strange face as he puffed on his cigar. "You mean ... when they were kids, right?"

"Sure." Dad shrugged, noncommittal. How could he possibly explain that there had been occasions when we were all locked in the house thanks to monsters ... and gargoyles ... and attacking wraiths? That wouldn't go over well. It was best to let it rest. "That's what I meant."

Clint didn't look convinced. "How many of them still live here?"

"Three," Griffin answered when my father suddenly feigned ignorance. "Redmond, Braden and Cillian still live here."

"They seem a bit old to still be living with their father."

"I don't mind." Dad met my gaze. "The house will be lonely once they're all gone."

"What about you and your wife?" Clint challenged. "Are you looking forward to having a break from your kids?"

Dad worked his jaw. In truth, we hadn't really talked about how we were going to explain Mom and Dad's relationship. They were still married. That didn't mean they were going to live happily ever after.

"Lily and I are ... on a different path," Dad said finally.

Clint shifted in his chair. "I don't understand."

"You don't need to understand," Griffin chided. "It's private, which means you need to mind your own business."

"I see." Clint went back to smoking his cigar, which was a relief. That allowed me to sip my whiskey without interruption, until I heard a familiar voice in the foyer and knew things were about to get even more uncomfortable.

"Hello, everyone." Mom breezed into the room, her brown hair perfectly styled. It was gray when she'd first returned, as if the life was slowly being sucked out of her through the roots. I never asked why when it turned brown again. I couldn't help but wonder if that was a mistake. "I'm sorry I'm late. I didn't realize Cormack was sending a limousine for everyone or I would've been here sooner."

She turned to Clint and extended her hand. "I'm Lily Grimlock, Aisling's mother."

"Clint Taylor, Griffin's grandfather." Clint didn't stop smoking as he shook my mother's hand. "None of your kids look like you. They all look like their father. How come?"

I always thought I was the worst when it came to conversation in party atmospheres. Clint blew me out of the water and took the top prize.

Instead of reacting with anger or annoyance, Mom merely smiled. "You know, it kind of bothered me when they were really little and wanted to be cuddled. When they grew older and started to talk — and beat up on each other constantly — it was helpful to blame their father for their antics, and their hair color made that easier."

Amusement crawled through Clint's laugh. "I can see that."

"Yes, well ... ." Mom's eyes slowly tracked to me. "Hello, dear. I didn't see you there. Are you getting excited for the big day?"

I forced myself not to cringe when Mom gave me a fake hug. It took everything I had not to recoil from her touch, especially because I wanted to start accusing her of any number of heinous things. "I am excited," I confirmed, leaning closer to Griffin. Touching my mother always left me cold all over, and he never minded sharing his warmth. "A wedding is a big deal."

I said the words, but I wasn't sure I believed them. A marriage *was* a big deal. As far as I could tell, a wedding was a huge show, but I wasn't keen on being center stage.

"It is a big deal," Clint agreed, his smile wide and engaging. "Pretty soon you'll be Mrs. Griffin Taylor. That's got to be exciting."

I stilled. "Excuse me?"

Griffin cleared his throat, his discomfort obvious. "Ignore him. He's trying to get a rise out of you."

Clint opted to play dumb rather than acknowledge that. "Oh, don't be shy, boy. It's exciting when a woman takes your name."

Ugh. He had to be joking. "I'm keeping my name."

"I told him that," Griffin said hurriedly. "He doesn't believe me, thinks I'm pulling his leg, but I swear I told him that."

"The reason I don't believe you is because it's insulting," Clint barked. "I can't believe you would agree to be insulted by the woman you plan to call your wife."

"It's not insulting," Dad countered, catching me off guard. "Just because Aisling chooses to keep the family name doesn't mean she doesn't love Griffin."

"That's easy for you to say," Clint challenged. "It's your name she wants to keep. It's my name she wants to shun. If she wants to marry into this family, she should take the name."

"Why do you think that?" Mom asked, taking the open chair next to Dad and focusing on Clint. "I mean ... I don't see anything wrong with taking a husband's name — I did when I married Cormack — but I don't think it's necessary. In this day and age, more and more women are choosing to keep their maiden name. There's nothing wrong with it."

"There is something wrong with it," Clint argued. "There's something very, very wrong with it ... and I don't like it."

I rubbed my forehead as Griffin tightened his grip on my waist and leaned close. "Don't listen to him. We've already talked about this and we both agree it's smarter for you to keep Grimlock because of ... well, everything that keeps happening. People fear the Grimlock name. The Taylor name strikes fear in no one."

"Right," I said dully as I rubbed my temple. "How soon until dinner?"

Griffin didn't answer because he was too busy being dragged into the argument. "Grandpa, I've explained this to you at least five times now. Aisling is keeping her name. I don't understand why this is such a big deal."

"I'll tell you why it's such a big deal," Clint persisted. "It's a big deal because my son is dead. Your father is dead. I only had one male child. The rest were females. Your father only had one male child. That means you're the only person left to carry on the Taylor name."

Griffin's expression was blank. "So?"

"So, what's going to happen when you have children?" Clint barked. "Are they going to be Taylors or Grimlocks?"

Huh. I hadn't even considered that. "Well ... ."

"They'll be Taylors," Griffin answered automatically. "Just because Aisling isn't taking my last name doesn't mean our children won't carry the name." He looked to me for confirmation. "Right?"

"Um ... sure."

"She doesn't look like she agrees," Clint groused.

Griffin narrowed his eyes. "Do you agree?"

"I haven't given it much thought," I admitted. "It makes sense. They'll be Taylors."

"Are you sure?"

"Yeah." The more I thought about it, the more certain I became. I was being forced to keep the Grimlock name (even though I had no inclination to shed it even if safety wasn't a concern) because it struck terror in the hearts of our enemies. I had no intention of letting my children join the reaping world, so they were much better off being Taylors. "I'm definitely sure."

"I think that's a bit down the line," Dad added, his expression hard to read. "They have plenty of time to talk about children when they're ready."

"Why wouldn't they be ready now?" Clint asked. I was really starting to dislike him. I generally enjoyed hanging around blunt individuals, so this was unusual.

"They're not even married yet," Dad insisted. "They have plenty of time for children. They should enjoy each other for a bit, just the two of them, before they consider expanding."

"Is that what you did?"

"No." Dad shook his head as his eyes drifted to Mom. "We started having children right away."

"Do you regret it?"

"No." Dad smiled as his gaze moved to me. "I don't regret any of it. Aisling is not me, though. She has plenty of time."

What he left unsaid was that we were constantly threatened by a force greater than ourselves and no one wanted to bring a child into that situation. Even though I wanted to lash out and rip Clint's head from his shoulders when he said something dismissive to my father that I didn't quite make out, I managed to keep my anger under wraps.

Now was not the time to explode. There was too much going on ... and there was a greater threat in this very room.

"We should talk about something else," Mom suggested, clapping her hands. "How about dinner? I hear Cormack is having an ice cream bar. That's always exciting."

"Yeah, let's talk about that," I agreed. "You got the gummy sharks, right?"

Dad nodded. "Have I ever forgotten the sharks?"

"No. I just feel the need to go on a rampage."

Dad's smile was enigmatic. "You'll be okay. We've all got your back."

I had no doubt that was true. Well, except for Mom.

Four

We could have stayed at Grimlock Manor. We bandied the idea about so that Griffin could be close to his family. Ultimately, he insisted we head back to our townhouse. His mother didn't look happy with the announcement.

For us, it was a good idea. It allowed us to spend two hours of quiet time watching television and then enjoy eight full hours of sleep. We both woke rested the next morning, although, in typical fashion, I decided to ruin things. "Can you call your department and find out what happened to Zake Zezo?"

Griffin cocked an eyebrow as he rolled on his elbow to meet my gaze. "Don't you think you should let this go? We're getting married in a few days. Now isn't the time to go on an adventure."

"I thought marriage was an adventure. Isn't that what you've been telling me?"

"Very cute." Griffin poked my side. "Do you really want me to call?"

"I really need to know," I insisted. "If something is going to happen, I want to get ahead of it. I have this horrible fear that wraiths are going to descend on our wedding if I don't get proactive."

Griffin's fingers were gentle as he stroked them down my cheek. "Do you really think that's going to happen?"

"Probably not. But I want to make sure it doesn't. We're so close."

He blinked several times, his mind clearly working overtime, and then he shrugged. "Fine. I'll call. I just have one question."

"Shoot."

"What are you going to do if he was murdered?"

"I have no idea." That wasn't a lie. "I just need to know. It's important to me. I didn't like the little ferret, but he was at the airport for a reason. I'd really like to know the reason."

"Fair enough."

I left Griffin to call his station and wandered into the bathroom to brush my hair and teeth. By the time I returned, he was sitting on the side of the bed staring at his phone, his body language giving me answers before I asked the obvious question. "He's dead, isn't he?"

Griffin slid his eyes to me and nodded. "He died at the hospital last night. Apparently there was no chance of him ever waking up once he hit the ground."

"How did he die? Was he shot?"

"It's interesting that you ask that because they're not quite sure how he died. His body shut down — the autopsy shows that — but they're unsure why. Right now there's no cause of death while they wait for toxicology reports."

"I'm not sure I understand."

"They can't find a reason for his death," Griffin explained. "His organs shut down, but they can't find an underlying explanation for it."

"Poison?"

"That's a fairly good guess, but I don't know."

I wanted to push him further even though I recognized he'd shared everything he had, but I didn't get the chance. The bedroom door burst open, causing my heart to leap, and my best friend Jerry strolled over the threshold as if he belonged there.

"Why aren't you dressed?"

I glanced down to make sure I had shorts and a T-shirt on (I couldn't remember if I'd tugged anything on before crashing the previous night) and then frowned at Jerry. "Why are you here so early?"

"Forget that," Griffin groused. "What did we say about knocking? You're supposed to knock before entering our bedroom."

"I thought the rule was that he was supposed to knock before entering the townhouse," I challenged. "Isn't that what we agreed on?"

Jerry gave a loud moan. "I can't believe you turned on me, Bug."

Even though the news of Zake Zezo's death left me feeling unsettled, I couldn't stop myself from smiling. "I would never turn on you, Jerry. How could you say something like that?"

"Because ever since this one showed up, I've been turned into a second-class citizen." Jerry jerked his thumb in Griffin's direction. "It's ... demeaning."

Griffin was used to Jerry's theatrics so he barely reacted, instead slipping his arms around my waist and pulling me to his lap. "I thought we were going to spend quality time together this morning. Why is Jerry here?"

Actually, that was a good question. "I don't know. Why are you here?"

"Oh, you can't be serious!" Jerry's expression turned dour. "If you're serious, you're in big trouble. Like ... grounded trouble."

Griffin snickered at Jerry's shrill threat. "I like the idea of Aisling being grounded. Can we be grounded together? I'll take the day off work and we'll spend it in bed ... thinking about what we've done."

"Oh, don't even." Jerry wagged a finger in Griffin's face. "Aisling has plans with me today. Neither of us has time for your perverted games."

"But I'm so good at them," Griffin protested.

"Shh!" Jerry slapped his finger against Griffin's mouth, earning a stern look from my soon-to-be husband. "You're getting Aisling for the rest of your life. She's mine for the day ... and up until the wedding ... and for the first day when you get back from your honeymoon ... and probably a lot of weekends after that."

Griffin let loose a weary sigh as he shook his head. "I have no idea how you managed it, Jerry, but you've totally sucked the fun out of our morning. Nice job." He flashed a sarcastic thumbs-up. "We're instituting new rules when we get back from the honeymoon, by the way. You're not allowed in here without knocking on the front door. Period."

He sounded stern, but I knew there was no way Jerry would follow anyone's rules but his own.

"Oh, yeah, right." Jerry rolled his eyes, causing me to smile. "Come on, Bug. We have to get going if we're going to make our appointment."

I racked my brain. "What appointment?"

"You'd better not be serious."

"Well, I am. What appointment do we have? It wasn't on my phone — and you said you uploaded everything to my phone to make sure I didn't miss anything. And I made plans to meet Griffin's mother for lunch. I don't think she'll take it well if I have to cancel at the last minute."

"You should be fine for lunch," Jerry supplied. "Our appointment shouldn't take more than thirty minutes."

"And ... where are we going?"

"The final fitting for your dress."

"Oh." Honestly, I had forgotten about that. "I've tried on that dress fifty times, Jerry. It fits."

"You still have to try it on today." Jerry refused to back down. "After that, the dress will be zipped into a garment bag, where it will be protected until the day of the wedding. This is tradition, Bug. You can't get out of it."

He said it with such force it was hard to argue. Still, I looked to Griffin for help. "Is that true? Is it impossible for me to get out of it?"

Griffin chuckled as he rubbed his hand over my back. "He looks serious. Look at it this way, once you have the dress that's one less thing to worry about."

"You still haven't seen the dress."

"And I won't until the ceremony."

I eyed him speculatively. "Since when did you become so superstitious?"

"Since I fell in love with a reaper who keeps getting attacked by supernatural monsters," Griffin replied without hesitation. "I want to make sure we don't tick off the fates so close to our wedding."

"Good plan." I gave him a quick kiss. "Did I mention I'm having lunch with your mother today?"

"You did."

"Do you want to join us?" I hoped I came off sounding lackadaisical as I averted my eyes, as if the invitation was an afterthought. "You know ... just an intimate meal for the three of us."

"I have work."

"Yes, but ... ."

"I have work," Griffin repeated before I could get a full head of steam and try to manipulate him. "I'm not being sent out to any scenes right now — which is actually boring — but I have a mountain of paperwork to get through before I'm cleared to head out on our honeymoon. Do you want me to risk not finishing?"

Oh, now he was simply playing dirty. "Fine. I'll have lunch with your mother alone."

"Good girl." He patted my butt and smirked. "My mother likes you. How bad could it be?"

"And now you jinxed me," I complained.

"You'll live." He gave me a small push toward the bathroom. "We need to get ready. We both have full days."

"I don't even know why I'm marrying you sometimes," I complained.

"Love is a strange and wonderful thing."

"Isn't it?"

JERRY WAS TEN TIMES more excited about the dress fitting than I was. Sure, I picked it out and preferred it to every overblown frock Jerry tried to wrestle me into, but there was only so much enthusiasm I could muster for a dress.

"What do you think?" Marion Dalton was the third dressing consultant to work with me since we'd started the process months before. I chased off the first two — although not on purpose — and Jerry warned me things would get ugly if Marion opted to bolt. That was the only reason I held my tongue now as she slowly circled me, staring at the dress.

"I think it's nice," I replied automatically. "I think it looks great. Can I take it off now?"

"Shut up, Bug." Jerry's voice was low and full of warning. "I told you this would take thirty minutes. You've been in the dress for two minutes. Shut your hole."

It was rare for Jerry to turn so forceful and snap at me. "Hey! I'm the bride. You're supposed to be nice all week."

"That's a rule you came up with," Jerry countered. "I didn't agree to that."

"You said that as the bride I get whatever I want this week. I can guarantee that I don't want to be yelled at so ... you shut your hole."

Jerry's mouth dropped open, but no sound came out.

Sensing trouble, Marion wisely took a step back and looked nervously toward the back of the shop. "I'm going to run to the storage room. I forgot ... something. I'll be right back."

I paid her little heed as she scurried away. I couldn't blame her. If I were forced to wait on someone like me I'd spend my afternoons drinking to forget the horror.

"You know, Bug, you're really on my last nerve," Jerry said finally, recovering. "You're supposed to be walking on clouds and smiling at butterflies, not doing whatever it is you appear to be doing."

I made a face. "Walking on clouds?"

"You know what I mean." Jerry, never the type to back down, wasn't about to start now. "You're being a pain ... and I'm sick of it. Why aren't you more excited about your wedding? Are you having second thoughts?"

I was beyond annoyed with being asked that question. "Do you really think I'm having second thoughts? After everything Griffin and I have been through, why would I change my mind now?"

Perhaps sensing a shift in my demeanor, Jerry took a long time studying my face. "I know you love him," he said finally. "It's clear you want to marry him. You're being a real pain, though. I think Griffin is worried, too. I catch him watching you when he thinks no one is looking and the fear is real."

I didn't want to hear that. "I don't mean to upset him. It's just ... something bad is going to happen, Jerry. I can feel it."

"At the wedding? Your father is paying for security at the wedding, reapers and stuff. You'll be fine."

"I'm not really worried about the wedding," I offered, rubbing my hands over the front of the dress as I stared at my reflection in the mirror. I really did love the design. It was simple and fit my personal style — which was always understated and never overblown — better than every other dress we'd considered. I was a big fan of the dress. Everything else was wearing me down.

"If you're not worried about the wedding, what are you worried about?" Jerry was dramatic and liked to be the center of attention, but he was also a good listener. We were close for a reason, and it wasn't all fun and games when we were growing up. We both felt like outsiders in our own families at times — Jerry because he was gay and, while he accepted it, others didn't. As for me, I was the lone girl in a sea of boys who did not want me to play the same games they were allowed to play — and our bond was something I knew would never break.

"It's my mother. She's evil."

Jerry rolled his eyes. "Not this again. You've been saying that since she got back. She's helped you several times now, Bug. I think you should let it go."

"I can't let it go."

"Why? I mean ... I know she's not the same mother who died eleven years ago, but she's not the evil being you originally thought came back either. Why can't you just take it as a win?"

"Because I can't. That thing is not my mother."

"Why do you keep saying that?"

I had no other option, so I told Jerry about what I'd witnessed at the cemetery the day we ended the storms. It wasn't that I was keeping it from him as much as I was trying to make sense of what I'd seen. Jerry lived with my brother Aidan, and Jerry was affected by the storms to the point he'd punched the man he loved. I knew he wouldn't take the news well.

"Wait a second ... are you saying your mother had a hand in causing those storms?"

I nodded, miserable. "There's no other explanation. She had one of the rounded talismans. She didn't destroy it until after we took everyone else down ... and she didn't toss the disc into the fire until she thought no one was looking."

Jerry was flabbergasted. "But ... why?"

"I don't know. I'm starting to think it's a game with her."

"It has to be something else." He was adamant. "There has to be a reason you're not seeing."

"I've been fixating on it for weeks," I argued. "There's no other reason. She's evil."

"But ... she came back from the dead and was reunited with her family," Jerry argued. "That deserves a happy ending."

"This isn't a movie or a book," I argued, stepping down from the raised platform and moving toward the dressing room. "Not everyone gets a happy ending, Jerry."

"I refuse to believe that. You're going to get a happy ending. I don't care how many monsters I have to kill, I'm going to make sure you get everything you deserve."

"Yeah, well, maybe this is what I deserve." I disappeared into the dressing room and stripped out of the dress, making sure to carefully zip it inside the garment bag before returning to the front of the store.

Jerry stood at the register talking to Marion in a low voice. I forced a smile as I handed him the dress. "Can you please take care of this for me while I finish paying? I know you'll make sure nothing happens to it."

Jerry held my gaze for a long beat. "Yes." He took the dress and gently draped it over his arm. "You're going to be happy, Bug. I promise."

I smiled. I couldn't help myself. "I think I am. The marriage part will be fine. It's the other stuff that's going to come to a head."

"I hope that's not true."

"I guess we'll have to wait and see."

I paid for my dress and bit the inside of my cheek to keep from laughing at the relieved look on Marion's face when I moved to leave the store. Even though my father spent a fortune in the shop, they wouldn't miss me.

I paused by the front door long enough to tuck the receipt in my wallet, and when I raised my eyes I focused on a woman walking past the glass panel. My heart practically stopped when I recognized the woman's face, and I almost stumbled forward I was so surprised.

It was my mother, only not the mother I saw the previous evening.

This was the woman who had left Grimlock Manor late at night to handle an emergency soul extraction and had died in a fire. This was the woman who had raised me, promised I would one day love my brothers even though they were all massive buttheads and listened to my laundry list of grievances whenever I fought with someone during my childhood.

This was the woman who had died eleven years ago ... and somehow she was on the other side of the door.

"Son of a ... !"

Five

I felt as if I was stuck in slow motion, unable to breathe as I watched the woman breeze past the door. I ordered my feet to work, but they didn't immediately acquiesce. By the time my muscles actually snapped to attention, I was already leaning forward and I almost tripped into the glass panel.

"Be careful," Marion warned from behind me.

I ignored her, and with shaking hands, managed to push open the door. My legs felt alien, as if they belonged to someone else, when I hit the sidewalk and turned left to follow the woman. I didn't immediately see her, but that didn't stop me from breaking into a run.

It was a workday, so the sidewalks weren't full of people. I caught a glimpse of a dark head — the one I was certain belonged to my mother — as it disappeared down a side street. I increased my pace and was at a full sprint when I rounded the corner ... and smacked headlong into another woman approaching from the opposite direction.

"Watch where you're going!"

I was so focused on following the woman who looked like my mother I barely glanced at the person I ran into. Unfortunately for me, I happened to recognize her face.

"Angelina?" I pulled up short, my heart hammering.

Angelina Davenport was my high school nemesis. No, true story. She was the Joker to my Batman, and she was as loud and annoying as the super villain.

"Oh, why?" Angelina twisted her face into a scowl as she smoothed her hair. "Can't I have one week when I don't have to interact with you?"

Funnily enough, I felt the same way. Unfortunately for Angelina, I didn't have time to deal with her. "Pretend you didn't see me. We'll both enjoy that." I shifted my eyes to the sidewalk where I'd last seen my mother only to find it empty. In fact, the entire sidewalk — other than Angelina and me — was devoid of bodies. "Ugh. Where did she go?"

Angelina made a big show of looking over her shoulder. "Where did who go? What poor soul are you chasing today?"

I craned my neck to get a better view, but there wasn't so much as a shadow on the sidewalk to indicate where the woman had been. "I'm not chasing anyone," I replied. Explaining what I was doing to Angelina was extremely low on my list of things to do. "Don't worry about it."

"I can't help but worry about it. You're a menace ... and bad things happen when you're around."

"Like what?"

"Like death." Angelina's voice momentarily cracked before she collected herself. "There's a lot of death that happens around you."

She wasn't wrong. In fact, a few weeks ago her mother had died and I was the one who collected her soul. I did it on the sly — we had rings that made us invisible, after all — but I recognized the moment Angelina became aware of my invisible presence as she sat vigil for her dying mother. Angelina was the only one with her mother when the woman slipped away. I waited in the back of the room as the older woman's soul separated from her body and then collected her while Angelina stared forward and pretended she didn't sense me. It wasn't exactly a warm and fuzzy moment, but it was as close to camaraderie as Angelina and I could muster.

"Yes, well, I have a way about me," I sniffed as I straightened my purse. "The funeral was nice."

"Yeah, I was surprised to see you there." Angelina's cheeks were hollow, as if she'd lost too much weight, and her eyes were dark as they snagged with mine. "I sent the invitation so Cillian could attend, not you."

Years before, Angelina and Cillian dated for several months. She'd cheated on him, ending the relationship, but she still held a torch for my scholarly brother.

"I don't think Cillian wants to be in your world," I offered. "He's been pretty clear about that."

"Are you saying you want to be in my world?"

"No." I was firm as I shook my head. "I thought about skipping the funeral, but it didn't seem right after ... well, after the storm incident."

Angelina narrowed her eyes. "Yeah, that was weird."

"I was trying to keep her safe."

Angelina looked away and swallowed hard. "Those storms have been the talk of several news cycles. People believe weird things were happening."

"I think calling what happened with those storms 'weird' is an understatement."

"A lot of folks were talking about how people turned mean and evil if they were caught unaware during the storms," Angelina pressed. "My mother acted exactly the same. She wasn't any different than she normally was."

And that was the only reason I could muster any sympathy for the woman. "Yeah, well, it's over now. You have nothing to worry about."

"I wasn't worried."

"Good."

"Yeah, well ... ." Angelina uncomfortably shifted from one foot to the other. Our conversations usually involved hateful words and rampant name calling. I couldn't remember the last time we talked for this length without the word "slut" being fired like an arrow into the heart. "What are you doing here? This isn't your usual shopping area. I thought I ceded Walmart to you and claimed the good shops for myself."

That was a weak attempt, but it was better than nothing. "I was picking up my wedding dress after my final fitting. You know, because someone actually wants to marry me. I'm sure your pimp won't allow you to get married, right?"

"I heard your father had to pay Griffin to marry you," Angelina countered. "Once he saw you naked he doubled his fee."

That dig was even better. "Yeah? I heard your pimp was making you wear a paper bag over your head so you wouldn't scare away the toothless customers. How is that going? Are you doing better on tips now?"

"And I heard Griffin was considering blinding himself for your wedding night!"

I made a clucking sound with my tongue as I shook my head. "Weak sauce."

"I know." Angelina was clearly disappointed with her effort. "I'll do better next time. I still feel off my game."

"I won't hold it against you."

"You hold everything against me."

"Mostly because you're a total whore and you like things held against you," I shot back.

Angelina's lips curved. "Yeah, things should be back to normal next time we see each other. I'm looking forward to that."

"You and me both."

"Who were you really looking for when you slammed your bovine hips into me while running around the corner?"

"I thought I saw someone."

"Who?"

"Someone I knew a long time ago." Something occurred to me. Angelina knew my mother before she'd died. She would've recognized her if they shared the same sidewalk. "You didn't see anyone you recognized before I accidentally almost tripped over your huge butt, did you?"

"I didn't see anyone."

Hmm. "You didn't see a woman with dark hair, no shopping bags and a black coat?"

"No. It's too hot for a coat. It's summer."

She had a point. That hadn't even occurred to me. "I guess she must have gone in another direction."

"I guess." Angelina gave me a long once over. "You should really try fasting until the big day. Those thick hips of yours are going to look terrible in a wedding dress."

"I'll consider it ... after lunch. I'm meeting my fiancé's mother for lunch, by the way. That's because I have a fiancé and you don't."

"Maybe I don't need a man to complete me," Angelina shot back. "Have you ever considered that?"

"I think you should go with that instinct. It will make ending up a spinster much easier. Although ... you'd make a fantastic cougar. Have you considered being a cougar?"

"Cougars are old women who date younger men."

"I know."

"I'm not old."

"That's not what your mirror told me."

"At least I don't buy my clothes from Hot Topic," Angelina spat, her temper ratcheting up a notch. "Are you going to wear Converse with your dress?"

"I'm considering it."

"Class all the way, I see."

"Oh, like you'd know class," I scoffed.

Angelina's eyes were nothing but glittery slits as she planted her hands on her hips. "I have to be going. I have an appointment. You'll have to schedule a meeting for later if you want to continue this particular argument."

"I'm good."

"So am I."

"Toodles." I offered her a taunting wave before giving the empty sidewalk another cursory glance. There was no sign of my mother, or any other woman, for that matter. I was probably imagining the resemblance anyway. That made the most sense.

Still, I couldn't quite shake the feeling that something important was about to happen.

KATHERINE WAS ALREADY SEATED at the small Mexican restaurant I'd chosen for lunch. She had a huge margarita sitting in front of her and had made her way through half a basket of tortilla chips.

"I'm sorry I'm late."

Katherine shrugged, noncommittal. "It's not the end of the world, although it would've been nice if you'd called to tell me you weren't going to be on time."

I tamped down my irritation at her passive-aggressive response. "I wasn't planning on being late. I ran into someone on the street and I had to insult her."

"You *had* to insult her?"

"Yup. It's part of our thing. We've been off our game since her mother died a couple of weeks ago."

"Oh, that's terrible." Katherine made a sympathetic noise. "I don't understand why you would insult a woman who just lost her mother."

"She's horrible. You don't need to feel sorry for her."

"I don't care if she's horrible. Her mother just died. You of all people should ... ." Katherine caught herself and switched gears. "Your mother was lovely at dinner last night. How are things going?"

I had to give Katherine credit. She absorbed the truth about my family relatively quickly even though she had no idea things like reapers and wraiths existed before a mirror monster jumped through a pool table lamp and tried to kill me. She'd recovered quickly, and that was enough to earn my respect.

"My mother is ... a unique individual," I said finally. "But I don't really want to talk about her. Let's talk about something else."

"Okay. What did you have in mind?"

That was a good question. "Tell me about Clint. He seems like a tool."

Katherine didn't bother to hide her snort. "He's not so bad. He's merely set in his ways."

"He's your father-in-law."

"He is. He was very good when Griffin's father passed. He helped us a lot around the house."

"That doesn't mean he's not a tool."

"I guess," Katherine agreed, grabbing another chip. "A family name is important to some people. You don't get it because you have four brothers to carry on your family name. It's really important to Clint that the Taylor name not die with Griffin."

"I already said that any kids we have will be Taylors."

"Yes, but you not taking the name seems like an insult," Katherine supplied. "Don't take it personally. I'm sure it seems antiquated to you — and Griffin went on a rampage about it last night — but Clint is from an older generation. He's allowed to feel how he feels."

"I get that." Honestly, I did. "I'm not keeping the Grimlock name to be a pain. I'm not doing it because of feminism, either."

"Then why are you doing it?"

"The Grimlock name inspires fear in our enemies, and I would like to cut down on attacks if at all possible."

"Oh." Realization dawned on Katherine's face. "I didn't think about that. It totally makes sense."

I found the irritation I'd been hoarding like a Kardashian does mirror time dissolving quickly now that Katherine saw my side of things. "Now simply isn't the right time to not be a Grimlock."

"Of course not." Katherine patted my hand. "You deal with a lot on a daily basis, and it's not always easy for me to remember that. I'm sorry if you felt pressured."

"It's fine." I waved off her apology with a flick of my wrist. "I'm sure I'll have much worse to deal with before I finally make it down the aisle."

"Yes, well, I'm here to help." Katherine brightened considerably. "Tell me absolutely everything. I want to take some of the burden off of you. Go ahead and load me up with wedding preparations. I'm here to serve."

That was an interesting offer. "Okay, but you asked for it."

THE REMAINDER OF LUNCH was a relaxing affair and Katherine was in good spirits when we parted. Dad sent a car for her, but mine was parked in the side lot, so I waved her off with a promise that we would touch base when I got to Grimlock Manor.

Once she was gone, I let my arm drop and exhaled heavily. Katherine was a nice woman — and I thought she was likely to be a decent mother-in-law — but she was a lot of work sometimes. The last thing I needed right now was more work.

I dragged a hand through my long hair, a tingle pricking along my spine as I sensed a set of eyes on me. I lifted my chin until I found what I was looking for, the woman who looked exactly like my mother. She stood on the opposite side of the street, her gaze trained on me.

I opened my mouth to call out to her, but thought better of it. Drawing attention to myself when I was convinced I was seeing a ghost didn't rank high on the intelligence meter. Instead, I slowly walked along the sidewalk.

Main Street in Royal Oak is too busy to jaywalk, so I had to find a crosswalk if I expected to make my way to her. She didn't move this time, instead staring directly at me, but she didn't look happy as I strode down the sidewalk.

"I'll be over there in a minute," I muttered under my breath as I waited for the light to turn. "Then I'll find out who you are. I'll shake the answers out of you if it's necessary. And why am I talking to myself? Only crazy people talk to themselves. Am I suddenly crazy? If so, I blame you, lady. This is your fault."

It took forever for the light to turn, and when it did I immediately moved to step off the curb. At that exact moment the woman started waving wildly, as if warning me not to step into the street. It took me a full beat to realize she was gesturing toward something behind me, not the crosswalk.

I swiveled quickly, my instincts taking over, and managed to avoid a white hand as it jutted out of the small opening between businesses. It wasn't an alley — not really, anyway — but there was enough space for one person to fit comfortably.

Even though I was stunned by what happened, I recognized two things at an initial glance. The first was that the being in the opening was a wraith, not a human. The second was that it was holding what looked to be an ornate dagger in its ghoulish hand.

I reacted out of instinct. This wasn't my first time facing off with a wraith. I knew how to kill them, and I'd taken to carrying a silver letter opener in my pocket just to be on the safe side. I drew the weapon now, casting a cautious look to the left and right. There were people on the sidewalks, but none of them were looking in my direction.

I had one chance to strike.

I ducked under the wraith's arm when it lashed out and tried to slice me with the dagger, using my elbow to slap the weapon out of its hand while simultaneously jabbing my letter opener in the creature's chest. I aimed for its heart — even though I wasn't certain it had a heart — and drew back the letter opener quickly.

The wraith, as was their way, turned to flaking ash the second I stabbed it. By the time the dagger hit the ground, all that was left was a pile of dust that would blow away the moment a strong breeze hit the narrow opening.

I bent over to pick up the dagger. It looked important, runes and carvings decorating the blade. I shoved it in the front of my hoodie to hide it before zipping, and then turned to face my mother.

It shouldn't have surprised me — part of me thought I was imagining her, after all — but the spot where she'd previously stood was empty. She was gone – again – and I had no idea what to make of any of this.

"This day just sucks," I grumbled under my breath, shaking my head. "I should've stayed in bed with Griffin."

Six

I headed straight to Grimlock Manor.

I wasn't worked up over my fight with the wraith. Sadly, those had become commonplace. Seeing a vision of my mother right before the creature attacked was another story. I was downright unnerved by that.

The house bustled with activity. One of Griffin's cousins — I think his name was Ted, but I'd met so many people the night before their names blurred — laughed like a loon when he hit the stairs in the foyer, my brother Redmond close on his tail. Redmond slowed his pace long enough to look me up and down.

I pasted a bright smile on my face, but it was for Griffin's relatives. I didn't want to melt down in front of them because talking about wraiths seemed like a surefire way for Clint to suggest locking me up.

"What's up, kid?" As the oldest, Redmond was often my rock. He spoiled me rotten when I was a kid. Also, he didn't care that he was older than the boys my age. He beat them up whenever someone broke my heart during my tumultuous teenage years. Sometimes I thought he could read me best.

"Nothing." I hoped my smile came off as pleasant rather than deranged. "What's going on here?"

"We're organizing a pool tournament upstairs. Do you want to join us? You can be on my team."

My brothers were sharks when it came to games and gambling, so I fixed Redmond with a dark look. "Don't take money from Griffin's relatives."

"That wasn't on the list of rules you passed around before they arrived."

"Yes, well, I'm adding it now." I rolled my neck until it cracked. When I pulled my chin up, that allowed Redmond to see the tip of the dagger I stashed in my hoodie poking out. I covered it quickly, but not fast enough.

"What's that?"

I slapped Redmond's hand away when he reached for the dagger. "Don't even think about it. Go upstairs and play pool ... but don't bet on the games. That's just begging for trouble."

"If we don't bet on the games there's no reason to play."

"Grimlock pride."

Redmond snorted. "Whatever. This family has no pride. Trust me." He glanced over his shoulder to confirm that Ted had disappeared before lowering his voice and leaning closer. "Did something happen?"

That was a loaded question. "I ran into a wraith downtown."

"Are you okay?"

"I'm fine. It happened fast. I killed it with the letter opener I've been carrying."

Redmond cocked an eyebrow, his expression hovering between concerned and amused. "You've been traveling with a letter opener? Since when?"

"Since I figured out that Griffin would worry himself sick if he found out I was carrying around a knife," I answered. "I'm fine. It was carrying this dagger. I'm taking it to Cillian. There are weird runes and symbols on it."

Redmond dragged a hand through his dark hair, his expression grim. "Do you think we're about to be attacked ... again?"

That was the question of the day. "I hope not. That's why I want Cillian to look at the dagger."

"Well ... be careful. The house is full of Taylors."

"How is that going?" I was concerned. My family is an acquired taste, and very few people want to go through the trouble of adjusting their palates. "You guys aren't being jerks, are you?"

Redmond shrugged, noncommittal. "No more than usual. Things are fine. They're nice people and they seem excited to stay in a castle. That's what they keep calling the house."

"Well, this might come as a bit of a surprise, but it's big enough to be a castle," I pointed out. "Not everyone grew up in a house big enough to have its own ZIP code."

"Fair enough." Redmond held up his hands in capitulation. He tried for a smile, but it didn't make it all the way to his eyes. "You're pale, kid. Are you sure you're okay?"

"I'm fine." I couldn't tell him about seeing Mom. He'd think I was crazy. Er, well, crazier than usual. "It happened fast and took me by surprise. I'm sure I'll be fine once I have a drink."

"Okay. Cillian is in Dad's office. Make sure you close the door before whipping out that dagger. The Taylors have been warned about going into the office. They're appropriately fearful."

"Good to know."

DAD WAS FOCUSED ON his computer when I let myself into his office without knocking. He glanced up, shaking his head when he realized it was me.

"There's a rule in the house while we have so many visitors," he intoned. "You have to knock before entering my private space."

"I'll keep that in mind when I'm hanging around your bathroom," I said dryly, flicking my eyes to Cillian sitting on the couch. "Why are you guys are holed up here?"

"Paperwork," Cillian answered simply.

"I'm doing paperwork," Dad corrected. "Your brother is hiding from Clint."

"Eastwood or Taylor?"

"I think they share the same attitude." Dad smirked when Cillian uncomfortably shifted on the couch. "Clint has been asking your brother about his intentions regarding Maya. It hasn't been going well."

"At least it's not just me." I unzipped my hoodie and removed the dagger. "I hate to add to our already full plate, but a wraith attacked me in downtown Royal Oak about an hour ago and it was carrying this." I dropped the dagger on the desk and took a step back. I had a knack for drama, and it was on full display.

"What?" Dad hopped to his feet as Cillian scrambled off the couch. "Are you okay?"

"I'm fine. I managed to deflect him. I was carrying a silver letter opener in my pocket. I stabbed him in the heart. No muss, no fuss. He left this behind."

"It looks old," Cillian noted as he grabbed the dagger before Dad had a chance to study it. "Like ... really old."

"Is that your professional opinion?"

"Yes." Cillian made an exaggerated face as he poked my side. "You're really pale. Are you sure the wraith didn't touch you?"

Because I'm a reaper, wraiths have a unique ability to suck the life out of me should they get their gross and disgusting hands on any part of my skin. I know what it feels like because I'd fallen prey to the ability before. That wasn't my problem today. "He didn't touch me. He just surprised me."

"How did it happen?" Dad was calm as he pressed his hand to my forehead. "You're not warm."

"Wraiths don't give reapers fevers."

"No, but if you get sick because of being drained, a fever is one of the first signs," Dad countered. "Sit down." He moved to the small refrigerator behind his desk and took a bottle of water from inside. "Drink this."

"I was hoping for something heavier," I supplied.

"You didn't even drink the whiskey Griffin poured for you last night," Dad argued. "You took two sips and then abandoned it. That leads me to believe you weren't feeling well then either."

Was that true? "I wasn't sick," I said hurriedly. "I was a little nervous about how our family would get along with Griffin's family —

and hoping Mom wouldn't eat any of them if she was feeling peckish — but I wasn't sick."

Dad didn't look convinced. "I think you've got a lot on your mind right now." He chose his words carefully. "You're getting married and you have a lot of people you don't know very well hanging around. Anyone would feel overwhelmed."

"I'm not overwhelmed!" I'm just seeing the mother who died eleven years ago hanging around downtown Royal Oak. That's different. I didn't say that, of course, but I wanted to. Instead, I rubbed my forehead. "I'm just tired."

"Then drink your water." Dad exchanged a weighted look with Cillian that wasn't lost on me. "Tell me about your run-in with the wraith. What happened?"

"I was leaving that Mexican restaurant on Main Street," I replied, cracking the seal on the water bottle and taking a long drink before continuing. "Katherine was already gone thanks to the car you sent. That worked out well today, by the way, so thanks."

"I don't want anyone getting stranded in an area they don't know," Dad said as he leaned a hip against his desk and crossed his arms. "Plus, I hired reapers to moonlight as drivers in case of an attack."

"I didn't know that." Cillian's surprise was evident. "That was smart."

"Everything I do is smart."

"Everything he does is humble, too," I teased.

Dad fixed me with a serious look. "Finish your story."

"There's not much to tell. I left the restaurant and was heading down the sidewalk. I stopped at the crosswalk and waited, and the second the light turned so I could start walking I heard something behind me."

That was an outright lie. The only reason I turned was because the woman across the way furiously gestured for me to do so. I couldn't tell Dad and Cillian, though. They wouldn't understand. Okay, Dad might understand — and I actually wanted to own up to everything for his benefit — but I didn't want Cillian to be part of the mix. He would tell our brothers and then it would turn into a big thing.

"And it was a wraith?" Cillian asked.

I nodded. "There was a gap between two buildings. Not a big one, but large enough so a wraith could stay out of sight. I saw the dagger moving, so I reacted out of instinct and stabbed it with a letter opener. Within a few seconds, all that was left was the dagger. I figured I should bring it to you guys."

"Definitely." Dad flicked his eyes to the item in question. "Any ideas, Cillian?"

"None so far, but I can conduct some research." Cillian looked happy at the prospect. "I need to sneak this up to my bedroom. I don't want any of the Taylors to see it."

"No, it won't be easy to explain," I agreed.

"Except they think we deal in antiques," Dad pointed out. "You could simply say it's an item we're considering for auction. Whatever happens, though, don't let them touch it. If Redmond and Braden's incessant need to turn everything involving the Taylors into a competition is any indication, someone might lose fingers if we're not careful."

"Good point." Cillian's grin was wide as he moved toward the door. "I'm going to scan the carvings into my computer and let the search run through dinner. If we get lucky we might stumble across some answers before the end of the night."

"I can't remember when we last got that lucky," I said.

"I can." Dad's gaze snagged with mine. "I believe it was a few weeks ago when a magical storm hit while you were alone with Griffin and he didn't attack you."

"That wasn't luck," Cillian countered. "That was love."

"And on that note ... ." Dad pointed toward the door. "I can take only so much schmaltz, Cillian. Be careful with that dagger and take it directly to your room."

"Yeah, yeah." Cillian rolled his eyes before disappearing through the door.

Dad made sure it was shut tight before returning to his desk chair and sitting. "Your brother is right. You're exceedingly pale. If I didn't know better I'd think you're sick. Do you want to tell me what's going on?"

I hated the way he regarded me, as if he was readying himself to start yelling even though he had no idea if I'd done anything to warrant a lecture. "What makes you think something is going on?" I decided to buy time before answering. I had an opening where it was just him and me. I didn't know if I would get another chance to tell him what really happened. Now that I had an opportunity I was nervous.

"Aisling, you know I love you, right?"

The conversational shift threw me. "Of course."

"Good, because I do. I love you, kid."

"I love you, too."

"You're full of crap, though," Dad snapped, causing my eyebrows to fly up my forehead. "You're hiding something. Don't bother denying it. I can see it. Tell me."

I didn't have a choice. Or, maybe I simply didn't want a choice. I was an adult. I was getting married in a few days, for crying out loud. I still wanted my daddy to fix my life. "I saw Mom."

"You saw your mother with the wraith?" Dad's face flushed with anger as he straightened his shoulders.

I shook my head. "Not like that. I saw Mom, as she used to look, right before it happened."

Obviously confused, Dad tilted his head to the side. "I need more information."

I didn't blame him. "I saw her twice today." I told him about the initial sighting at the bridal boutique, wringing my hands the entire time as I tried to calm myself.

"You probably saw someone who looked like her," Dad countered.

"No, it was too exact." I told him the rest, including my run-in with Angelina because it somehow steadied me, and when I was done, he didn't look happy. "It was her. I swear it looked exactly like her."

Dad opened his mouth, but no sound came out.

"You think I'm crazy, don't you?"

"No." Dad's answer came fast and hard. "I don't think you're crazy. I think you're under an unbelievable amount of stress."

"So ... you think I imagined her."

"I think you saw a dark-haired woman who reminded you of your mother and your mind filled in the gaps," Dad clarified. "I don't think you're crazy. Not even a little. I do think you thought you saw something that you didn't."

"I can accept that answer for the first time. I chased her down the street, although I'm not really sure it was her. She would've passed Angelina, but she said she didn't see anything. But the second time she was looking right at me."

"A woman was looking at you," Dad corrected. "A woman you thought resembled your mother."

"She warned me about the wraith," I persisted. "She motioned for me to turn at the exact right time."

"How can you be sure what she was motioning toward?" Dad challenged. "You said yourself that the area was dark. How could she see the wraith?"

"I don't know."

"Aisling, it's all right." Dad grabbed my hand and gave it a hard squeeze. "You're going through a lot right now. You're getting married, and I'm guessing you and your mother planned out a lot of things before ... well, before everything happened."

"You mean before she came back from the dead and started eating people to stay alive?"

Dad shot me a look straight out of my childhood. It was almost enough to make me laugh. If my nerves hadn't already been shot I would've given in to the chuckle.

"Before she ... returned," Dad stressed. "She's not your mother, at least not in the way we all want her to be. Part of her is still in there. I see it from time to time."

"So ... you think I imagined all of it."

"I think you saw someone who looked like your mother because you've been spending a lot of time wishing you had that mother back the past few weeks," Dad replied. "I think that's normal. Do I think that woman saw the wraith behind you? Maybe. Perhaps she only saw a shadow and thought it was a mugger and was trying to warn you."

It was plausible, but I wasn't certain I could buy it. "I guess."

"I think you need some rest, kid." Dad rested his hands on my shoulders and forced me to look up. "You need to calm yourself, maybe take a bath and go to bed early with a good book and some pizza."

I rolled my eyes. "How is that going to work with all of Griffin's relatives in town?"

"They're staying here. You don't have to entertain them. Why do you think I had so many kids? And why do you think I allow three of them to stay here without paying rent? Entertaining the Taylors falls under Redmond, Cillian and Braden's job descriptions."

I pursed my lips, amused despite myself. "You're probably right."

"I am right."

"I just want to point out, so it's on record and everything, that you thought I was nuts when I told you about the zombies, too," I noted. "Who was right then?"

Dad let loose one of those sighs only a father can muster. "I will lodge your complaint on record and revisit it if you turn out to be right again."

"Good deal." I downed the rest of my water. "What's for dinner tonight? I'm officially starving."

"Only you could think about food after what you just told me."

"It's a gift."

"It's ... something."

Seven

I took my father's advice and went upstairs to take a bath in my old room, the huge ceramic tub beckoning me. I stripped out of my clothes as I crossed the room, filled the tub with steaming water and bath salts, and climbed in to close my eyes for a bit.

I wanted to push thoughts of my mother out of my head. I mean ... the mother I saw on the street. Okay, I wanted to push the mother I was forced to contend with in real life out of my head, too. It was the woman on the streets giving me fits, though.

No matter what my father said, I couldn't refrain from wondering if I was losing my mind. It couldn't be normal to see a woman who had died eleven years ago on the street at every turn. It was craziness. Like a Kardashian when she sees a camera and it's not pointed at her craziness.

Griffin found me in the tub when he entered the house thirty minutes later. I was readying myself to get out when he shook his head and started adding more warm water. "Not yet. I need twenty minutes in there, too."

"I'm already a wrinkled prune."

"I like you that way."

I watched with a bit of amusement as he speedily stripped out of his clothes and climbed into the tub with me, pushing me forward so he could get comfortable behind me. Steam hung in the bathroom like a damp curtain when he was done adding water, and the feeling of his hands on my back was calming enough that I was almost lulled into a nap.

Then he spoke.

"Why did your father meet me at the front door and suggest I needed to come up here and make you feel better?"

My eyes sprang open as I internally cursed my father. "He's a worrywart. You know that."

"Why really?"

Son of a Grimlock! I was going to make him pay. "It's nothing."

"It's something and we both know it. I'm going to melt down if you don't tell me."

I had no doubt about that. "I had an incident with a wraith today." That wasn't a lie, but it was hardly the thing my father worried about most.

"Are you all right?" Griffin leaned over my shoulder so his eyes could roam my body. "Are you bruised anywhere?"

"It happened fast," I assured him. "I was leaving the restaurant where I had lunch with your mother and it was there, waiting. I took it out really fast. It never touched me. It was carrying a dagger, so I brought it home for Cillian. It wasn't a big deal."

"I think it's a big deal any time you get attacked by a creature that can kill you."

"Yeah, well ... I'm okay."

Griffin brushed his lips against my shoulder as he wrapped his arms around me. "From your father's reaction I thought for sure you were hurt. I practically ran up the stairs. My grandfather was waiting to talk to me, but I ignored him, so we have that to look forward to tonight."

I smiled. "Your grandfather is wacky enough to fit in with this family."

"He's set in his ways," Griffin clarified. "Your family knows all about that." He poked my side and caused me to squirm. "You especially know all about that."

"I'm not set in my ways."

"You're the worst." Griffin's hands were gentle as they stroked my stomach. "I was worried when I saw your father's face. I'm glad you're okay."

"That makes two of us."

"I bet I'm more glad than you."

"It's not a competition."

"I thought everything in the Grimlock world was a competition."

He had a point. "We'll call it a tie."

"Fair enough."

GRIFFIN AND I REMAINED holed up in my room until dinner was ready. By the time we descended the stairs I'd changed my clothes and taken a nap. The sleep did me good. I was well rested and raring to go when we hit the parlor.

"There you are." Mom practically pounced when she saw me, grabbing my arm and tugging me across the room before I had a chance to greet anyone. "I have a present for you."

"It had better not be a body part in a box," I grumbled under my breath. "I've seen that movie and it never ends well."

Mom ignored my sarcastic tongue. "This is Annabelle Blythe."

A smartly-dressed woman in a pantsuit sat in the chair between Redmond and Braden. She looked to be in her late twenties, with shiny black hair and big brown eyes. She was pretty, and clearly thrilled to have my brothers throwing themselves at her. She barely looked up when Mom stepped in front of her.

"She's my present?" I couldn't help being disappointed. "If you're going to gift me with a human, go with a hot dude who will massage me all the time."

"You already have that," Griffin pointed out as he walked to the drink cart where Aidan was mixing cocktails. "Baby, what do you want to drink?"

"Just iced tea."

Griffin stilled, his eyebrows drawing together as he slowly lasered his eyes. "You don't want alcohol?"

He made me sound like a lush. "My stomach is still mildly upset."

That was true. More importantly, though, I wanted to keep a clear head while my mother was in the house. It seemed silly on the surface, but I couldn't shake the idea. "I'll have something to drink when it settles."

"Are you sure you're all right?" Dad ignored the awkward stares he earned when he leaned forward and pressed his hand to my forehead. "You're not warm, but you've been off all afternoon."

"She was fine at lunch," Katherine interjected from behind me. I had no idea when she'd entered the room, but clearly my spatial awareness was off. "She ate a full meal, an appetizer and a bunch of chips and salsa ... although she made a big stink about being allergic to avocados so she couldn't have guacamole. Did you accidentally eat some guacamole?"

"Since when are you allergic to avocados?" Mom asked.

"She's not allergic," Dad countered. "She just tells people that because she hates guacamole and most Mexican restaurants don't listen when she says she doesn't want it on her plate."

He knew me too well.

"Ah. That makes sense." Mom pressed her hand to my cheek. "Your father is right. You don't feel warm."

"I'm not sick." I slapped their hands away, my temper getting the better of me. "You don't have to worry about me being sick because it's not going to happen."

Dad looked dubious. "You were pale when you got back to the house and now you're not drinking. If those aren't signs of illness ... ."

"Tell me about my gift." I gestured toward Annabelle, who was busy blushing furiously as Redmond whispered something in her ear. "Knock that off." I kicked my brother's shin, causing him to yelp. "She's supposed to be my gift, not your gift."

"I think she's a gift for us all," Braden drawled, winking.

"And I think you guys are pigs. I still don't understand what I'm supposed to do with her." I flicked my eyes to Mom, suddenly suspicious. "She's not really a gift for Griffin, is she? If you're pulling your crap from a few weeks ago I'll beat the snot out of you."

The Taylors congregated in the room sucked in huge mouthfuls of oxygen. They weren't used to children talking to parents that way. I didn't care. I knew what my mother was capable of. She kept trying to separate me from Griffin, and she wasn't above hiring a professional to make sure it really happened. She was running out of time and it would be just like her to track down a high-priced prostitute.

"I most certainly did not buy her for Griffin," Mom snapped.

"Wait ... what did she say?" Annabelle jerked her attention from Braden long enough to focus on me. "Did she just say what I think she said?"

"She didn't say anything," Mom countered. "You imagined it. Look over there. Braden has his hand on your thigh. Focus on that."

"Yes, focus on that," I drawled, shaking my head. "Why would you possibly get me a gift that's meant to entertain my brothers? That's, like, the worst gift ever."

Dad chuckled as he leaned back in his chair. "I told you she wouldn't like it, Lily. You should have listened to me, but no. You knew better."

"She doesn't even know what the gift is," Mom countered. "She can't dislike it until she knows what it is."

"Then tell her what it is," Griffin suggested as he returned to my side.

I wordlessly took the iced tea he offered and downed half the glass, rolling my eyes when he made a face. "That game we played upstairs dehydrated me."

"Drink up, baby." Griffin ran his hand over my back as he regarded Annabelle. "Seriously, who is this?"

"She's your new wedding coordinator." Mom looked so happy with herself I was surprised she didn't sprout wings and float toward the ceiling with her halo on full display. "She's here to help with the wedding."

I rubbed my forehead and focused on my father. "I don't know what that means."

"Think of her as an assistant," Dad offered. "She'll handle the seating chart, food, music, ice sculptures, traffic to and from the church, bartenders and the like. That will free you up to do whatever you want ... including rest."

Griffin brightened considerably. "That is a great idea."

Mom preened. "I thought so."

"I'm on the fence," Dad countered. "Aisling isn't good at ceding control."

He was right. I hated it when anyone had control over me. Because I was more excited about the marriage than the wedding, though, I liked the idea of a wedding coordinator ... especially because I knew exactly who to put in charge of her.

"You're right about me having control issues," I offered. "I do. It's terrible ... but I do. There's no getting around that."

Dad narrowed his eyes, suspicious. "Uh-huh."

"I think having a wedding coordinator is a great idea," I added. "It'll free me up to focus on ... um, bride stuff. Also, it'll give Jerry a little thrill when I put him in charge of Annabelle."

Dad snickered as Mom's smile diminished.

"I think that's a fabulous idea," Dad noted. "Maybe you can even put in a caveat that your brothers are not allowed to participate in wedding tasks."

"Oh, come on," Braden complained, his lavender eyes flashing. "This is a wedding. It's supposed to be fun for everyone."

"Everyone but you," I sneered.

Braden ignored me and focused on Dad. "Why are you trying to ruin my fun?"

"It's one of my little pleasures," Dad replied, unruffled. "As for you, Aisling, I think putting Jerry and Annabelle together will ease much of your burden ... and you need that."

I didn't touch on his worry, instead finishing my iced tea. That allowed Mom to give her opinion.

"Why would you have Annabelle work with Jerry instead of you? That's not why I hired her."

"Yes, but Jerry is in charge," I said. "He's been in charge for weeks. I stopped being in charge when he got that little headset thing and ordered special software so he could be more organized. He'll handle Annabelle's duties."

"But ... ."

I ignored her and grinned at Annabelle. "I can't wait until you meet Jerry. You two are going to have loads of fun."

DAD WENT SIMPLE FOR dinner. Steak, vegetables, potatoes and cake for dessert. The Taylors "oohed" and "aahed" appropriately and the members of my family wolfed down their food as if they hadn't eaten in days.

I excused myself from the table long enough to wander into the kitchen when I was half done with my meal. I had a hankering for capers and wanted to add them to my mashed potatoes. I found what I was looking for and closed the refrigerator door, a hint of movement catching my attention through the big window over the sink. It looked out on the backyard, and I recognized the creature sitting in the middle of the landscaped space right away.

"Oh, good grief."

Even though I wasn't keen to talk to the little scamp, I forced myself through the back door and scuffed my feet against the ground until I was directly in front of the taciturn gargoyle I'd grown to know and ... well, tolerate.

"Bub."

"Female Grimlock," he acknowledged, bobbing his head.

I scowled, frustrations bubbling up. "I have a name."

"There are too many of you. I can't keep your names straight."

I knew that wasn't true. "What are you doing here? Are you looking for my mother?" I could never decide if Bub was working for my mother or simply tolerating her existence. In a weird way, I trusted him more than her ... but that wasn't saying much. It didn't help matters that he looked like a strange rubber animal mutation. A dog-owl with attitude, if you will.

"I was merely out for a walk," Bub countered, his eyes busy as they tracked to the window. "You have a lot of people inside."

I furrowed my brow. "How do you know that?"

"It's hardly a secret," Bub scoffed. "People have been watching the house for days. Your upcoming nuptials are the talk of the town."

"I'm guessing that's only in certain circles."

"Fair enough." Bub shifted from one foot to the other, his tail lashing back and forth to indicate his mood. There was a time I thought that tail was something else, so I had trouble focusing on it without picturing something pornographic. "Everyone knows you're entertaining guests right now, that your focus is split and you're distracted."

"I'm not sure what I'm supposed to say to that," I said, confused. "You can tell your friends that my focus isn't split, though. In fact, I have a shiny new gift that allows my focus to be more ... um, well, focused ... than ever. How does that sound?"

"Confusing," Bub replied. "Having a new gift doesn't mean that you won't be distracted from what's going on."

"And what's going on?"

"Big things."

The creature was always cryptic, but his answer this time set my teeth on edge. "Do you want to be more specific than that?"

"I can't." Bub was matter-of-fact. "I don't know all the specifics. Even if I did, I couldn't tell you. That's not how the game is played."

My frustration bubbled up and threatened to take over. "What game are you playing? I often think it's different from the one I'm playing. It's like you're playing Risk while I'm stuck with Monopoly."

"The stakes are much bigger than that."

"Oh, geez." I slapped my hand to my forehead. "I don't understand what you're trying to tell me. For once, can't you just tell me the information and we'll pretend I figured it out on my own?"

"No."

"Then why are you even here? I already know things are weird. I figured it out myself. I didn't need to find you skulking around my backyard to give me a heads-up."

"I'm here because I need to make sure you grasp the big picture," Bub replied. "A war is coming. It's not a little fight or skirmish, which is what you've faced so far. It's a war."

"Oh, you're so freaking dramatic," I complained, rubbing the back of my neck. "My father thinks I'm dramatic, but you really take the cake. Wait ... do you eat cake? I'm guessing you eat grubs and worms and stuff, right?"

Bub was obviously offended. "I don't eat worms."

"Don't take that tone with me. How was I supposed to know?"

"Do you eat worms?"

"Dad made me eat escargot once. It was like worms."

"Escargot is delicious. You're simply ridiculous when it comes to food."

"Whatever." I cracked my knuckles as I regarded him. "Are you going to give me another hint? I mean, telling me a big battle is coming is fun and everything, but I need more information if I expect my brothers to stop fighting over the new wedding coordinator and focus on me."

"I can't tell you what's to come," Bub said simply. "It's not set in stone, though I have a feeling I know how things will go. You must stay alert and ... listen to your heart instead of your head for a change. In this one instance — and only this one — it won't lead you astray."

I wasn't sure if that was a dig at Griffin, but I opted to ignore it. "Does this have something to do with the wraith that attacked this afternoon?"

"I don't know anything about that," Bub replied. "All I know is that things are about to shift, and you have to be ready for it."

"I'm always ready."

Bub snorted. "You might want to run some drills or something, because you've never faced anything like this."

"I'll keep that in mind."

Eight

G riffin decided to drink with my brothers, so we spent the night at Grimlock Manor. Somehow, given Bub's vague words, it seemed safer. I kept his warning to myself. Once the booze started flowing, I figured it was a bad idea to attempt a serious conversation.

Griffin woke with a groan, his hand immediately going to his face as he rubbed the sleep from his eyes. "Ugh. I feel as if I've been run over by a tractor-trailer."

I'd been expecting that, so I'd collected bottles of water and aspirin before retiring. "Take this."

Griffin downed the aspirin and a full bottle of water before turning his attention to me. His hair was a mess, his eyes heavy, and he seemed confused. "Why aren't you hungover?"

"Because I didn't drink."

"You didn't?" Griffin screwed up his face in concentration. "I could've sworn you were drinking with us."

"No. I watched you play pool with my brothers and your cousins. That chest-thumping thing you did when your team won was particularly sexy. It made me fall in love with you all over again."

Griffin turned sheepish. "I'm sorry about that. At least I think I'm sorry about that. It's kind of a blur."

"You don't have to be sorry. You beat Redmond and Braden. They didn't take it well."

"Grimlocks are poor losers."

"I take offense to that."

"It's the truth." Griffin grabbed my hand and flipped it over so he could stare at my palm. "You really didn't drink?"

"I wasn't in the mood."

"Why?"

I shrugged. There was no easy answer to that. "I don't know. I just wasn't."

"Are you feeling okay?" His hand was on my forehead before I could slap it away.

"I wish people would stop asking me that. I'm not sick."

"You're not warm," Griffin supplied. "That's something, I guess. Why did we stay here if you were capable of driving us home?"

"Because I can't drive two vehicles and Dad promised an omelet bar this morning. Apparently it's going to be just us because your family is going to the Henry Ford Museum."

"I vaguely remember talk of that," Griffin acknowledged. "I know it sounds selfish, but I'm actually glad it will be just us for breakfast."

"Yeah. It will be quieter."

"And you'll have a chance to tell everyone what's bugging you."

I stilled, thankful my gaze was already on the wall so I wouldn't have to see what I was sure amounted to fear in Griffin's eyes. "Why do you think something is bugging me?"

"Because I've met you."

"But ... ."

"Please don't. I know you're hiding something."

I found the courage to shift my head and stare at him. "I saw my mother yesterday." I blurted out the words without thinking better of it. "She was on the street when the wraith attacked."

Griffin bolted to a sitting position, his hangover forgotten. "Your mother was there when you were attacked? Did she try to help?"

"The thing is ... it wasn't my mother. Er, well, not the mother you've met. It was my other mother."

Griffin pressed the heel of his hand to his forehead. "I'm going to need you to explain that in more detail."

That's what I did. I told him the story, from the beginning, and waited for him to react. When I was done, he seemed more confused than curious. "I'm not sure I understand."

"My father thinks I'm imagining it. He called it stress, but I can tell he thinks I'm losing my mind."

Griffin gently moved his thumb over my cheek, considering. "What do you think?" he asked finally. I could tell he was struggling with the appropriate response.

"I don't know. I think there's a chance I'm losing my mind."

Instead of reacting with sympathy and fear, Griffin chuckled.

"It's not funny!" I slapped his leg. "We're supposed to be getting married in a few days. Heck, I only have two days left of work. You won't think it's funny if you go on that surprise honeymoon my father has waiting for us with a crazy person."

Griffin caught my hand before I could slap him a second time. "You're not going crazy."

"I'm seeing a woman who died eleven years ago."

"True, but you don't know why you're seeing her," Griffin countered, his tone soothing. "The thing is, I happen to cross a lot of people struggling with sanity in my line of work. You're not supposed to say 'crazy,' by the way. That's considered rude."

"Oh, well, good. I just love a manners diatribe first thing in the morning."

Griffin poked the lower lip I jutted out and grinned. "Those struggling with sanity don't know it's happening. They think they're perfectly sane. If you think you might be losing it, that means you're not."

"Is that your professional opinion, Doctor?"

"That's a game we haven't played in a while." Griffin's smile widened. "Do you want to be my naughty nurse?"

"I'm serious!"

"Okay." Griffin held up his hands in mock surrender as I turned shrill. "Baby, you need to calm down. I was kidding."

"I'm not. I saw my dead mother."

"Not your dead mother," Griffin stressed. "You saw someone who looked like the mother you remember, which I think is totally normal given the circumstances."

"And what circumstances are those?"

"You're getting married." His voice softened as he stroked his hand over my leg. "You're getting married and you want your mother. You know the woman who came back isn't the same person and you can't help being bitter about it. It's okay to want her. I only wish I would've realized that's what was going on a few days ago. It would've saved me some worry."

My eyes burned at his earnest response. "She warned me about the wraith. How would a strange woman who just happened to look like my mother know to do that?"

"I think your mind works at a fantastic rate." Griffin chose his words carefully. "I think somehow you registered the danger behind you, so you assumed the woman was warning you when it simply might have been something else."

"Like what?"

"Like maybe she was waving at someone else on the sidewalk and you assumed she was gesturing at you."

Was that possible? It didn't seem likely. "I don't know." I chewed my bottom lip. "I swear it looked exactly like her ... and I saw her twice. That seems too weird to be random."

"You saw the same woman twice in Royal Oak," Griffin clarified. "There's a lot of foot traffic on the street, shopping. You were on the main drag the entire time. I don't think that's out of the realm of possibility."

Well, when he said it like that. "It's just ... if you asked me to swear in a court of law that it was her, I would've had to do it. It looked just like her."

"I know." Griffin wrapped his arms around me and tugged until I was on his lap, swaying back and forth as he pressed kisses to my neck. If he was suffering from a hangover, he was doing a good job of hiding it while focusing on me. "I'm sorry. I wish you could have the mother you want."

"You don't have your father," I pointed out. "That has to be hard for you."

"It is, but I have my grandfather. And, well, you might not want to hear it, but I kind of think of your father as a surrogate father now. He'll be there."

I was dumbfounded. "You think of my father as your father?"

"A surrogate father."

"That means you think of me as a sister."

"Not even close." Griffin tickled my ribs, causing me to gasp as I choked on a laugh. "I simply feel close to him. I don't think that's a bad thing."

"Definitely not," I agreed when I managed to breathe again. "It's kind of nice."

"Especially after he threatened to kill me the first time we met."

"He'll threaten you again before the wedding. He'll pull you aside and make a big speech about how if you hurt me he'll kill you. You know that's coming, right?"

"I do." Griffin nodded his head. "I also know I'm fine with it because I would cut off my own arm rather than hurt you."

"That's sweet ... and kind of gross."

"It's true." Griffin slipped a strand of hair behind my ear and smiled. "In a few days the wedding will be over, but we'll have a marriage to contend with. You have no idea how much I'm looking forward to that."

He wasn't the only one. Still, Bub's words burned in the back of my brain. "There's something else I have to tell you. We should move the conversation into the shower so we're not late for breakfast, though. I need to tell my father what happened last night. He's going to be furious."

"Something tells me I'll be furious, too."

"You can't be furious. I would've told you last night but you were drinking with my brothers and there were witnesses all over the house. That's not on me."

"Fair enough."

This time the smile I mustered was legitimate. "I can rarely say something isn't my fault and mean it. Is it wrong that I'm excited about that?"

"No." He gave me a soft kiss and pointed me toward the shower. "Come on. You can't drop a bomb like that and leave it hanging. I need to know what's going on. And for the record, I would appreciate it if you didn't keep secrets any longer. We agreed to share everything. That's why we're getting married."

"Even if I think I'm going crazy?"

"Especially if you think that."

"Huh. You learn something new every day."

"WAIT ... WHAT?"

Dad practically jumped out of his chair when I related my conversation with Bub in the backyard the previous evening. I waited until I had my omelet, hash browns, tomato juice and what looked to be a fresh doughnut on my plate before launching into the story.

I swallowed the huge mouthful of food I was chewing before responding. "I already told you the entire story. It's not going to change. Bub didn't give me any actionable information."

Thankfully Griffin's family was already up and out of the house. Even though Grimlock Manor boasted almost sixty rooms (including bathrooms and storage closets), my father's voice tends to carry. They would've come running if they heard the verbal explosion in the dining room.

"Why didn't you tell anyone?" Aidan asked, splitting a doughnut in half so he could share with Jerry. My best friend believed carbs didn't stick to his hips if Aidan was the one to share food items with him. "We could've gotten more information if you'd told us right away."

"First, you guys started drinking two hours before dinner yesterday," I reminded him. "Second, he wasn't going to wait around and let you nab him. He was waiting to talk to me. He took off when he was done."

"Bub always seems to be waiting for you," Cillian noted as he forked part of his omelet onto a slice of toast. "He tries to avoid the rest of us like the plague."

"I've seen him," Aidan argued.

"Me, too," Jerry echoed. "I was there the first night he appeared, in case you've forgotten."

"Bub only approached that night because it was necessary," I argued. "He was trying to talk to me and I was attacked. He helped and interacted with you guys because he had no choice."

"That's true." Griffin was thoughtful as he mashed his omelet with his hash browns. "He almost always approaches Aisling when she's alone unless he's on a timetable. He tries to avoid the rest of us whenever possible."

"Which makes him suspect," Redmond supplied.

"Or simply shy," I said.

"No, he's definitely suspect," Dad argued, his anger obvious as he leaned back in his chair. "I don't like this. Why is he making his presence known at this juncture? It seems suspicious."

"I don't think it seems more suspicious than anything else he's done," Griffin countered. "The little monster likes to hide in the shadows and entice my girlfriend outside. I'm more worked up about that than his timing."

"Except Aisling was attacked on the street yesterday," Dad persisted. "She could've been killed. She acted quickly and protected herself. Then Bub shows up out of nowhere? I don't like it."

Hmm. He had a point. I hadn't even considered that. "What about the dagger?" I focused my attention on Cillian. "Have you found out anything about the dagger?"

"As a matter of fact, I have." Cillian flicked his eyes to the door, as if to assure himself that the Taylors were really out of the house, and then continued. "Two of the carvings were flagged during the computer search. You're never going to believe where they originated."

My appetite quickly flagged. "Oh, I'm not going to want to hear this, am I? If we have to save the world — or at least Detroit — right before my wedding, I'm totally going to turn into Bridezilla."

Griffin patted my knee under the table but kept his eyes on Cillian.

"I want to know. I always feel behind when it comes to this stuff. I don't want that to be the case this time."

"Well, then brace yourself." Cillian's eyes sparkled. He really was a fan of research. To him, a good book was better than chocolate. It was one of the only things that drove me crazy about him. "The carvings signify soul walkers."

No one at the table spoke.

"Soul walkers," Cillian repeated, as if we'd somehow misheard him. "Am I the only one who knows what a soul walker is?"

"Apparently," I replied, abandoning my fork on my plate. "I think you need to explain it to us."

"And you need to eat," Griffin interjected, pointing at my plate. "Your eating habits have shifted drastically over the past few days and I don't like it. The reason people keep asking if you're sick is because you're pale. You wouldn't be pale if you ate a full meal."

"I ate a full meal last night."

"No, you didn't," Dad said. "You ate a third of a meal and then mixed capers with your mashed potatoes and called it a night."

Hmm. I didn't realize he was watching me that closely. "Well ... ."

"Shh." Dad pressed a finger to his lips. "Your brother is talking now. I want to hear what he has to say."

"Right now I don't have a lot to say," Cillian offered. "I have more research to do. The main thing I found was that the carvings were created by a group of soul walkers who were local to the area at the turn of the century ... and by that I mean 1900 and not 2000."

"I figured that," Dad noted. "I don't think I've ever heard that term. What is a soul walker?"

"It's a group of individuals — many with Native American blood, although that's not a prerequisite — who believe you can extend your life by separating your soul from your body," Cillian explained. "The practice was fashionable for a few years, but then most religious groups abandoned it."

"Isn't that what already happens when someone dies?" Aidan asked. "I mean ... the souls separate from the bodies. We collect them and handle the transport to the great beyond."

"Yes, but soul walkers believe that they can remain behind without their bodies and not cross over," Cillian explained. "We know that souls go crazy if they're not collected in a timely fashion. That's how poltergeists and ghosts occur. Soul walkers believed there was a way to avoid that."

Dad knit his eyebrows. "How?"

"That I don't know." Cillian turned sheepish. "I'm still doing some research. That's my big goal for the day, aside from our charges. Luckily we have a rather light load."

"Definitely." Dad stroked his chin, his expression thoughtful. "Maybe the wraiths are trying to prolong their lives in a different way. That could be why the one that attacked Aisling yesterday had the dagger."

"Wraiths have already given up their souls," I pointed out. "As far as I know, once that happens there's no getting it back."

"True. We definitely need to conduct further research. I'll see what I can find out from the home office. I've never heard the term 'soul walker' before and I'm intrigued. Even if it's impossible for these souls to achieve the state of reasoning they're hoping for, that doesn't mean people won't try. They could be dangerous depending on what they feel they need to accomplish their goal."

"Good point." Cillian wiped his hands on his napkin. "Right now, the only thing we know is that a wraith attacked Aisling and it had a dagger. I suggest everyone be careful out there."

"That's the plan." I shoved a piece of doughnut in my mouth to keep Griffin from harping on me about my eating habits, waiting until I swallowed to speak again. "I wonder if reapers somehow play into the soul walker mystique."

"That's my guess," Cillian said. "I just need to confirm it."

"Then focus on that," Dad said. "I'll take care of the rest. Figure out what that wraith was doing and why it wanted Aisling. I don't care about the rest of it."

"I'm on it."

Nine

Dad gave me one job, which rankled.

"Seriously? Another crotchety old lady. Are you trying to punish me?"

Griffin chuckled as he slipped on his shoes in the foyer and watched the show.

"Not last time I checked," Dad said dryly. "I've been trying to give you an easy load to make sure you don't find trouble."

"I was attacked by a wraith yesterday."

"Not while working."

"Good point." I took my iPad from him and slipped it into my bag. "You know, you still haven't told us where you're sending us on our honeymoon. All you told me was that I didn't need a passport and I would be enjoying tropical weather. I'm going to need more than that."

"It's a surprise."

"I hate surprises."

"You hate not being in control of information," Dad corrected. "That's not the same as hating surprises."

I fixed him with my best "I'm your little princess and you have to do what I say" look. It was part of my regular rotation when I was a kid. "Can't you please tell me?"

"No."

"Puh-leez."

"No."

"You suck." I abandoned my interrogation attempt and flicked my eyes to Griffin. "Are you okay to go to work?"

"I'm fine. I have a bit of a headache, but that's my own fault." Griffin leaned over and pressed a kiss to my forehead. "I need to get through this paperwork so I can enjoy the honeymoon your father is surprising us with."

I scowled. "You're just trying to irritate me."

"It's easy." Griffin turned serious as he snagged my fingers and gave them a squeeze. "I know your father has been going out of his way to give you jobs that are easy and free of danger, but I would appreciate it if you were careful all the same. I don't want a bruised bride."

"I'll be careful. Dad keeps giving me mean old ladies who like to yell. There's nothing safer than that."

"You always seem to find trouble."

"It's a gift."

"I would appreciate it if you put that particular gift on layaway." He tugged me close and gave me a soft kiss. "Soon, baby. Soon we'll be married and I won't have to ask you to do things, I'll be able to order you to follow directions ... and you'll do it."

My mouth dropped open as he broke out a sly grin and easily evaded my slapping hand. "That's not even remotely funny."

"I have to get my jollies somewhere."

I watched him go, a myriad of revenge possibilities floating through my head. When I risked a glance at my father, who I'd forgotten was still there, I found him smiling. "It's not funny."

"It's kind of funny," Dad countered. "I remember what it was like right before I got married. I thought I was going to be the boss, too."

"Yeah? How did that work out for you?"

"Not well."

"Then why do you look so happy?"

"Because you're starting out on a new adventure, Aisling," Dad replied, matter-of-fact. "You're going to marry the man of your dreams, although I was hoping you'd remain celibate until you were fifty and I wouldn't have to see the flirting. You'll eventually start a family. I can't wait to see karma rear its ugly head when you have a daughter of your own."

My stomach rolled at the prospect. "I think we're going to wait a bit before adding kids to the mix. It's not exactly safe now."

Instead of agreeing, Dad merely shrugged. "When will it ever be safe?"

"When Mom isn't around eating people and potentially working against us."

Dad's smile slipped. "You're adamant about this. You think she really is up to something, don't you?"

I nodded without hesitation. "I'm worried that you don't think she's up to something," I admitted. "You were the most suspicious when she first came back, even more than me. Now you don't even issue a token complaint when she drops in without calling first."

"I ... guess that's true." Dad didn't look happy with the realization. "I didn't even think about it. You're right, of course. She has fit rather seamlessly back into our lives in recent weeks."

"What if that's on purpose?"

Dad worked his jaw. "You think Bub visiting has something to do with your mother, don't you?"

"Yes." I saw no reason to lie. "He always shows up when she's working an angle. I don't think his timing last night was coincidental."

"What would you have me do? Should I ban her from the house? Are you going to disinvite her to your wedding?"

"I didn't technically invite her in the first place. Jerry is in charge of the guest list, and he discovered pretty quickly that I don't have many friends. In fact, he made a list for me. Seventy-five percent of them are members of this family. Two of them are Griffin and Maya. Apparently I'm not very likeable."

Dad took me by surprise when he chuckled. "You're likeable. You're simply picky. You surround yourself with people you love and don't need a wide circle. That's not necessarily bad."

"My maid of honor is a man. He's insisting on being called my macho man of honor, but it's the same thing."

"Your macho man of honor is your best friend," Dad corrected.

"Jerry has always loved you. When you were a kid, part of me wished he was straight so there was a chance you would end up together. Now, don't misunderstand, I'm not unhappy with the way things worked out.

"Jerry and Aidan are well-suited for each other," he continued. "Jerry allows your brother to be silly when he wants to be. Aidan is rarely silly. He was far too serious when you were children."

"That's because he was gay and didn't initially realize it," I volunteered. "He knew he was different from Braden, Cillian and Redmond when he was younger, and he didn't like feeling separate. When he got older and realized he was gay, he was terrified of telling you guys."

"You mean telling me."

"I mean all of you," I clarified. "You were great with him, though. You didn't even blink when it came out. You simply nodded and said that was fine, that nothing had changed. I don't think you realize what a relief that was for him."

"Your mother knew before I did, but once I gave it some thought it became obvious. Aidan is my son. Nothing could stop me from loving him."

"Braden, Cillian and Redmond were good, too. I knew they would come around, but they were good from the start. They never ostracized him."

"Did you think they would?"

"No. I also didn't think he would end up with Jerry," I admitted. "I was upset at first, because it felt like Aidan was stealing my best friend. I see now that I was a big baby over that situation. They are good together. You're right about that."

"Aidan and Jerry's relationship came at the right time," Dad noted. "You and Jerry were ready to let go, at least a little. You'll never fully let go, and that's good. Jerry and Aidan found each other when you were struggling with your feelings for Griffin. To me, it seemed fate had a hand in all of that because it worked out so well and no one felt left behind."

I licked my lips as I debated how much to say. "I wasn't sure you would ever like Griffin. This morning, when we were talking about things, I asked him if he was upset his father wasn't going to see him get married."

"What did he say?"

"He said he had his grandfather and you, so it was fine."

Dad's eyebrows migrated up his forehead. "Me?"

"He says you're like a surrogate father to him. That makes me uncomfortable because I'm his sister in that scenario, but I've decided to ignore it."

Dad's hearty chuckle was back. "Well, I think that's the nicest thing I've heard all day. Griffin is like a son to me, too. Sure, he's a handsy son I occasionally want to smack around, but he's a good man. I couldn't have asked for a better partner for you."

"You fought our relationship at the start."

"That's because I didn't think he was good enough for you. I was wrong about that. He's the best thing that ever happened to you, mostly because he dotes on you while still putting his foot down when necessary. You've so rarely heard the word 'no' growing up, it's a wonder I didn't ruin you for all men."

"I liked being spoiled."

"And I liked spoiling you."

"That's not going to stop once I get married, is it? I would hate to lose my power over you."

"It will never stop, kid." Dad pulled me in for a hug, briefly resting his cheek against my hair. "We'll figure this out. If your mother is behind it, believe me, I'll take care of it. I'm not blind to what she is. I know it might not seem that way, but I'm always watching."

"I know." I patted his back. "I should get going. Connie Portwood is set to expire soon and I don't want to keep her waiting."

"Just suck and run. That's the one lesson you've yet to learn."

"I'll do it today – for you."

"That's my girl."

I DIDN'T SUCK AND RUN.

It seemed Connie Portwood was furious about her lot in life. She started talking before I could even pull the scepter from my pocket.

"Back, demon!" She arranged her hands in the shape of a cross before her. "I will not be tempted by Satan!"

"Oh, geez." I rubbed my forehead as I regarded her. "Why don't I ever listen to my father? Wait ... don't tell him I said that. I'll never live it down otherwise."

"You can't have my soul," Connie hissed. "It's the Lord's to do with as he pleases, and you are not the Lord."

"Yeah, yeah." I flopped into the floral print chair at the edge of the room and pulled out my iPad so I could study Connie's details. She seemed religious, overly pious even. Hopefully that meant she was going to a good place. "What the ... ?" My mouth dropped open when I read the special notes at the end of her file. "I'm going to bet Dad didn't read the whole thing before he gave you to me."

"I cannot hear the evil words spewing from your forked tongue," Connie intoned.

"Then why did you answer?" I expanded the notes section and continued reading. "Did you really get arrested for trying to blow up a Baptist church?"

"They do not follow the teachings of our Lord and savior."

"I don't even recognize the religion listed for you," I mused. "Is it some form of cult?"

"It's the only true path to salvation," Connie barked.

Connie's final resting place wasn't Heaven, so I had some bad news for her. "You probably shouldn't have kicked those Girl Scouts last week. They were just selling cookies. I'm not saying that was the final nail in your coffin — which is a bad pun, I admit — but I don't think it helped. I would've barred you from Heaven for that alone."

"They were selling sin," Connie spat.

"In the form of thin mints and samoas," I countered. "If Girl Scout cookies are wrong, I don't want to be right."

"Sugar is sinful."

"Oh, geez." I shook my head. "You're a real piece of work, aren't you? My Dad is a big believer in karma. I have to wonder if you're mine. I should've told him right away when Bub showed up for a visit. I guess that's on me ... thanks to you."

"I am not listening to you, harlot!" Connie lifted her hands over her head and made weird finger figures that I couldn't quite identify. "Save me, Lord!"

Something occurred to me. "You're faking this, aren't you?"

Connie stilled, the only movement coming from her twitching mouth. "I have no idea what you're talking about."

"You're faking it," I repeated. "You don't believe what you're spouting. You've attacked, like, three churches, according to your records. There's no way you think you're going to Heaven."

Connie blinked three times in rapid succession as she stared at me. "What are you?"

"A reaper. What are you?"

"A warrior for God."

"You're full of crap." I crossed my ankles and leaned back in my chair. "You're evil and you know it. What's most interesting about this is you don't seem to care. You're putting on an act for my benefit — which is entertaining, I'll grant you that — but you don't really believe anything you're saying."

"I believe it all."

"No." I chewed my bottom lip as I studied her. "You're a sociopath. Maybe a bit of a narcissist, too. This is all a game to you."

"I don't play games."

"You don't even care that you're dead."

Finally, Connie abandoned her act and shot me a withering look. "I'm seventy-five and I've been in poor health for years. What did you expect?"

I shrugged, noncommittal. "I don't know. Some remorse wouldn't hurt."

"I'm not remorseful. And as for those Girl Scouts, they should've just given me the cookies and run away. Instead, one of them kicked me."

"You were trying to steal her cookies."

"So what?"

"Yeah, you're a total jerk. I'm sure you'll be glad to know you're going to Hell."

"I don't believe in Hell."

"That doesn't mean you're not going."

"I won't be staying." Connie sounded so sure of herself that I abandoned what I was going to say next and changed course.

"You recognized what I was from the start. How?"

"I know things."

"Like what?"

"Things I'm not going to share with you."

"I'm guessing you weren't the life of the party when you were alive, huh?"

"I would rather be boring than a harlot."

"Whatever."

"I'm bored with this conversation," Connie announced. "You're the ferryman, right? You should get to ferrying."

I wasn't used to a charge who understood the process. "I'm a woman, but you're basically right."

"So ... ferry. I'm sick of being here. This place is depressing."

The house was so run down I couldn't argue. "Fine." I rummaged in my pocket for my scepter. "You're my only charge of the day. I was hoping you'd be more entertaining."

"You should learn to entertain yourself. Life will be better if you stop being reliant on others."

"What do you know about life being better? You seem pretty miserable to me."

"I know things."

"Like what?" I wasn't ready to let it go. There was something odd about the woman. "What do you know?"

"I know there's a woman waiting for you on the front walk."

The simple statement caused my heart to stutter. "What?" I slowly got to my feet and moved to the front window, my stomach twisting when I saw my mother — the young version from the previous day — staring at the house from forty feet away. "You can see her?"

Connie made a derisive sound in the back of her throat. "Of course I can see her. She's not invisible."

I wasn't sure of that until Connie pointed her out. "What do you think she wants?"

"I think she wants you to follow her," Connie replied without hesitation. "She's waiting for you to get your head out of your rear end and stop dilly-dallying."

I remembered where I was and straightened my shoulders. "I'm not dilly-dallying. I think that's a stupid saying, by the way. I never dilly-dally."

"Then prove it."

"Fine." I pressed the button on my scepter, but not because Connie dared me to do it.

Her last words were "it's about time" before she disappeared. The scepter was in my pocket and my attention on my mother within seconds.

She remained standing in front of the house, hands on hips. She was clearly waiting.

"This can't be real," I muttered, shaking my head. "I have to be imagining this. Maybe I've already been locked up and this is all in my head."

As if listening from afar, Mom tilted her head to the side and crooked her finger. Connie was right. She wanted me to follow.

"Well, if I am in a nuthouse, I guess it makes sense for me to go with the friendly neighborhood ghost," I said to nobody in particular. "And if I'm not crazy, I should probably stop talking to myself."

There was no one there to answer. I heaved out a sigh and moved to the door. I had only one option. I had to follow her. If I didn't, she would continue haunting me until I cracked.

No one wanted that.

Ten

The woman — my mother, although it felt weird to think so — waited for me to escape the house. Once I hit the front walk, she started along the sidewalk.

We were in Royal Oak — mostly because my father wanted me to stick close to home right before the wedding — and I had left my car parked on a side street as I gave chase. The woman kept a block ahead of me, never glancing over her shoulder to make sure I trailed behind. She was sure of herself, a fact that grated.

I followed anyway.

She walked for a good ten minutes before she changed course, turning swiftly down a sidewalk that led to an abandoned theater. I recognized the building. People had been trying to renovate and relaunch the property for what felt like forever. Five years before, in fact, it had opened briefly, and Jerry dragged me to several movies, including a midnight showing of *The Rocky Horror Picture Show* (one of his favorites). The interior was old and kitschy ... and fairly run down.

The woman disappeared when I got close to the door. It was shut, and looked to be locked, but she was nowhere to be found. I searched for her for ten minutes before giving up, stopping long enough to snap screenshots of the sign at the front of the building and a few points of interest before departing to collect my car.

For the entire walk back to Connie's house I found myself looking over my shoulder and down every side street. My mother didn't show her face again, so I hopped in my car and headed toward Woodward Avenue. For some reason, I knew exactly where I was headed ... and why.

I needed help. My father and Griffin wanted to help. In fact, they were going above and beyond to offer the reassurance they felt I needed. But they didn't believe me. They thought stress was causing me to see things.

At first I believed that was a legitimate possibility. The past few weeks had left me feeling beaten down, something I wasn't used to. As the only girl in a family full of boys, I could've been treated differently during my adolescence. I could've been lifted to a pedestal or even dropped to the bottom rung of the hierarchy.

My father never pretended to treat me exactly as he did my brothers. He was careful to make sure they didn't hurt me while roughhousing, but he was also adamant that I couldn't be cut out of the action. That meant if he went golfing I was often invited. Sometimes I was forced to go with the rest of the family even though I was convinced golf was a game for bored people.

He played video games with us, allowed Jerry and I to dress him up for make-believe parties and snuck me candy when he thought no one was looking. I wasn't the only one to get candy. I knew from secondhand accounts that all my brothers were spoiled in the same manner. My father went out of his way to treat each of us as if we were the only child in the universe when he had a few minutes to spare. Individual time was a biggie — with him and my mother — and we were all spoiled in our own ways.

That didn't mean my standing in the family was always solid. There were times I fought with my brothers, tattled, and they hated me for it. Other times they felt like big bullies and I cried myself to sleep on my father's lap.

It might sound like my mother had very little to do with my upbringing, but the opposite was true. She was a force in Grimlock

Manor until she died when I was a teenager. Before that, she was the smarter disciplinarian who picked her battles and seemed to grasp our individual needs better than we did. After she passed, lost in a fire that didn't really claim her, my father became the indulgent one. Oh, he would claim otherwise, swear up and down he was going to bring down the hammer, but he was a big pile of mush. After my mother died, things changed.

Dad's personality was larger than life. He always made me laugh. The weeks surrounding my mother's death were enough to cripple anyone, but he realized right away that he couldn't crumble. If he did, we would've followed. He had five children, and it was his job to keep us going.

Things didn't always work out as he planned — we were all arrested a time or two, individually and together — but he learned to be flexible. Before Mom died he wanted things his way and had to be cajoled into bending. After, he did his best to be mother and father to a brood of basket cases, which frequently meant he had to be ready to bend. He was good at it, better than he'd anticipated.

When I first discovered there was a chance my mother was alive, he was the one I worried most about. To be fair, Braden was a worry, too. Braden suffered more than anyone after my mother died. They'd had a strong bond. Dad spent a lot of time with Braden in the aftermath to make sure he didn't retreat, but of all my siblings, Braden was the one who refused to see that Mom could be up to something upon her return. He wanted to forgive her, let bygones be bygones. Everyone else was leery.

I was the last to warm to her, to accept that maybe trust wouldn't open me to attack. I never fully got over the hump no matter how hard I tried. That's why it wasn't much of a surprise when she cast the disc into the fire and pretended she'd helped rather than hurt during our previous escapade. I hadn't told anyone about that but Griffin, and he struggled with keeping the secret. He thought I should tell my father everything, but I wasn't sure how that would work out. My mother could easily lie to explain away the situation. I would never believe those lies, but my brothers were a different story. And my father? He would cast her out on principle, but it would start a war.

I didn't want a war right before my wedding.

I parked in the lot for Tea & Tarot, a kitschy shop that boasted a powerful fortune teller named Madame Maxine. I wasn't sure what term to use to describe Madame Maxine. Witch. Bruja. Voodoo queen. Sorceress. She was powerful, but her origins were murky. She was tight with my brother Redmond, and had a good relationship with my father, but our interactions were markedly tense.

She liked it that way.

The store was empty when I entered, the chimes above the door announcing me. Madame Maxine sat at her tarot table, almost as if she'd been waiting for me. She smiled when she saw who darkened her doorstep.

"Hello, littlest Grimlock."

I hated it when she called me that. "Madame Maxine." I gritted back my annoyance. She wouldn't help me if we got off on the wrong foot. My attitude wasn't exactly warm and welcome where she was concerned. "How are things?"

"Busy. How are things with you?"

I loitered close to the sun catcher display at the front window and shrugged. "Confusing."

"I know."

"How do you know?"

"You might not believe this, but I've felt your uncertainty building for days," Madame Maxine replied. "I knew you'd come. I didn't know you'd come alone, which shows you're growing as a person, but I knew eventually you'd have no choice."

I forced myself closer to the table. "You felt my uncertainty?"

"Your feelings aren't nearly as bottled up as you'd like people to believe. Sit." She gestured toward the table. "You need a reading."

That was the last thing I wanted. "Can't you just tell me what I need to know instead of making me jump through hoops this time? You can consider it a wedding present."

Madame Maxine chuckled, the sound low and throaty. "I can't do that."

"You mean you won't do that," I grumbled, throwing myself into the open chair across from her. "I know your game."

Madame Maxine's sigh was long and pronounced. "Little Grimlock, we all have rules we have to follow in this world. Even you. I know you like to believe otherwise, but all of us are governed by someone."

"I'm not governed by anyone."

"Oh, really?" Madame Maxine cocked a challenging eyebrow. "Who signs your paychecks? Whose ring do you wear?" She inclined her chin toward my left hand. "Whose wellbeing do you put above your own?"

The questions felt invasive. "My father is my boss, not my king. As for Griffin, he's going to be my husband. That doesn't mean he's the boss of me."

"No, and he's not interested in being your boss," Madame Maxine readily agreed. "He's your partner, not your superior. What's interesting is that you're not trying to be his superior. I thought that might eventually become your downfall when it came time to mate, but apparently you picked a man strong enough to survive your personality. That's no easy feat."

I was fairly certain she meant that as an insult. "I don't want someone I can boss around."

"Definitely not," Madame Maxine agreed. "You might think you want that, but in truth you like a good fight. Growing up with four brothers taught you that."

"I don't always want a fight."

"No?"

"No."

"Then why are you here today?" Madame Maxine challenged. "If you're not looking for a fight, why not bury your head in the sand and hide until your wedding day?"

"Because I happen to believe there are some things you can't hide from."

"Like?"

It was now or never. "What do you know about soul walkers?"

Whatever she was expecting, that wasn't it. Madame Maxine couldn't hide her reaction fast enough and her mouth dropped open. "What?"

"Soul walkers," I repeated, intrigued by her reaction. "What do you know about them?"

"I'm not sure there is anything to know."

"There has to be something," I persisted. "I was attacked by a wraith yesterday, and the dagger it carried had carvings that pointed toward soul walkers. Cillian is still researching, but that has to be significant."

"I haven't heard that term in a long time," Madame Maxine mused as she held out the deck of cards for me to cut. "I wasn't aware anyone was still practicing that particular ritual."

"That means you do know something about it." I handed back the deck.

"I've heard stories," she volunteered. "I don't know how truthful they are. I've never met a soul walker. They were supposedly extinct long before I was born."

"Which was when?" The woman zealously guarded her age, so I was mildly curious to see if she would slip.

Instead, she chuckled. "So funny, Grimlock daughter."

"I hate it when you call me things like that," I groused as she dealt the cards.

"Why do you think I do it?"

"Because you've got a mean streak. If I didn't hate you so much I might respect you."

"You don't hate me. You want to hate me, but you can't force yourself to do it."

"You don't know. I could hate you."

"So funny." Madame Maxine rapped my knuckles as she finished doling out the cards. "As for the soul walkers, I only know what I've heard from stories, more lore than fact. The soul walkers were local to this area before expanding to other locations, but they originated here. By that I mean the first soul walker supposedly sprang from Detroit. They grew to be a national phenomenon for a bit, but then they faded away."

"Do you think it's true that they could keep their minds intact once separated from their bodies?"

Madame Maxine held out her hands and shrugged. "Stories have a way of taking on a life of their own over time. You know that. I don't think it's impossible. I guess that's the best I can offer."

"And the soul walkers in this area? Where did they hang out?"

"I don't know. I believe a group took up space at a Royal Oak business, although it was a village back then and not the city you know today. Why they picked Royal Oak is anybody's guess, but they were prevalent for only a few years."

"Do you know which business?"

"No."

My disappointment was a bitter pulse of acid reflux. "Well, that sucks."

"It does indeed." Madame Maxine studied the cards as I tapped my fingers on the tabletop. "You have something else on your mind. Why don't you spill that while I make sure your future isn't about to go off the rails?"

"Maybe I don't want to tell you what's bothering me. Have you ever considered that?"

"You never want to tell me."

"Good point." I rolled my neck. "Okay, here's the thing ... here's the thing." I trailed off, uncomfortable. "I keep seeing my mother, only it's not the mother who came back but the one who left Grimlock Manor the night she died. Three times now she's come to visit. My father thinks I'm crazy, but I'm starting to think I'm really seeing her."

Instead of laughing, Madame Maxine's eyes widened. "Do you think she's a soul walker?"

"No." I answered before really considering. "I mean ... I don't think so. Obviously my mother survived the fire. Whether her soul did is another matter entirely. At least part of her soul has to be in that thing that keeps inviting itself to dinner, right?"

"I honestly don't know. Madame Maxie rubbed her chin, thoughtful. "Does she speak to you? The woman you keep seeing, I mean."

"No. One time she walked past a window and disappeared. Yesterday she gestured from across Woodward and alerted me that a wraith was about to attack. Today she sat outside a charge's house until I was finished and led me to an abandoned theater."

"Which theater?"

"The Dunmore, although that's not its name these days. They've changed it fifty times over the past ten years, but none of the names have stuck."

"I know the place." Madame Maxine was flummoxed. "Did she go inside?"

"I lost sight of her. I don't think so. The doors are chained."

"Did you go inside?"

"I'm not an idiot. With my luck the place will be crawling with wraiths. Do you have any idea how much yelling my father would do if I made the mistake of walking into an abandoned building after everything that's been going on?"

Madame Maxine's smile was back. "Since when do you listen to your father?"

"Since I don't want to make a mistake that could possibly hurt someone I love."

"You really are growing." The clucking sound Madame Maxine unleashed set my teeth on edge. "You've always been intriguing, Aisling." I couldn't remember the last time she used my real name. "Even as a child, you were courage personified ... even though you were a mouthy little monster."

"Yes, I'm an absolute joy," I deadpanned.

"I worried you would never grow into your own. You have, though, and you've turned into an amazing woman."

The compliment threw me for a loop. "Why are you suddenly being nice to me? Do you see death in those things and want to soften the blow?" I peered closer, although I had no idea how to read the cards. "I really don't want to die, so if you could keep that from happening that would be great."

Madame Maxine barked out a laugh that echoed throughout the store. "Still funny."

"Yes, I'm a laugh riot."

"I don't see death here," she said after a beat. "I do see a big fight. Do you see this? That's the tower card. It means you'll face a big battle."

"Will I win?"

"Don't you always?"

"Yes, but ... will the people I love win, too? I don't want to lose any of them."

Instead of answering, Madame Maxine posed her own question. "What about your mother? Do you want to lose her?"

"I don't think she's my mother."

"Part of her is."

"But the bigger part of her isn't. I'm more worried about my brothers. I want my father to be safe ... and Griffin ... and Jerry."

"I can't answer specific questions, and it's not because I'm being stubborn but because I don't have the answers. I think your immediate future is fluid, which is probably not what you want to hear."

"Definitely not."

"The good news is that you're the strongest person I know," she continued. "I'm not blowing smoke or pumping your ego. You are extremely powerful and strong ... and I believe you will bring your family through this."

"That's it? That's all you have to tell me?"

"I want you to have faith in your family," Madame Maxine stressed. "I also want you to have faith in yourself. Don't second guess yourself. That will be a mistake.

"When the time comes, you'll know what to do," she said. "Don't think it over. Do what feels right. You'll know what it is when it's time."

I understood she was trying to be soothing, but I still wanted to smack her. "You make me want to drink," I complained. "I mean ... seriously. I want a big bottle of whiskey and I want to drink it all."

"I have a way with people. I can't help it."

"It's annoying."

"So are you."

"Yeah, well, you didn't have to remind me."

"I'll remember that for next time."

I could only hope there would be a next time.

Eleven

Griffin surprised me with takeout for four at home. The table was already set and fresh beer was in the refrigerator. He went through the trouble of lighting candles and everything, which wasn't part of our normal dinner hour.

"What's all this?" I kicked off my shoes and shuffled toward the table. "Why are there four places set? You're not bringing dates for both of us, are you?"

"Ha, ha." Griffin poked my side as he tugged on a pair of oven mitts. "It's too late for that. You're stuck with me forever. You might as well get used to it."

"Well, it will be difficult, but somehow I'm sure I'll struggle through."

"I'm sure you will, too." Griffin planted a solid kiss on my mouth before opening the oven. "I got baked spaghetti from that place you love over on Main Street. I figured that would put you in a good mood."

He had no idea. Still, I was suspicious. "Why aren't we eating at Grimlock Manor with your family? Won't your mother be upset that we're hiding out here?"

"No."

He sounded so sure of himself that I almost tabled my doubt. Almost, but not quite. "What's really going on?"

"Your father is taking my family to a fancy restaurant in the Renaissance Center. He suggested we take advantage of his giving nature and spend the evening together ... and alone."

"In other words ... he's worried about me."

Griffin heaved a sigh as he carried the tin to a big bowl on the counter and dumped the contents inside. "I don't think being worried is something that deserves derision. He's your father. He's allowed to worry."

"Because he thinks I'm seeing things."

"He thinks you're stressed."

"Yeah, well, I was stressed again today." I'd considered lying to Griffin about my afternoon, but it didn't seem fair. If the situation was reversed, I wouldn't be happy if he lied, so I figured being upfront was my only option.

Griffin didn't flinch or start yelling. Instead, he scraped the contents of the takeout container into the bowl and kept his eyes focused on his task. "Oh, yeah? Tell me about it."

He sounded calm, but I recognized he was putting on an act. "I had one soul today. She was a real loon, by the way. She was clearly a sociopath and a narcissist."

"She didn't have a body stuffed in her refrigerator, did she?"

"No, she was too old to carry around a body. She might've been capable in her younger years, but if that's her thing, she's well past that now."

"That's a relief."

"I was talking to her when I saw someone on the front walk. It was my mother."

"And we're talking about your other mother, right? The younger one."

"Yes. I'm considering calling her Mom Beta so there's no confusion."

"At least you have a plan."

I had to bite back a hot retort because the anger bubbling up threatened to overcome me. "Mom Beta wanted me to follow her, so I did. She led me to that abandoned theater that's on the outskirts of the business district and then she disappeared."

That was enough to cause Griffin to fix his full attention on me. He was done playing it cool. "You didn't go inside, did you?"

"No. I'm not an idiot."

"It's not a question of intelligence. You're extremely smart ... except when we're watching science fiction movies and you insist on pointing out plot holes that don't exist."

"Oh, come on." I made a face. "How can there be an end of the universe when it's ever expanding? I don't care what you say, that fifth *Star Trek* movie makes no sense."

"That movie has a lot more problems than the end of the universe."

"Marsh melons?"

"Among other things." A hint of a smile ghosted Griffin's mouth. "I'm glad you didn't go inside. Thank you for that. You have no idea what could have been waiting for you."

"Plus, if there's a woman out there who looks exactly like Mom trying to entice me into an abandoned building, chances are that's on purpose," I added. "Like ... maybe someone is trying to unnerve me and purposely created a woman who looked like Mom."

"How do you create a woman?"

"You're not asking because you want to see if you can try it yourself, are you?"

"I'm pretty happy with my woman ... except when she picks apart *Star Trek* movies."

"Yeah, well, get used to that. We're going to be married for a long time."

"That's the plan." Griffin took me by surprise when he grabbed me by the waist and bent low to plant a lavish kiss on my lips. "Look at that. Still happy ... and still fine with the whole marriage thing."

I couldn't stop myself from smiling. "That was fairly cute."

"I do my best." Griffin straightened and brushed a quick kiss against my forehead before releasing me. "Tell me about the building."

"I don't know much about it. It's a theater. I've been inside. It was years ago. It has a retro feel. Jerry made me see *The Rocky Horror Picture Show* there."

"That's not really what I was talking about," Griffin said dryly. "What's the situation with the location?"

"Abandoned."

"Aisling." All traces of mirth vacated Griffin's tone. "I think I'm being extremely patient here. Can't you please just tell me what I want to hear and we'll go from there?"

That seemed fair enough. "It's empty, as far as I can tell. The windows are all blocked, so you can't see inside. I tried looking through the front windows but didn't risk going to the rear because there's an alley back there that is cut off from the world. Someone could easily grab me if I wandered behind the wall."

"Good girl."

"The front door is chained, but it's one of those padlocks that you can pick with a bobby pin."

"How do you know that?"

"Redmond taught me how to pick locks when I was a kid. That's how I always knew what I was getting for Christmas every year."

"Ah, so you're a criminal in your free time," Griffin intoned. "I had a feeling, but I didn't want to accuse you of anything without proof."

"I don't know what's inside."

"Okay."

"I want to know, though."

"I figured." Griffin ran a hand through his hair as he considered the situation. "Aidan and Jerry are coming for dinner. I wanted it to be just the two of us, but Jerry insisted that wasn't possible because he has things to go over with you. I figured it would be easier to have dinner together and then kick them out."

"Good plan."

"After that, we'll go on an adventure," Griffin offered. "I want to reward you for not investigating on your own."

"If you wanted to reward me, you should've brought cake."

"Jerry is bringing something spectacular – his words, not mine – so you won't be left hanging for dessert."

"Score!" I pumped my fist. "I bet it's the gummy shark cake I've been angling for. I wanted it for the wedding, but he vetoed it."

"I bet it is."

I stared at him for a long beat. "Are you really going to break into an abandoned building with me?"

"Yes."

"Thank you." I threw my arms around his neck at the same moment I realized Aidan and Jerry were already in the townhouse ... and watching the scene with unveiled interest. "Oh, hey." I stumbled as I tried to recover. "How long have you guys been standing there?"

"Long enough to know we're all breaking the law together later," Jerry answered as he carried the gummy shark cake of my dreams to the counter. "I can't wait to hear why we're doing it."

Crap. I looked to Aidan for help. "You don't want to break into an abandoned building, do you?"

"On the contrary. I can think of nothing I'd rather do a few days before your wedding," Aidan drawled. "I can't wait to hear the details either."

Well, it looked like my secret mental illness was about to become public. That's not how I was expecting the night to go.

IN THE END, I HAD to tell them everything.

Jerry reacted by instantly believing me, saying he had no doubt that the universe was conspiring to make me nutty and it was all outside forces responsible for the things I'd been seeing.

Aidan was more reticent.

"How could it be Mom?" He was dressed in dark colors (as were we all) as we walked to the theater. Parking in a spot close to the theater seemed like a bad idea in case anyone was watching the lots. "Our mother would be eleven years older than what you're describing."

"I didn't say it made any sense," I grumbled.

Griffin squeezed my hand as he walked at my side. "Don't get worked up."

"Do I sound like I'm getting worked up?"

"A little."

"Just a little." Jerry held his thumb and forefinger an inch apart. "You don't have to worry about me trying to put you in a straitjacket.

It won't go with your wedding dress, so it's really far down on my to-do list."

"Thank you, Jerry."

Griffin tried to hide his smirk by staring at the traffic, but it was obvious he found Jerry's reaction entertaining.

"I'm not saying that I don't believe you," Aidan said hurriedly. "I'm just suggesting that ... maybe ... um ... you might want to see a mental health professional."

"And thank you, Aidan," Griffin growled, his eyes flashing.

"I was trying not to insult her."

"Try harder next time," Griffin snapped. "This is hard on her. You don't need to act like a Grimlock."

"I don't have any choice in being a Grimlock."

"Maybe you should try harder on that, too."

I cleared my throat to cut off the potential argument. "There's no reason to fight. I'm the first person who believes it might be a good idea to lock me up."

"We already talked about that." Griffin was calm as we turned the corner that led to the theater. "Those struggling with mental issues don't know it."

"That is true, Bug," Jerry offered. "I've never met a crazy person who knew he or she was crazy."

"Just out of curiosity, how many crazy people have you met?" Griffin asked.

"You'd be surprised."

"Well, it doesn't matter." Griffin's presence was solid and warm at my right as he slowed his pace and eyed the theater. "Aisling is fine. I'm starting to warm to her idea that someone wants her to believe she's seeing her mother."

"How does that work?" Aidan looked legitimately curious. "Do you think one of our enemies paid someone to get a bunch of plastic surgery to make her look like Mom?"

"I guess that's possible, but I was thinking the answer may be more magical," Griffin replied. "Is there a spell that can change someone's appearance?"

"I don't know, but it's definitely something to ask Cillian to look into," I answered. "That's not a bad idea."

"It's better than the plastic surgery theory," Aidan admitted. "That leads to another question: Who would want to knock Aisling off her game?"

"Mom." The single word was out of my mouth before I gave thought to what I was saying.

Instead of being upset, or immediately jumping to Mom's defense, Aidan's expression was quizzical. "Why, though? Why would she want to go after you this way?"

"I don't know."

"Maybe it's because she's never liked me," Griffin offered. "It could be that she believes if she shakes Aisling enough she'll postpone the wedding ... or maybe even call it off."

"She should know me well enough to know that's not a possibility," I countered. "Even if I was crazy, I'd still marry you."

"Oh, so sweet." Griffin grinned and gave me a kiss before sobering and staring at the theater. "This is the place, right?"

I nodded. "Yeah."

"Where did she disappear?"

"Right by the front door. I didn't see exactly how she managed it ... but she was gone within seconds. It was almost as if she just disappeared."

"Okay, well ... let's see what we've got." Griffin made sure to keep me close as he moved to the closest window. He squinted as he tried to look through the glass, but it was too dark inside to see anything. "If anybody is in there, they're sitting in the dark."

"Nobody enjoys sitting in the dark," Jerry said. "That must mean Aisling was mistaken and the building is empty."

I didn't miss how shrill his voice had turned. "Jerry, you don't have to go inside."

"I don't think anybody should go inside."

"Yes, well, I'm going inside." I had no intention of backing down. "I need to see. That's the only thing that will convince me I'm not crazy ... or maybe that I am crazy. I need to see either way."

"You're going to see." Griffin dug into his pocket and came back with what looked to be a fancy lock pick. "Let's open this place up, shall we?"

I widened my eyes. "What is that?" I leaned closer, agog. "Is that a police thing? Like ... can you magically open doors with that?"

"It's not magic, and it is a police thing." Griffin grinned when he shoved the device into the lock. "As much as I would've enjoyed watching you show off your law-breaking skills, we're on a limited timetable. I think we should get in and out without wasting time."

"I hear that's how you approach everything," Aidan teased, his eyes on the lock as Griffin pulled it off the chain.

"If you think you can get to me in the usual Grimlock way, think again." Griffin opened the door and pulled a flashlight from his pocket, swinging its beam over the walls before sliding his gaze to me. "It's dark. Are you sure you want to go inside?"

I nodded.

"Okay. Stay close."

Griffin took the lead, forcing Jerry and me to huddle together in the middle of the line as Aidan brought up the rear. It wasn't a long trip. We headed straight for the main theater – it made the most sense – and when we pushed open the doors we found the room well-lighted and on display.

"Look at this place," Aidan said, shaking his head as he looked around. "It's falling apart."

"I think it's sad," Jerry lamented. "It was beautiful when we were here a few years ago, wasn't it, Bug?"

"I don't know if 'beautiful' is the word, but it was definitely nicer than this." I made a face as I took in the dilapidated surroundings. The velvet chairs were dusty, many of them ripped, and I had no doubt critters were probably living inside if some of the animal noises I was certain I heard were to be believed. "This is horrible."

Aidan shifted his eyes to the balconies that overlooked the main floor and shook his head. "The wood is rotting. I think there's been some water damage."

"Since when are you a construction expert?" I challenged.

"You can smell the water damage."

He wasn't wrong. I moved to step farther into the room, but

Griffin extended an arm to stop me, his gaze on the far wall. I followed the path of his eyes and let loose a low growl when I saw the markings painted on the wall.

"Those are the same carvings I found on the dagger," I said after a moment. "There are more of them, but those two in the center are the same."

"Yeah." Griffin dug into his pocket and retrieved his phone. "I'm going to take some photos. Look around and see if there's anything else of interest. But don't leave this room."

"What about checking the second floor?"

"We're not staying that long." Griffin was firm. "I don't think it's safe to stay here. You have five minutes and then we're gone."

"But you said ... ."

"I said I was going to make sure you were safe," Griffin said, cutting me off. "That's what I plan to do. You have five minutes. That's it. I don't want to hear a word of argument."

I mustered a sarcastic salute. "Yes, sir."

"If you want to play that game, we'll do it later. For now, take photos and don't touch anything that might have mold on it. I'm serious."

"Okay." I held up my hands in defeat. "We'll do it your way."

"That would be a nice change of pace."

Twelve

When I'd met Griffin, I equated the emotions I felt with falling. The first time he showed up at my door after realizing what I was, a mixture of lust and future love fueling him, I fell ... although we separated the next morning. At the time, I was fairly certain I was the only one who fell. When he came back, confident he could deal with the reaper stuff, we'd fallen together.

Other than a misunderstanding about his relationship with his sister (don't ask), we'd fallen together on pretty much everything ever since.

Perhaps that's why his insistence that we stay in the main theater grated so badly. There were things I needed to see and he either didn't care or wouldn't allow himself to acquiesce to my needs. Both options frazzled me.

"Aisling, what are you doing?"

Aidan kept his voice low as he appeared at my elbow. Griffin was busy snapping photos and Jerry refused to get too close to the seats because he was convinced they were infested with black mold, which forced him to stick close to the walls (which he was convinced were rotting, thanks to asbestos). That allowed Aidan and me to wander as we pleased, but the place I desperately needed to visit was only accessible via shadows.

"I need to look upstairs."

Aidan swallowed hard and glanced over his shoulder before shaking his head. "Griffin won't like that."

"Griffin isn't the boss of me."

"Close enough."

Aidan's insistence on doing what Griffin said grated. "Just ... distract him."

Aidan's eyebrows migrated up his forehead. "Distract him?"

"You heard what I said." I took a step toward the dark corridor that I was certain led to the stairwell. "I'll be back in a few minutes. If you do your job correctly, he won't even notice I'm gone."

"Oh, he's going to notice." Aidan's hand snapped out and grabbed me around the wrist. "You're not going alone."

I tamped down my irritation, but just barely. "I know how to take care of myself."

"You're not going alone," Aidan repeated, firm. His eyes — mirror images of my own — meant business. "If some thing or someone tried to lure you here, I'm pretty sure the exact wrong thing to do is to allow you to wander around in the dark by yourself."

Oh, he had to be kidding. "You're not the boss of me, or my protector. I don't need either."

Aidan was stubborn, so when he jutted out his lower lip, I recognized he had no intention of backing down. "I'll yell out for Griffin. Don't think I won't do it. You can act as tough as you want, but we both know you'll crumble if Griffin starts barking orders."

I wanted to argue with the statement on principle alone, but he wasn't wrong. If Griffin caught me and started melting down, I'd turn away. "You listen here ... ."

"No, both of you shut up," Griffin snapped as he strolled to my right and eyed Aidan and me with annoyance. "No one is going anywhere, and that includes the dark hallway that's probably teeming with monsters."

"You don't know that," I challenged. For some reason, the stairway was calling to me. "I just want to take a quick look."

"No."

"Just ... thirty seconds."

Griffin wrapped his fingers around my wrist. "No."

"I need to see." I opted for honesty. "I feel like I need to look in that stairwell. If you stop me ... ." I left it hanging. There was no appropriate threat. It wasn't as if I was going to end things with him because he was worried about my safety. On the flip side, I was getting a bit old to threaten a scene ... and Griffin was the sort of man who wouldn't care if I did start whining and crying to get my way. That was one of the reasons we fit.

Griffin waited for me to finish the sentence. When I didn't, he simply licked his lips and stared.

I decided to take a different tactic. "If I don't see, I will be haunted by this memory until the end of time."

Griffin rolled his eyes. "Oh, geez."

"That was a little overdramatic," Aidan noted.

"I know. It's how I feel. I need to look."

Frustrated, Griffin blinked several times in rapid succession. Finally, he shook his head and nodded. "Fine." He rummaged in his pocket and handed me the flashlight before pulling his gun from his holster, causing me to widen my eyes. "Where is your letter opener?"

Dumbfounded, I patted my hoodie pocket until I came up with the item in question, swallowing hard when I couldn't pull my eyes from the gun. "Isn't that your service weapon?"

"Yes."

"Won't you lose your job if you discharge it here because we're technically breaking and entering?"

"Yes."

My heart painfully flopped. "I changed my mind. We don't need to go to the second floor."

Griffin searched my face for a long beat. "We're going," he said finally, putting his hand to the small of my back. "Aidan, I want you and Jerry to wait here. Watch your surroundings carefully. If I tell you to run, do it. I'm not kidding."

Aidan balked. "I'm not leaving my sister behind."

"If something happens, you're to escape." Griffin refused to back down. "Someone needs to call for reinforcements, and that falls to you."

"I think you should let me go upstairs with you," Aidan argued. "Three is better than two. We can send Jerry out front with his phone and he can call for help if necessary."

"Yes, let's send Jerry to do it," Jerry said dryly. "And what happens if monsters are waiting for me out there?"

"The odds of that are slim," Aidan replied.

"Oh, well, you can carve that on my tombstone. 'The odds of him dying were slim.' That sounds fan-freaking-tastic."

I bit the inside of my cheek to keep from laughing at Jerry's theatrics. He was my best friend for a reason, and that reason was because he always made me smile ... even at the most difficult of times. "Jerry and Aidan should stay here together," I volunteered, making up my mind. "Griffin and I will be quick. I don't think anything is waiting for us in the stairwell."

"Then why do you have to look?" Aidan challenged. "Why can't we just leave like Griffin wants?"

It was a fair question ... but I didn't have a good answer. "I don't know."

"She needs to see," Griffin supplied, prodding me forward. "She won't sleep if she doesn't. That means I won't sleep ... and not for a fun reason."

"Oh, you're so gross." Aidan made a face. "She's still my sister."

"And she's also my wife," Griffin said. "Wait here. Be ready. If all goes well, we'll be out of here in three minutes."

Aidan acquiesced, although it was obvious he wasn't happy. "Make it quick."

Griffin kept me close as we hit the hallway, his body pressed against mine as I swung the flashlight beam so I could see the walls that led to the stairwell.

"More symbols," Griffin noted. "Hold the light so I can take photos."

I did as he instructed, making sure to hit each wall before we arrived at the stairs. Griffin held out an arm to stop me from climbing, taking a moment to test the ancient wood before shaking his head.

"Baby, this wood isn't sound. I don't think you should climb the stairs."

I swallowed hard. "Griffin ... ."

"I know. You need to see." Griffin dragged a frustrated hand through his brown hair, which desperately needed a trim before the big day. "I don't think it's safe for both of us to climb those stairs."

"Then I'll go myself. I'm lighter anyway."

"Aisling ... ." He looked pained.

"I'll be quick. I won't be able to let it go if I don't try. We both know it."

"Yeah. I do know that." Griffin was resigned as he leaned forward and kissed me. The gesture was hard and quick, and promised a potential argument when we got home. "Be careful."

"I will."

"Be quick."

"I will."

"Remember I will fall apart if something happens to you."

My heart pinged at his serious expression. "I'll be right back."

I was determined to keep Griffin from regretting his decision to let me out of his sight, so I made good on my promise. I tested the first two stairs and then ascended quickly. Each step groaned thanks to my added weight, but they didn't give.

Once I hit the second floor, I turned the flashlight beam to every corner and came up empty. No one was on the second floor. The hallway that snaked off to my left was so dank and dark there was no amount of chocolate in the world that could entice me to brave it.

I don't know why I believed it would be different. It was quiet, and I abandoned my insistence on searching the space relatively quickly the moment I saw a spider that looked to be the size of my head. I took a moment to snap a few photos from the balcony and waved at Aidan to get his attention. "I'm coming down. We're getting out of here."

Aidan nodded in relief. "Good. Is everything okay?"

"It's even grosser up here, and the wood is definitely rotting. I know Jerry loves this place, but I think it would be better if they demolished it and started from scratch."

"Yeah, let's talk about architecture at home," Aidan said. "I don't like this place. It's creepy."

"Okay." I took another minute to search the small balcony and vestibule behind it before moving back to the stairs. There was absolutely nothing here ... yet I couldn't shake the feeling that I was missing something important. Worry about what that "something" was fled when I hit the bottom of the stairs and Griffin pulled me in for a long hug. "I'm okay." I awkwardly patted his back. "I was quick. I promised I would be and I followed through."

"It felt like ten years."

"Yeah. You're starting to sound like my father when you say things like that."

"I can live with that. They say girls want to marry their fathers."

That was a sobering thought.

WE DROPPED AIDAN AND Jerry back at their townhouse – conveniently located next door to our townhouse – before letting ourselves inside and checking all the doors and windows.

Griffin drew a bath because we both felt dirty after our tour of the abandoned theater, and neither one of us spoke until we were both in the tub, up to the neck in steaming fragrant water.

"Did you see anything on the second floor?"

"No." I shook my head as he massaged my stiff shoulders. "Someone was clearly up there because more of those symbols were painted on the walls. I took photos, by the way. I don't think anyone was hanging out there, though."

"Why do you think you felt such a strong need to go up there?"

"Maybe I'm simply crazy for stairs. Did you ever think of that?"

Griffin's lips curved against my ear. "You need to let that go. You're not crazy."

"I might be crazy."

"What does that say about me if you are? Apparently that means I like crazy women. Perhaps I'm crazy, too."

"That would be a relief. I like it when we have things in common."

Griffin chuckled as he wrapped his arms around my waist and

pulled me close. "I'm glad you can still laugh in the face of all this. I know it's hard for you, but we'll get through it ... just like we've gotten through everything else."

"It's weird, but I was thinking about how we hooked up when I was trying to figure a way to get upstairs without upsetting you."

"That was never going to happen."

"I had to try."

"Right." He ran his hands up my arms before moving them back to my neck. "What were you thinking about? I remember the start of our relationship as a delightful romp."

I couldn't stop myself from snorting. "Oh, that was ... just unbelievable."

"You remember things differently?"

I nodded. "I remember falling."

"You fell? I don't remember you falling. You're talking about the day I found you and Aidan in the alley with the body, right? I thought for sure you guys must've had something to do with the body because there was no other reason for you to be in the alley. Little did I know the weird girl with the purple eyes and attitude galore actually had a reason ... and I would grow to understand it."

"I wasn't really thinking about that day," I said. "I was thinking more about the first time you came to the townhouse to ... you know."

Griffin's lips were warm as he kissed my neck. "I could never forget that night. Everything changed for me that night."

"No, everything changed for me," I corrected. "You were still undecided. You left the next morning."

Griffin stiffened. "I didn't want to leave. I had to."

"I wasn't attacking you because of it. I thought I'd never see you again. I didn't think anyone could put up with me for the long haul. I remember I was a little morose that day. Dad thought I was being a pain. I think I had a broken heart, although I wasn't really sure about anything because I was too numb."

Water sloshed as Griffin tightened his grip. "I didn't want to leave. I needed to think. The thing is, I already knew I wanted you. I tried to talk myself out of it. I mean ... I tried hard. But it was already too late. I think it was too late from the moment I laid eyes on you."

"I thought you didn't believe in love at first sight," I teased.

"I don't. Whatever happened in that alley that first day was chemical. I felt something inside me. It was like fireworks in my head."

"I felt the fireworks someplace else."

Griffin's laugh was so loud it echoed throughout the small bathroom. "Is it any wonder I fell for you that first day?"

"Did you think we'd end up here?"

Griffin pursed his lips and sobered. "I don't know. I always figured I'd get married one day, but I thought it would be down the road. I wanted to focus on my career and worry about a wife and family later."

"And now?"

"All I want is you."

His simple answer warmed the cold parts inside of me that had yet to warm since we'd left the theater. "I didn't think we'd make it this far," I admitted, running my fingers over his. "I thought you'd get annoyed with me. Heck, I thought you'd get annoyed with my father and brothers. You took all of it on, though, and you never looked back."

"Your father and brothers aren't as bad as I initially believed."

"Oh, they're bad."

"Okay, they're bad," Griffin conceded, his grin lightning quick before he pressed a kiss to my cheek. "But once you realize why they're bad, it's impossible to dislike them."

"And why are they bad?"

"Because they love you," Griffin replied. "All they want is to protect you. Sure, that irritates you, but that doesn't stop them from doing everything they can to protect you. They'll never stop.

"As someone who understands the need to protect you, I'm grateful for their help," he continued. "Your father tries to be this big, tough guy, and I truly was a little afraid of him at first. But the more I watched him, the more I realized it was an act."

"You should probably never tell him your theory."

"I'll keep that in mind." Griffin shifted so he could get more comfortable before exhaling heavily and going back to my massage. "I have no doubt your father would've considered killing me if I'd ever hurt you. He would do the same for any of his kids. That's why he encourages you to go after Angelina so much. She hurt Cillian, and you're absolutely awful to her, so it's as if your father has a hand in the punishment when he lets you run free."

Hmm. I hadn't ever considered that. "When did you stop being afraid of him?"

"When I realized we were on the same team. He would die for you. I'd do the same. We recognized that in each other."

"You also realized he was a big marshmallow at some point, right?"

"I did," Griffin confirmed. "I believe it was the first time I watched you fake tears to get an ice cream bar and he immediately gave in. That's when I knew who he was."

"Who do you think he is?"

"A father. At first I thought he was a businessman, maybe even a protector. He's a father first, though, and that means he will always put you guys ahead of work, money and his own needs. That's how I want to be one day. He's a great role model."

I wasn't much of a crier, so the tears pricking the backs of my eyes took me by surprise. "You'll be a great father. Don't worry about that."

"And you'll be a great mother."

I wasn't so sure about that. "I had a great role model ... until she came back from the dead and started eating people."

"We'll figure it out. Close your eyes for now. Rest. We'll talk more about it in the morning."

"Okay." It wasn't difficult to do as he asked because I was exhausted. "Can we have breakfast at the Coney Island tomorrow morning?"

Griffin chuckled. "Apparently I'm a big marshmallow, too. Yes, we can have breakfast at the Coney."

"Thank you."

"You're welcome."

I waited a beat. "It's okay to be a marshmallow. I like you that way."

"That's because you're addicted to getting your own way."

"You say that like it's a bad thing."

"Shh. It's quiet time."

"Fine, but we're going to talk about this later."

"I look forward to that."

Thirteen

I had gummy shark cake for breakfast.

Griffin made sure I slept hard thanks to a little romance before bed. Then he woke me with some more romance. Coupled with our evening excursion, I needed the sugar buzz to charge my power banks.

"Good morning, baby." Griffin was in a good mood when he pressed a kiss to the top of my head. "How are you feeling on this, your last day of work before the wedding?"

I shoved a forkful of cake into my mouth and thoughtfully chewed as I regarded him. "We need to talk."

Griffin arched an eyebrow as he poured a mug of coffee. "About what?"

"The fact that you're so chipper in the morning. I've put up with it until now because I didn't want to seem like a terrible person, but the only way this relationship is going to work is if you're as crabby as me in the morning."

Griffin chuckled. "Why can't you be the one who changes? I think we'd both be better off if you woke up happy."

"That's not true. It's common knowledge that morning people die sooner. You need to get over this 'I'm happy in the morning' crap and join me on the dark side."

"Uh-huh." Griffin took the chair to my left and watched as I bit into a gummy shark with extra zest. "Should I be worried you're eating cake for breakfast?"

"We have nothing else."

"There's oatmeal."

"Again, we have nothing else," I repeated. "It was your bright idea not to shop so we wouldn't leave a bunch of food behind when we left for our honeymoon."

"A honeymoon destination your father has yet to reveal."

"He's enjoying that." I took another bite of cake. "I'm sure it will be lavish. He doesn't do anything small."

"I'm sure, too." Griffin grabbed a napkin from the holder at the center of the table and wiped the corners of my mouth. "Are you stress-eating a bit? Is that what's going on here?"

I narrowed my eyes until they were nothing but lavender slits. "Are you going to give me grief about my weight now?"

"No. I think your body is perfect."

"Uh-huh. And what if I get fat? I mean ... you mentioned kids last night. I'm going to get fat if I have kids."

"Okay, I see your head is in a really good place this morning." Griffin moved to pull the cake from me, but I growled, causing him to snap his hand away from the platter. "That is neither cute nor attractive."

"I need the sugar." I gripped my fork tighter and met his concerned gaze. "It's my last day of work before the wedding."

"I know. I can't tell you how happy I am about that."

"Why? Because you're afraid I'll keep seeing things if I'm out on my own?"

"Because you were attacked by a wraith the day before yesterday."

"Right." I'd almost forgotten about the wraith. I was more interested in my other mother. Yeah, I decided "other mother" was better than "mom beta." It rolled off the tongue easier. "Dad gave me only two charges today. It should be quick."

"I'm glad for that."

Instinctively, I reached over and feathered my fingers over Griffin's cheek. "It's your last day of work, too. Are you worried?"

"No. I'm looking forward to a break. Do you know when my last vacation was?"

I shook my head.

"I don't either. It's been that long. I have a lot of days saved up, probably more than I can ever use."

"Oh, I'll find a way to use them." I was certain of that. "In fact, I think you should save them until we have kids and then you can be the one who stays home with them when they're cranky. By the way, I'm a big believer in karma. That means we're going to get some really rotten kids because I was a terror."

"I'm already expecting that. I think we'll survive."

He was awfully calm for a guy about to get married. "Why aren't you more worked up about this? I mean ... you're about to be a husband and say goodbye to your bachelorhood. Do you know what that means?"

"I know what it means to me," Griffin clarified. "I'm mildly interested in hearing what it means to you."

"It means that I'm the last woman you'll ever see naked."

Amused, his lips curved. "That's not a deterrent. What else have you got?"

"It's going to be just you and me forever," I pointed out. "Sure, we'll have kids, but when they're gone it will be just you and me again."

"I'm looking forward to that."

"Are you sure?"

Griffin's eyebrows drew together. "If you've decided to turn insecure out of the blue, I've got to tell you I don't like it."

"It's not that. I know I'm a joy and you're lucky to have me."

"I feel the same way."

"It's just ... look at my parents." I grabbed another gummy shark from the cake and bit into it. "What's going to happen to them when my brothers finally move out? How will they deal with being alone?"

"First, I think the odds of Braden and Redmond leaving anytime soon are slim," Griffin replied. "I like your brothers — at least some of the time — but those two aren't ready to settle down and they're not leaving the family castle until they find wives of their own."

He had a point. Still ... . "What do you think is going to happen with my mother? I mean the one who keeps popping up and inviting herself to family events. You don't think my father will try to make a go of it with her again, do you?"

Griffin shrugged. "Probably not, but I can't completely rule it out."

"I'm afraid."

"For him?"

"For all of us."

"Oh, Aisling, you can't let this eat you alive." He took the fork from me even though I put up a token struggle. "You're also done with cake for breakfast. I don't want to send you out on your final shift hopped up on sugar. You'll likely pick a fight with someone at every turn."

"You usually like it when I pick a fight with people."

"Not really. That's something you've told yourself that isn't really true. I don't mind it when you fight with Angelina because I know you can take her."

"She is easy."

"I want you clearheaded and on top of things today. It's important."

"You think something bad is about to happen, too, don't you?"

"I ... ." Griffin worked his jaw as he debated how to answer. "I think that something might happen," he said finally. "Given your track record, it's an inevitability. I'm hoping whatever it is won't affect our wedding. Believe it or not, I'm looking forward to being your husband."

"Even if I stress eat until the honeymoon?"

"Even if."

He hadn't said anything I didn't already know, yet I was relieved all the same. "I'll be careful today. I promise."

"Thank you."

"You be careful, too."

"I'm doing paperwork."

"Don't get a paper cut."

"I'll do my best."

I leaned forward and rested my forehead against his. "I love you."

"I love you, too." Griffin stroked the back of my head. "I'm not giving you the fork back so you can keep eating the cake."

"The love is fading."

MARY LOU HARRIS WAS MY last charge as a single woman.

I wasn't much for marking the time in that manner — it seemed like clock-watching and that was always a waste of time (pun intended) — but I couldn't stop myself from marking the day in increments.

My last breakfast on my last day of work as a single woman.

My second-to-last charge on my last day of work as a single woman.

My last chance to annoy a soul as a single woman.

I was counting down, although it wasn't as if I was counting down to doomsday or anything. It was more that I was looking forward to something.

"Oh, you should wipe that stupid look off your face." Mary Lou, on the other hand, wasn't looking forward to anything, even though I'd informed her upon our initial meeting that she was going to a good place. Apparently she didn't believe me ... and she was nowhere near ready to leave this world in favor of the next. She had a lot more complaining to do.

"I don't have a look on my face." That was a damnable lie. In truth, I couldn't hide the expressions chasing me as I looked over the wedding photos spread across Mary Lou's mantel. "We're you really married eight times?"

Mary Lou's sneer told me she wasn't a fan of the question. "Why do you care?"

I shrugged, noncommittal. "I was just curious. You have eight different wedding dresses. I could barely pick one."

"The dresses were the easiest part."

"Uh-huh." Curious despite myself, I pressed further. "What was the hardest part?"

Mary Lou tilted her head to the side, thoughtful. "Marriage."

Hmm. It wasn't the answer I expected. "I thought the wedding was the hardest part."

"The wedding is a party, and I happen to like a party ... especially when it's held in my honor."

"Right." I trailed my eyes over the photos again. "You liked the party better than the hangover."

"Excuse me?"

"I didn't mean that the way it came out," I said hurriedly. "It's just ... you liked the party and didn't care about everything that went with it, including the people. That's why you married and divorced eight times."

"I only divorced six times," Mary Lou corrected. "Two of my husbands died."

"You didn't kill them, did you?"

"Of course not! I married them when they were sick. I knew they were going to die, so it wasn't hard to hang on."

I barely managed to hide my grimace. "That is ... lovely."

"Oh, look who is all high and mighty." Mary Lou wrinkled her nose as she bopped her head back and forth in a mocking manner. "You haven't even been married once and you're telling me how to live my life. That is ... ridiculous. Talk to me when you've got a divorce or two under your belt."

"I don't plan on that ever happening. I'm only getting married once. It's going to stick."

Mary Lou let loose a snort that sounded like a pig rolling around in the holy grail of slop. "Oh, you're so cute." She mimed pinching my cheek and giving it a good shake. "Don't you think everyone who has ever been divorced believed at the start that they were marrying for life? Why else would they say the words?"

That was a fair question. "I think that most people do mean it," I acknowledged. "I think most of the people who marry do so with the best intentions." My eyes drifted over the photographs again. "Maybe not you after the third or fourth time, but I bet in the beginning you thought you were going to live the fairy tale."

"I did think that," Mary Lou agreed, nodding. "I thought that the wedding would be superb, the honeymoon a dream, and then we would slip into domestic bliss. It turns out domestic bliss isn't real."

"I think it's real," I countered, "but realistic expectations are a must. Domestic bliss isn't really domestic bliss. It's more of a compromise between two individuals who desperately want to make something work and are willing to put in the time to make sure it happens."

"Ugh." If Mary Lou had a body, this was about the point I'd expect her to start throwing up. Secretly, I was glad she couldn't because my stomach was a bit stretched thanks to the huge amount of cake Griffin let me eat before cutting me off. I expected him to be more strict. "You're an idiot if you think things are going to work out in some neat and happy way."

"I don't think anything in this world is neat," I countered. "That's why you hire maids ... or marry a man who enjoys picking up after you."

"Did you select a man who enjoys picking up after you?"

"Not really, but we spend an hour each week picking up together. It's essentially a bonding ritual," I explained. "Sometimes Griffin bribes me with a night out if I do the cleaning without complaining."

"That's ... not so bad." Mary Lou leaned forward, intrigued. "When I married the first time, men didn't help with the chores. Women stayed home, did the housework and took care of the children. Men went to work, had drinks with their friends and told women how to keep the house clean."

"That sounds ludicrous."

"It was. Why do you think I divorced so often?"

"I think you got divorced because you were just as set in your ways as the men you married," I answered without hesitation. "They didn't want to change and neither did you."

"Nobody wants to change."

Was that true? "I think most people want to better themselves. That's not changing just for the sake of changing. The problems arise when someone — or maybe both people — don't want to better themselves. I won't have that problem. I always want to be a better person, and Griffin is the same."

"You seem sure of yourself."

"I am."

"Then I won't rain on your parade," Mary Lou said. "That still doesn't mean I'm willingly going with you. I have plans for my life — I was just getting close to Hank Bivens at the senior center — and there's a chance I could get to marriage number nine. I prefer that to eight. It's a better number because threes are lucky."

"Well, you don't really have a say in the matter," I said. "In fact ... ." I trailed off when a hint of movement caught my attention through the front window. I turned away from the mantel to stare at the fluttery shadow.

"Did you forget what you were saying?" Mary Lou snapped her fingers in my face to get my attention. "Focus. You'll never survive marriage if your attention span doesn't improve."

"Do you live alone?" I asked, scratching my cheek as I stared at the shadow. It belonged to a human — or at least a humanoid being, because I couldn't rule out a wraith — and I was certain that who or whatever owned the shadow waited in the bushes for a very specific reason.

"I just told you that I was working on a new husband," Mary Lou replied, disdain practically dripping from her tongue. "Do you listen to anyone but yourself?"

"Not usually." My mind was moving at a fantastic rate as I moved from the living room to the kitchen. I leaned over the sink to peer out the window there, my heart skipping a beat when I saw an actual human moving across the patio.

"Who is that?" Mary Lou's eyes widened when her gaze landed on the man in question. He wore denim jeans, a raggedy T-shirt and a leather jacket. "It's too hot for that jacket."

"He's a rogue reaper," I replied as I dug in my pocket for my cell phone. "That essentially means he thinks he's Fonzie."

"Do you know him? Do you work with him?"

"I know him," I replied, rolling my neck to assuage some of the tension building there. "I definitely don't work with him." I punched in my father's number and waited for him to answer. "Just ... hold on."

It took three rings for my father to greet me. "Hey, kid? Are you done for the day? If you want to take off and do bride stuff, that's fine. You can bring the souls by later."

He was far too accommodating these days. I almost missed the way he used to yell and threaten me. Apparently you can't scream at a bride because it's frowned upon, at least according to Miss Manners. I had no doubt he would be over it by the time Griffin and I returned from our honeymoon.

"I have a problem." I didn't stand on preamble. He wouldn't want it and, quite frankly, I didn't have time. "There are rogue reapers outside this house — front and back — and I'm pretty sure one of them is Xavier Fontaine."

The only sound on the other end of the call was a slow hiss, which told me my father was sucking in a breath.

"I don't think I can get out of here without them grabbing me," I admitted, shifting from one foot to the other. "I know there are at least two people here, and I saw Xavier through the back window. He probably wants to kill me for what I did to his brother."

"What did you do to his brother?" Mary Lou asked.

"I left him to die in a fire."

"Aisling, please tell me you're not talking to the soul," Dad barked, finding his voice.

"Fine. I won't tell you that."

"Why can't you just suck and run?"

"Because I was told a lady never did that."

Dad's growl was low and made me smile despite my dire circumstances. "We'll talk about your filthy mind later, young lady. As for now, sit tight. Cillian and I are on our way."

"What if they come after me?"

"Then I'll find you. I promise."

The words were meant to be comforting, but the gummy sharks and cake sitting like a ball of lead in my stomach threatened to revolt all the same. "Hurry. I don't like this."

"Oh, I'm going to hurry. Make sure you suck that soul before we get there. We won't have time for two bouts of nonsense. Do you understand?"

"I get it."

"Good. We're on our way. We'll be there in ten minutes."

"You live twenty minutes away."

"We'll be there in ten minutes. Count on it."

Fourteen

I paced Mary Lou's small living room and cursed the day I was forced to join the family business for what felt like forever. In real time, it was probably five minutes. Still, I couldn't shake the feeling something was about to go very wrong.

"Don't you have a sword or something?"

Mary Lou's question caught me off guard. "Why would I have a sword?"

She shrugged. "I just thought monster hunters always carried swords."

"I'm not a monster hunter." That was mostly true, although I'd dispatched my fair share of monsters since becoming a reaper. "I'm supposed to collect souls and that's it. I don't understand how this keeps happening."

"My guess is it's karma," Mary Lou offered, seemingly innocent. "You seem like the type of person who would have karma constantly biting her on the ass."

"Oh, well, thank you for that," I said dryly, rolling my eyes. "I can't tell you how helpful that is."

Mary Lou held her hands up in a placating manner. "I'm just saying ... a sword could only help."

"Yeah, well, I don't have a sword." I positioned myself behind the curtains to stare at the front porch. It was empty, which either meant the rogues were going to enter from the back or wait to grab me when I exited. "My father is coming. He'll know what to do."

"Sure. I can see that."

"He'll know what to do," I repeated, more to comfort myself than convince Mary Lou. "He always knows what to do."

"I'm not saying you're wrong, although your husband-to-be can't be happy at your hero worship for your father."

"I don't have hero worship."

"Really? That's not how it looks to me."

I slowly drew my attention from the front porch and extended a warning finger. "Do you want me to absorb your soul right now? I'll do it."

Mary Lou rolled her eyes. "You're going to do it anyway. You have a job to do. I've resigned myself to the fact that I'm not going to see that ninth wedding."

"You didn't need a ninth wedding anyway."

"I wanted one."

I often wanted things I didn't need, so I opted to let it go. "My father will be here soon. He's bringing my brother. It'll be okay."

"I'm already dead," Mary Lou noted, gesturing to the body on the floor. She had choked while eating Girl Scout cookies. As far as deaths went, there were worse ways to go. "You're the one who should be worried."

"I am worried."

"That's why you should take my sword."

I stilled, surprised. "What?"

"My sword," Mary Lou repeated. "You should take it. You'll need protection when you run."

"I don't understand." In truth, I was utterly flabbergasted. "Why do you have a sword?"

"I think the better question is, why doesn't everyone have a sword?"

My father owned ten swords, so I couldn't come up with a reasonable answer. "Where is your sword?"

"Hanging above my bed."

That seemed an odd place for it, but I wasn't in a position to offer decorating opinions. "Great." I ran down the hallway, turning into what I thought would be a normal bedroom. Instead I found a huge metal bed with *Game of Thrones* banners hanging from the walls and a replica of Ned Stark's huge sword "Ice" mounted on the wall. "What the ... ?"

"I'm sad I'll never see the end of the show. I was so close."

"I'm sure they have television in Heaven," I murmured, distracted. "Where did you get that thing?"

"The internet."

"You can get swords over the internet?"

"You can get anything over the internet. I bought a special tea blend to go with my sword."

"Huh." With few other options, I strolled to the display and carefully reached for the sword, letting loose an inelegant grunt when the heaviness of the blade took me by surprise. "Good grief."

"Yeah. It's got some heft to it." Mary Lou seemed pleased with herself. "It's sharp, too. You should be able to stab someone good."

"I don't want to stab anyone." That was the truth. "I just want to get away from here and figure out what those rogues are doing outside."

"I think they're clearly here for you."

"Yeah, but that won't stop them from absorbing you." I cast the enthusiastic soul a rueful look. "I need to absorb you now. If I don't, I could lose you in the melee when my father arrives."

"But ... I want to see the fight." Mary Lou adopted a pitiful expression. "You'll be using my sword."

"If I don't absorb you and somehow screw up, they could take you." I opted to be truthful. "If they take you, getting to the other side isn't a guarantee. Rogues sell souls, and you could be used to feed a wraith or something."

"What does that mean?"

"You'll never get to Heaven. You'll simply cease to be."

"Oh." Mary Lou didn't look happy at the prospect. "Well, I don't want that."

"Definitely."

"I guess you can absorb me." She didn't refrain from pouting. "This is disappointing."

"Tell me about it." I dug my scepter out of my pocket and pointed it at her. "I hope *Game of Thrones* ends the way you want it to."

"Thanks."

"Maybe you'll find a ninth and final husband in Heaven."

"That would be nice."

I flicked the button and forced a smile as Mary Lou's soul dissolved, only letting it slip when I shoved the scepter back into my pocket and carried the sword into the living room. The front porch remained empty when I checked, but my anxiety ratcheted up a notch.

I practically jumped out of my skin when my phone rang.

"Dad?"

"Who else? Are you ready?"

I nodded before I remembered he couldn't see me. "I'm ready. I have a sword."

"Where did you get a sword?"

"Mary Lou had one. Big *Game of Thrones* fan."

"You made friends with the soul?"

"I think that's a gross exaggeration," I countered. "She pointed me toward the sword and I took it. That's hardly the stuff of a lasting friendship."

"You absorbed her, right?"

"I did."

"Aisling." Dad's voice was low and full of warning.

"I absorbed her," I snapped. "I explained what would happen if the rogues got their hands on her and she willingly went."

"She doesn't have a choice in the matter. That's not how this works."

"Yeah, yeah, yeah." I dismissed his words. "Where are you?"

"We're on the street. We're going to park directly in front of the house. I want you to run out when you see us."

"What about my car?"

"Already taken care of. The home office is retrieving it."

That was a relief. I swallowed hard as I gripped the sword tighter.

"If something happens, tell Griffin ... ." Tell him what? There was nothing I could say to ease his pain.

"Nothing is going to happen." Dad was firm. "I won't let it, kid. I'm here and I want you to come straight for me."

I smiled when I saw my father's BMW roll to a stop in front of the curb. "I see you're traveling in style."

"Nothing but the best for you, kid. Come out now. Don't stop until you get to me. Do you understand?"

"Yes. I'm coming."

I paused by the front door long enough to take a bracing breath before flicking the lock and opening the door. I kept my wits enough to remember to close it. If I left it open, whoever responded to Mary Lou's death might be suspicious. Police intervention was the last thing we needed.

I gripped the sword as I hurried down the steps, my eyes widening when Xavier Fontaine hurried from the side of the house. Our eyes met, recognition sparked, and a slow smile spread across his face.

"I've been waiting for you."

"Good," Cillian barked, taking Xavier by surprise when he slammed his fist into the man's face from the side. "We've been waiting for you, too."

The blow wasn't enough to cause Xavier to lose consciousness, but he did teeter to the side and drop to a knee. Dad was busy dealing with a second rogue, one I didn't recognize, so I increased my pace and raced toward the car. I was almost there when I recognized a shadow swooping in at my left.

I reacted out of instinct, swinging the sword as hard as I could. Instead of the tip going into someone, the broadside smacked a large woman in the face. She groaned as she reared back, her heavily-lined eyes going narrow as she let loose a string of curses that could've made a sailor blush.

"In the car," Dad ordered, giving me a hard shove when I stopped to give the woman a long once over. "Now!"

He practically roared the order, so I had no choice but to acquiesce. I hopped in the back seat, smirking at the furious woman through the window when the door slammed shut. Dad was in the passenger seat bellowing orders for Cillian as we drove away.

"Are you all right?" Dad's eyes were searching as they snagged with mine.

I nodded. "I have a new sword."

"I see that."

"I also collected my last soul as a single woman."

"Yes." Dad's eyes roamed my face. "How do you feel about that?"

"Pretty good."

"I'm glad."

"I could use something to eat. I'm hungry."

"Consider it done."

INSTEAD OF IMMEDIATELY taking me back to Grimlock Manor, Dad selected one of my favorite Middle Eastern places for lunch. He waited until the three of us were safely ensconced in a corner booth, our orders placed and a raw vegetable tray with garlic dip in front of us, to ask the obvious question.

"What happened?"

I shrugged. "I have no idea. I looked out the window and noticed a shadow. I couldn't see a body attached to it, but it was far too human to ignore. Then I went to the kitchen and saw Xavier on the back patio. I almost didn't recognize him. It's been a long time since I saw him."

"I didn't even know he was in the area," Dad groused, leaning back in his seat. "I never disliked Xavier as I did Duke. He was much younger and raised by his brother, so it was almost like he was forced into the life and never willingly chose it."

"He seems pretty willing now," Cillian lamented as he rubbed his sore hand. "He's got a jaw like a pile of bricks."

I grinned at him, amused. "That was a nice shot."

Cillian returned my smile. "Thanks. It felt good to unload. I'm feeling a little tense this week."

"Clint?"

"Pretty much."

"Yes, that man is an ass," Dad said, tapping the side of the vegetable plate. "Eat up. You're still pale."

I made a face. "Why does everyone keep saying I'm pale?"

"Because you are."

"Well ... I don't feel pale."

"That's good," Dad said. "You need more than cake for breakfast, though."

I narrowed my eyes, suspicious. "Did Griffin call you?"

Dad shifted in his chair. "I called him when we were en route. I thought he should know you were in trouble but we were extracting you."

That sounded ... absurd. "Extracting me?"

"You know what I mean." Dad refused to back down. "He loves you. He had a right to know you were in danger."

"But ... he's probably freaking out."

"I texted him once we were clear of the house. He knows you're fine."

Now it was my turn to freak out. "He knows I'm fine, but I didn't call him to say there was an issue. He's going to be angry."

"So what?" Cillian challenged. "He's not your keeper."

"Yeah, but ... ."

"He's fine, Aisling." Dad made an annoyed sound. "He understands that you called me for obvious reasons. He's not upset. He simply wants you to be all right ... and you are."

"I guess." I wasn't convinced. "At least I got a new sword out of it."

"Yes, stealing from departed souls is always something to crow about," Dad agreed.

I glared at him as Cillian disguised a chuckle. "Let's change the subject," I said finally. "Cillian, have you made any headway on the dagger the wraith left behind?"

"As a matter of fact, I have." Cillian brightened considerably. He loved talking about research and books. "I was about to head downstairs to talk to Dad about what I found when he informed me you needed help. I think the Taylors are probably confused given the way we raced out of the house, so we need to come up with an appropriate lie."

"Good point." Dad grabbed a cucumber slice from the vegetable platter. "What did you find out about the dagger?"

"I managed to identify the third symbol, the one I was having trouble with."

"I remember."

"It refers to a chosen one."

I wrinkled my forehead. "You've got to be kidding me. Isn't that a little Harry Potterish?"

"I don't think 'chosen one' means the same thing," Cillian explained. "Although, now that I think about it, they're not that far off. The actual description refers to a traveler, someone who can move between planes with the help of magic and one of the marks that is carved into the dagger."

"We'll need more information," Dad prodded.

"The practice of soul walking was abandoned for a reason," Cillian explained. "It was considered dangerous."

"I would think that was obvious before they started doing it," I argued.

"Yeah, well, apparently they needed to face quite a few tragedies before they let that sink in," Cillian countered. "The thing is, from what I can tell, soul walking is how we ended up with wraiths in the first place."

My mouth dropped open. "What?"

"Don't talk with your mouth full, Aisling," Dad instructed, his gaze fully on Cillian. "How did you figure that out?"

"They never come out and say it," Cillian cautioned. "But the books I've found refer to two sorts of soul walkers. The first manage to keep a sense of self while separating from their bodies. The second don't. They're described as soulless beings who must feed on others to survive."

"That sounds like wraiths," I offered.

"Wraiths have physical bodies," Dad argued. "I thought soul walkers didn't."

"True soul walkers don't," Cillian corrected. "In the instances where the practice got out of hand, the soul tried to wedge itself back into a previous body because it couldn't survive. When that happened, it fractured the soul. The soul got the benefits of living longer, but it was in a physical body that required food ... and only one kind of food would do.

"Over the years, wraiths have evolved a bit," he continued. "They started out as an offshoot of soul walkers, though. I'm positive about that."

"It makes sense." Dad rubbed his chin, thoughtful. "What else did you find? I mean ... what's the deal with this chosen one crap?"

"I think I'm going to regret using that term," Cillian complained. "Don't think of this individual as the chosen one. Think of him as more of a champion, a traveler, as I mentioned before. The soul walkers and wraiths split at some point, and I think we can all agree why. Part of the legend is that one faction believed a traveler would balance the scales and fight the wraiths."

"Don't you think that's a bit ridiculous?" I challenged. "I mean ... it's kind of like a fable or something. It can't be real."

"It very well might not be real or the legend may have grown to the point it can't possibly be true," Cillian readily agreed. "I'm not saying I think it's real."

"What are you saying?"

"That wraiths sprang from somewhere, which means we might be able to use that information to more easily kill them," he answered. "Maybe there's a hint in this champion legend, which I haven't been able to track down in its entirety yet."

"You don't really believe one person can end all the wraiths, do you?"

"No." Cillian was firm. "Even the few writings I've managed to find on the subject say that's not possible. The champion isn't supposed to kill all the wraiths."

"What is he supposed to do?" Dad asked. "If not end the wraiths, why make up the legend?"

"That's a very good question," Cillian answered. "I don't know. A fight is mentioned regarding a split soul. I don't know what this champion is supposed to do. I don't know how the dagger plays into it. More importantly, I don't know why some random wraith would have possession of the dagger. It seems to me that's the sort of weapon that would be tucked away by a zealot."

"Maybe it was," I said. "Maybe the wraith was the former owner and he was a zealot. While soul walkers might no longer be a thing, wraiths are. That means people keep trying to perfect the soul walking ritual ... and failing. That's how wraiths are born.

"We always assumed wraiths were born because people wanted to live forever," I continued. "It turns out that's a rather simplistic explanation. It's not altogether untrue, but it's not a complete reason. The end goal was the soul walking, not being a wraith. Turning into a wraith was the consequence of soul walking incorrectly."

"It does change things," Dad mused, shoving a tomato in my direction. "Eat."

"I'm eating."

"Keep eating until your color is back."

"That might never happen at the rate we're going."

"You'll survive."

"Fine." I bit into the tomato. "But you're starting to bug me with the hovering."

"Apparently you need it." Dad flicked his eyes to Cillian. "We need to dig deep into this research. We might need more books than we have at our disposal. I'll make some calls when I get home."

Cillian broke out in a wide smile. "That sounds like a great idea."

"Only you would think that, son." Dad patted his arm. "That's why you're my favorite."

I made a horrified face. "What about me?"

"You won't be my favorite until you stop being pale."

"Yeah, yeah. I'm working on it."

Fifteen

I spent the rest of the afternoon hanging around Grimlock Manor. Dad refused to take me home — instead hiding my keys and insisting I stay close to him. He opted to bribe me with candy, just like when I was a kid, but I made him work for it. He had to send out for Red Vines because Twizzlers simply wouldn't do.

Griffin's family was in the main parlor when he arrived. I saw him on the monitor in Dad's office. He made a show of greeting them, promising he would have more time to spend with them later, and then excused himself to find me. He didn't have to look hard because it was clear he knew exactly where to find me.

"I need something to entertain me," I complained.

"I've heard adult coloring books are soothing," Dad noted. "I'll have Braden pick up a few on his way home."

He had to be kidding. "I don't want a coloring book."

"Then you're getting a gag." An afternoon alone with me had forced Dad to embrace his normal curmudgeonly attitude. It was a blessing.

"Whatever." I folded my arms over my chest. "You'll have to sing or something. I can't take much more of this."

Thankfully, Griffin picked that moment to save me from my boredom. "Hey, baby." He didn't wait for me to respond, instead pulling me into his arms and giving me a long hug as Dad pretended he didn't care and focused on his computer. "Are you okay?"

"I'm fine," I assured him, patting his shoulder. "Nobody laid a hand on me. Cillian punched Xavier, though, and I smacked a chick in the face with a sword."

Caught between amusement and annoyance, Griffin drew his eyebrows together. "Where did you get a sword?"

"My soul gave it to me. She was a big *Game of Thrones* fan."

"Ah, well, that totally makes sense." Griffin scooped me out of the chair and lifted me so he could sit, settling me on his lap as he ran his hands over my back. It was a sweet gesture, until I realized he was looking for bruises that didn't exist.

"I'm not hurt. I just told you that."

"You tend to cover up your maladies," he countered. "I'm just making sure. You're going to be mine full time in a few days and I want to make sure I don't regret my purchase."

Oh, well, that was insulting. "Are you insinuating that I'm your property?"

Griffin refused to back down. "Yes." He grinned as he kissed the tip of my nose and ignored the dirty looks my father shot his way. "You seem none the worse for wear. Not even a chip or small scratch. That's good."

"That means you can stop petting her and separate to two chairs," Dad prodded.

"I think we're fine sharing a chair." Griffin refused to be drawn into an argument no matter how my father goaded him. "I guarantee Aisling's brothers will be here any minute and they're going to need chairs. It would be rude to take two when we only need one."

I pressed my lips together to keep from laughing as Dad rolled his eyes.

"You're smooth," Dad said finally, shaking his head. "You're a pain in the ass, but you're smooth."

"Thank you."

"I didn't mean it as a compliment."

"You'll live."

Despite himself, Dad's lips quirked as he shook his head and focused on the report in front of him. "The home office tried to round up the rogues. They managed to take one into custody — the one you hit across the face with your sword, Aisling — but the rest got away."

Well, that was disappointing. "Xavier is the one we want," I said. "He was clearly in charge."

"Xavier Fontaine?" Redmond asked as he strolled into the room, with Braden, Cillian and Aidan close on his heels. "I just heard he's back in town. What's up with that?"

"Close the door," Dad instructed.

Aidan did as ordered, although I didn't miss a curious glance from one of Griffin's cousins on the other side of the door as it slowly swung shut.

"For those who weren't part of the excitement this afternoon, here's a brief rundown of what happened." Dad was calm and precise as he explained things to my brothers. When he was done the fury was palpable.

"I don't get it," Braden said finally. "Xavier Fontaine never wanted to be a reaper. He only did it because Duke raised him and said he didn't have a choice. Xavier was the least annoying of that group."

"Well, he's clearly changed his stance," Dad said dryly.

"But ... why?"

"Maybe because I killed his brother," I automatically answered, my mind busy. "Maybe he somehow found out about it and he's trying to pay me back."

Griffin tightened his grip, although he made sure not to cut off my air supply. "Is that possible?"

"I don't see how." Dad chose his words carefully. "Everyone who was at the cemetery that day is dead."

"You filed reports," Redmond pointed out. "Did you include the part about Aisling killing Fontaine? I know you don't want to hear it, but there's always a chance that there's a mole in the office, someone the rogues are paying off to share information. We've considered that for a long time."

"And I'm not ruling it out," Dad said. "I think that a mole makes sense. How else would the rogues know exactly where to be at the wrong time?"

"But?" Aidan prodded.

"But I didn't include the part about Aisling killing Fontaine in my report," Dad replied without hesitation. "I didn't think it was important who did what. Fontaine's death was recorded, but I didn't say who did the deed ... and if questioned, I would've taken responsibility myself."

I jerked up my chin, surprised. "Why?"

"Because you did what had to be done that day, but I don't want you facing retaliation for it."

I grasped right away what he was leaving out. "And you didn't think I could take it at the time because I was worked up about what I did."

"That is not true." Dad wagged a finger. "You were upset — you had a right to be — but I didn't think you were fragile."

Now it was my turn to furrow my brow. "Who said anything about fragile?"

"I think we're getting off track here," Griffin said quickly, shifting beneath me to get more comfortable. "What's the deal with this Fontaine guy? I understand he's the other guy's brother, but I want to know why I should be more worked up about this than any other attack."

"I don't know that you should," Dad cautioned. "The thing is, while I considered Duke Fontaine the ultimate enemy — even more dangerous than wraiths sometimes because money was his motivating factor — Xavier is another story. He wasn't someone to ignore, but he wasn't openly dangerous either."

"Except he was lying in wait outside of a charge's house to grab Aisling," Griffin argued. "That means he's dangerous."

"Apparently he's dangerous *now*," Dad said. "We have to figure out why."

"Until then, I suggest we keep Aisling locked down here," Braden suggested. "The house is big, so she won't feel penned in, and we'll always have somebody close in case someone tries to attack."

I balked. "I don't need a babysitter."

"Of course not." Dad smiled indulgently. "We're not looking after you. You're looking after us."

I knew exactly what he was doing and made a disgusted face. "That's not going to work on me. I'm not five, so you can't manipulate me the same way you used to. Jerry has a spa day planned for tomorrow. He will absolutely melt down if you don't let us go. He says my toenails are a travesty and he's got some facial thing that he claims will make my skin glow. If you stop him from taking me to the spa, he will make everyone in this house pay and you know it."

Dad narrowed his eyes. "I don't think the spa is more important than your life."

"Neither do I, but Jerry is the important one here. If you want to cancel the spa day, you have to explain it to him."

My father was a strong man, a tough negotiator and leader. He enjoyed bossing people around and laying down the law. He was fine with a few tears (as long as they weren't mine), and he got off on telling people "no" and watching them turn bitter. The look on his face when I mentioned the prospect of telling Jerry his meticulously planned afternoon was out the window was priceless.

"Fine, we'll figure out a way for you to go to the spa tomorrow," Dad finally conceded. "With backup. I don't want to hear a single word about it."

I had to bite the inside of my cheek to keep from laughing. "I'm sure Jerry will be thrilled that you're taking control of the situation."

"Don't push things."

Just for show, I jutted out my lower lip and pouted. Dad held out a good five seconds before pushing the Red Vines closer and prodding me to take one.

"This is why you're spoiled," Griffin said, disgusted. "You know exactly how to play everyone in your life."

"Does that include you?" Dad asked pointedly.

Griffin nodded. "I'm the worst. I don't know how it happened, but she can play me like her favorite video game."

"She's a master." Dad winked at me. "The good news is, Aisling is done with work. It will be easier to keep her safe. The bad news is that the house is crawling with Taylors and I'm worried they'll start asking questions."

"It will be okay." Griffin sounded sure of himself. "I'm done with work now, too. I can entertain them."

"That doesn't change the fact that this house is overflowing with big personalities," Dad noted. "We're due for an explosion."

"It will be fine." I offered a dismissive wave. "Griffin's family is easier to get along with than our family."

"That's exactly what I'm worried about."

DINNER WAS SUPPOSED TO BE A HUGE AFFAIR.

Dad arranged for a seafood buffet that included some of my favorites, like lobster, crab legs, scallops and fettuccine Alfredo. Griffin's family was floored by the spread, gushing and making happy gasping noises, but I understood it was for my benefit.

"I'm going to eat my weight in lobster!" I rubbed my hands together and performed a giddy little dance. "This is going to be awesome."

Dad's smile was fond as he stroked the back of my head and gave me a quick kiss on the temple. "I thought you'd enjoy it. There's blueberry and blackberry pie for dessert."

"Awesome!" I continued swaying my hips as I pumped my fist in the air. "This is, like, the best day ever."

"That's not what you said a few hours ago."

I refused to let him bring me down. "Things change. In fact ... ." I studied the dining room setup through the open door as my brothers and Griffin poured drinks for the Taylors in the parlor. "I'm going to run upstairs and change my shirt. Seafood is bound to be messy and I don't want to stain this one."

"You should've bought those bibs, Dad," Braden drawled, adopting his "I'm going to annoy Aisling" voice and setting my teeth on edge. "That way Aisling would've been fully covered for dinner."

Dad was horrified. "Adult bibs are never allowed in this house."

"I think you're missing out on a great idea," Cillian teased.

"And I think I need another drink."

I left my family to mingle with Griffin's and took the stairs two at a time to my old room — which looked to be my current room again, for the foreseeable future — and pulled up short when I found my mother standing in the open doorway. She stared into the room, as if looking at something only she could see, and she appeared lost in thought.

"Do you need something?" I tried to keep the accusation from my tone, but it wasn't easy.

"What?" Mom shifted her eyes to me and smiled. "Oh, Aisling, I didn't see you standing there. I was just looking around."

Suspicion wrapped itself around my heart and gave a vicious squeeze. "Why were you looking around when you knew we were downstairs?"

"The Taylors are nice people, but I miss our quiet family time."

"Right." I strolled past her and headed into the room. "I'm changing into an older shirt because Dad is having a seafood bar. I think it's going to be messy."

Mom chuckled, low and throaty. "I take it he's spoiling the crap out of you this week."

"He's spoiled the crap out of me my entire life. I like it that way."

"You always were a daddy's girl."

I stilled as I pulled a T-shirt from the dresser drawer. She sounded whimsical, wistful even. That didn't mean I trusted her.

"Why did you have one of the storm discs?" I blurted out the question without thinking about ramifications. The time was long past for playing coy. I didn't trust her. There was a reason for that.

"What?" Mom widened her eyes, adopting an innocent expression. I didn't miss the slight pink tone taking over her cheeks. "I have no idea what you're talking about."

"At the cemetery a few weeks ago," I prodded. "Once we finished off everyone, we had to cover up our activities. That included a fire. I was on the hill with Griffin. He wasn't keen on being close to anyone because he wasn't sure he would be able to maintain his composure and refrain from attacking."

"He managed it quite handily with you," Mom pointed out. "He did what no one else managed and found a sense of self in the middle of the madness. That must make you proud."

"I don't think 'proud' is the right word," I countered. "I was terrified that day. I thought he might rip me apart with his bare hands because he couldn't control himself. The thing is, I was more worried about him than me. I knew he would never get over it if he laid a hand on me ... whether he was in control or not."

"He is an oddly moral creature," Mom agreed.

I didn't like her tone. "He's a good man," I corrected. "He's a great man, in fact. That's why I'm marrying him."

"He seems very fond of you."

There was an insult buried somewhere in there, but I was too weary to search for it. "I was on the hill," I repeated. "I watched the cleanup efforts. You had one of the discs in your hand and you threw it in the fire when you thought no one was looking."

"You're mistaken." Mom was a masterful liar. That was something she picked up over the years she was separated from us, because she was a solid truth-teller during my younger years. "I did throw one of the discs into the fire, but I took it from Detective Green."

Mark Green was a local police officer who worked against us during the storms. He was adamant about taking us out, until Mom supposedly turned against him and tipped the scales so we could take him down. It was a convenient story ... and I didn't believe it.

"Dad threw in the disc that he found on Green," I countered. "I saw him."

"Then I must have thrown in the disc you found."

"No. Cillian handled that one." Events of that day were seared in my mind, probably forever. I'd never been so terrified in my life ... and for once it wasn't because I was worried about myself. I thought Griffin's life would end if he didn't somehow stop himself from killing me. That I managed to get through his confused mind barriers was still something of a miracle. "You had another disc, one you didn't want us to know about."

"You're mistaken." Mom met my gaze without blinking. "I did throw in one of the discs, but it wasn't something from my collection. It was one of the other discs that needed to be destroyed. I'm not sure which one, but you're mistaken thinking it was something else."

I had a choice. I could push her to the point of no return, explain that I was never going to believe her and kick her out of the house. That would fire up my brothers — especially Braden — and create a war. I wasn't in the mood for that. Only one option remained, and I really hated it.

"I guess I was mistaken," I said finally, dragging my shirt over my head and tossing it on the bed before replacing it with the older T-shirt. "I can't imagine how I got so turned around."

Mom merely smiled. "It happens."

"Yeah."

"I see you still have the sleigh bed we picked out together." Mom was eager to change the subject. "You hated it when we bought it, but you clearly like it now."

"It's big enough for all of us to play shark attack in. That's its more endearing quality."

"It's a beautiful bed." Mom's expression reflected thoughtfulness before she shook her head and gestured toward the door. "Shall we head down to dinner?"

I nodded. "I'm eating my weight in seafood tonight."

"That sounds fun."

"Oh, it's definitely going to be fun."

Sixteen

The spa day turned into a female extravaganza and I wasn't sure how it happened.

"Wait ... what?"

"All the women are going," Jerry explained as I stood at the bottom of the stairs in my yoga pants the next morning, my hair pulled back and my face makeup free. "That's part of the deal."

How did I not know that? "But ... I thought it was going to be just you and me."

"No." Jerry's answer was succinct. "Katherine and Maya are going, too. Griffin's aunt and two of his cousins, as well. Your brother is demanding to be part of it, too, although he hates the spa. Oh, and your mother."

My head screamed at the prospect. "My mother?"

Jerry shrugged, unbothered by my tone. "She heard us talking about it last night. I could hardly leave her out."

There were a hundred different ways he could've omitted her from the festivities. Unfortunately, I couldn't bring them up now because Katherine and Maya were descending the opposite staircase. "Well, great."

Behind me, still in his boxer shorts and T-shirt, Griffin grinned at my discomfort. "I think you're going to have a fabulous day."

His tone grated. "I'm sure you would think that."

"Your father and I are taking my male family members golfing. It only seems fair that the women should have an outing of their own at the same time."

I swiveled quickly and grabbed the front of his shirt, narrowing my eyes as I hissed. "This is going to be a disaster."

Griffin carefully unhooked my fingers from his clothing. "The bigger your group, the better it will be. I don't want you leaving this house, but I understand it's something you need to do. You were looking forward to it yesterday."

That was a gross exaggeration. "I was willing to tolerate it yesterday," I clarified. "That's when I thought it would be Jerry and me. Alone."

"You'll survive." Griffin patted my hand. "It will give you time to bond with my mother."

"I think we've bonded enough."

"And I think you need to suck it up." Griffin lowered his voice so only I could hear. "This is happening, so get over it."

I wanted to smack him around. "What if something happens?"

"Aidan will be there to help you."

"What if your mother and Maya see?"

"They already know."

"And your aunt and cousins?"

"I'm sure you can come up with a lie if it becomes necessary." Griffin was firm as he brushed his thumb over my cheek. "The more people with you, the less likely you are to be attacked."

I had news for him. That wasn't always how it worked. "Fine." I blew out a resigned sigh. Apparently there was no getting out of this. "I'm not happy with you right now. I hope you know that."

"Ah, married life." Griffin shot me a mischievous grin. "I can't wait to make up later."

That made one of us. Well, okay, two of us. Making up is fun. What can I say?

JERRY'S FAVORITE SPA WAS in downtown Royal Oak. It was close to our adjacent townhouses, so much so it was convenient to walk from there thanks to the ungodly parking situation in downtown Royal Oak. We left two vehicles in the lot and walked the three blocks to the Main Street business.

Griffin's family members found the downtown area delightful. I was used to it, so I spent my time searching each alcove and shadow for hidden enemies. I was an agitated mess by the time we hit the spa and found my mother waiting for us in front.

"Isn't this a fun outing?"

If I didn't know better, I'd think she was actually excited about the invasive procedures we faced.

"Yes, there's nothing I love better than being poked and prodded by strangers for an entire afternoon," I drawled. "I'm sure it will be the highlight of my week."

Mom ignored my sarcasm. "This was a great idea, Jerry. I'm so glad you invited me."

"We could never leave you out."

WE HAD OUR CHOICE OF pampering procedures. Dad was paying for everything and left a card on file, so we were instructed to enjoy the facilities and not worry about money. For me, that started with a pedicure.

"You seem stressed," Aidan noted as he sat beside me and removed his shoes. "You need to chill out. This is supposed to be a relaxing day."

"It was going to be relaxing when it was just Jerry and me."

"Yeah, well, things change." Aidan smiled at the woman who moved his feet into the basin of steaming water. "I think you're looking at this the wrong way. What's better than getting a pedicure?"

"Um ... just about everything." I ignored the woman working on my feet and tried not to squirm. "I wish I was still in bed."

"You'll be fine." Aidan closed his eyes and drifted. "But if you're going to complain, pick a different seat. I don't need your negative energy harshing my vibe."

"I'm going to harsh something worse than your vibe," I muttered under my breath.

"You need to relax, Aisling," Mom said as she and Katherine moved into the room and took massage chairs across from us. "This is supposed to be fun. You need to unclench a bit. I know you're nervous about the wedding, but there's really no reason to work yourself into a frenzy. Your father and Jerry have everything under control."

"And the wedding planner your mother hired to pick up the slack seems quite capable," Katherine added helpfully. "You have nothing to worry about."

That was easy for her to say. She didn't have rogue reapers and wraiths hunting her. Because talking about that seemed the exact wrong way to go, I did my best to push it out of my mind. "I'm allowed to be stressed if I want," I said finally. "I'm getting married. It's a big deal."

"Of course it is." Katherine's smile was kind. "I remember when I got married. I was convinced that Griffin's father would change his mind at the last minute and leave me stranded at the altar. I had reoccurring nightmares about it and everything."

"I had that dream, too." Mom smiled indulgently at Katherine, as if they were best friends out for a day of bonding. "It was ridiculous to worry about that — Cormack would never do anything of the sort — but it was an irrational fear I couldn't shake."

"Are you worried about that, Aisling?" Aidan asked, his eyes still closed as the technician pumiced his feet. "If so, you need to let it go. There's no way Griffin would take off and leave you stranded."

The thought hadn't even occurred to me until these ninnies brought it up. "I'm not worried about Griffin leaving me at the altar." At least not much. "I'm more worried about tripping over my dress train or spilling food on myself."

"Those are much more likely to happen." Aidan grinned when I poked his side. "I'm sure you'll be fine. Even if those things happen, they're not the end of the world."

He had a point. I forced myself to try to relax, hitting the massage button on the chair and settling in as I regulated my breathing pattern.

"It's not that I'm worried about the wedding as much as it seems like there's still so much to do."

"Jerry is handling most of it," Mom pointed out. "You're lucky. I had to do it myself. Jerry is pretty much a godsend as far as you're concerned."

"I've thought that since I was five," I said dryly.

"Yes, you two were adorable that first day." Mom smiled at the memory. "He adopted you because he said your style was tragic and you needed help. You were inseparable after that."

"Did you worry about them being so close as children?" Katherine asked. "I know he's gay — and that's cool and I think his relationship with Aisling is magnificent — but you had to worry about them being so close when they were children."

"Not really." Mom shook her head. "When they were very young it simply wasn't a worry. Aisling needed someone who could direct all his attention to her. With five children in the house, my greatest fear was always that they wouldn't get enough one-on-one attention. Jerry picked up the slack with Aisling."

"I didn't even think of that." Katherine nodded encouragingly. "Obviously it worked out.. They all seem like well-adjusted adults."

"I'm well-adjusted," Aidan offered. "Aisling is a mess. She always has been."

"I will pull your bottom lip over your head and force you to swallow if you're not careful," I threatened.

Mom and Katherine chuckled in unison.

"That's basically what it was always like," Mom explained. "As for Aisling and Jerry, I know this sounds horrible to say, but I knew before he was ten that I had nothing to worry about. Cormack wasn't as easily convinced, although he picked up on some obvious signs, but he spent a lot of time with Jerry and Aisling and came to the same conclusion.

"In some ways I often thought it would be easier for Aisling if Jerry was straight because he was used to our nutty family and eager to hang around the house all the same," she continued. "I always knew it would be difficult for Aisling to find a match because her father and brothers were so overprotective. I thought I would serve as a buffer for that ... although it didn't actually turn out that way."

I cleared my throat, uncomfortable. Katherine knew the truth about Mom. We were forced to tell her when the mirror monster popped up and there was a question regarding Mom's involvement with the attack. His cousins and aunt weren't aware, though, and I was keen to keep it that way.

"Things worked out fine," I said, eager to change the subject. "Griffin and I managed to find each other with no help from anyone else. We made a few mistakes but muddled through the relationship together. Everything is good."

"I was there when they met," Aidan offered, his eyes twinkling. "I saw the initial sparks and everything."

"Really?" Katherine's smile was wide. "Did you know right away that they would end up together?"

"No. I didn't even know they liked one another. They both played it cool."

"Griffin played it cool?"

"He threatened to arrest us."

"Right." Katherine bobbed her head. "Tell me that story again. I think it's adorable."

Aidan winked. "I'd love to."

I leaned back in my chair and closed my eyes, more than willing to revisit the start of my relationship with Griffin from Aidan's point of view. That was a story I would never tire of, even if Aidan did turn things theatrical for no good reason at points.

"Well, it started when we were in an alley," Aidan started. "Aisling was complaining nonstop — which is normal — when things took a turn for the worse."

AN HOUR LATER MY toes were dry and I was debating between a massage or a facial when I noticed a familiar figure standing on the other side of the lobby window. My other mother, the younger one, stared directly at me, waving.

"I've had enough of this."

I didn't care if I ruined my pedicure. There was no way I intended to let that woman out of my sight a third time. I was going to chase her down, wrestle her to the pavement until she cried for mercy and demand she answer my questions. I had a plan and I intended to stick to it.

"Where are you going?"

My other mother — the real one — gave me pause when she appeared in the lobby and glanced around. My hand was already on the doorknob and I was ready to race into the real world on bare feet, wearing nothing but yoga pants and a tank top with a built-in bra.

"I was going to get some air," I replied lamely. As far as alibis go, it was a weak one.

"I think you're trying to run." Mom made a tsking sound with her tongue. "I think that's a mistake. It's just a spa day, Aisling. There's no reason to panic. If you need some alone time because the female togetherness is too much, simply volunteer to get your massage next so you can take a breather."

She sounded so much like the mother I remembered, so practical, I couldn't stop myself from sliding my gaze to the window. Mom Beta remained where she stood, her eyes dark as she focused on my real mother. She didn't bother to race away in an effort to make sure nobody saw her. Instead, she remained rooted ... and glared.

"I ... ." My mouth went dry.

"What are you looking at?" Annoyed, Mom flicked her eyes to the window. "Do you see something out there?"

I blinked several times as Mom stared right through her other self. "Don't you see ... ?" I didn't have time to finish the question before the woman on the other side of the glass slowly shook her head and raised a finger to her lips. The admonishment was clear.

"Were you going to say something, Aisling?" Mom looked concerned as she reached out a tentative hand to touch my forehead. She rarely touched me — which I encouraged — but apparently she was feeling courageous today. "You're not warm. I don't think you have a fever. You look a little pale."

I was beyond annoyed by the statement. "Perhaps I should go to a tanning booth before the wedding, huh?"

"I'm sure your father can arrange for one of those spray tans." Mom didn't as much as glance to her right when the second woman made derogatory hand gestures in her direction. She clearly didn't see her. "They're much better than they used to be and there's no orangey color."

"I'll consider it." I felt sick to my stomach as my younger mother flipped off my current mother, the mad urge to laugh bubbling up in my stomach. "I think you're right about getting a massage. I need to zone out for a bit."

"Katherine just left the room." Mom's smile was benign. "It's a good time for you to enjoy an hour to yourself."

"I'll get right on it."

THE MASSAGE ROOM WAS dark when I entered, the only light coming from a small lamp in the corner that was turned to the dimmest setting. I immediately reached for my shirt the second the door was closed, eager to climb under the sheet and get comfortable, when a flash of movement in the corner caught my attention.

"I'm sorry. I thought the room was empty."

It took me a moment to focus, and when I realized the figure in the corner wasn't a masseuse but a wraith — one that was moving fast and extending a pair of ethereal hands in my direction — I had to bite back a scream as I stumbled backward to avoid the creature's touch.

"Son of a ... !" I swore viciously under my breath as I ran my hands over my yoga pants. They didn't have pockets, which wasn't a concern when I'd dressed because I didn't think I would need to protect myself from being eaten at the spa. Then I remembered that I turned the letter opener into a fancy hair pick of sorts and jerked the small metal item out of my hair, allowing the black tresses to fall in waves over my shoulders.

"I'm sorry to interrupt." Katherine opened the door without knocking, a bright smile on her face. "I forgot my purse in here. I don't want to misplace it with so many people going in and out."

"Get out of the way." I reacted out of instinct, flinging my future mother-in-law away from the door and plunging the letter opener into the wraith's chest with one fluid motion.

The creature let loose an otherworldly scream that wasn't loud enough to draw attention. It was more of a weak hiss than a raucous roar. The wraith's hands turned to ash first before the effect moved up its arms. Within seconds, the entire thing was nothing more than a pile of ash on the floor.

"What was that?" Katherine's voice was shrill.

"Trouble," I replied, regaining my senses as I glanced around. "Shut that door."

"What?" Katherine's eyes widened. "Shouldn't we call the police?"

"No." I was firm. "We need to clear up this ash, get it in the garbage can. The masseuse won't even know if we hurry."

Katherine was dumbfounded. "Are you kidding me? That's what you're worried about?"

I always worried about exposure. I could hardly explain that to her, though. "Yes. We have to get rid of it."

Katherine moved her head from side to side, her mouth open. Finally, she snapped her jaw shut and simply nodded. "Okay, you're the boss."

"I wish everyone in my life believed that," I groused as she shut the door. "We need something to use as a dustpan. See if you can find a magazine."

"I'm on it." Katherine paused. "That was kind of exciting, huh? You moved really fast. Is your life always like this?"

"No. It's a special occasion."

"Neat."

I had trouble mustering the same enthusiasm. "Yeah. Neat. It's totally the highlight of my day."

Seventeen

Once the spa shenanigans were finished, I forced Aidan to load everyone into his vehicle with the lie that I had "bride" things to do in the townhouse. He wasn't happy — and I could tell he would be placing a call to Dad as soon as he had a moment alone — but I refused to back down.

The second everyone was gone, I grabbed my purse and headed out. I knew exactly where I was going, and this time no one was going to stop me from searching the theater to my heart's content. I wouldn't be rushed this go-around. I would find ... something. I knew it.

I walked to the theater, my mind busy with what had happened at the spa. How had the wraith managed to get inside without anyone seeing it? How did it even know we would be there? Did my mother tip it off? Heck, did either of my mothers tip it off?

I was in front of the theater when a familiar Ford Explorer pulled to the curb. I internally cursed my bad luck — and my brother — when Griffin jumped out. He was dressed in khaki shorts and a polo shirt, his golf shoes still on, and he didn't look happy when he approached.

"If you're going to give me crap ... just don't," I warned, my temper flaring.

"What makes you think I'm going to give you crap?"

"You've got your crap face on."

"I'll try not to be offended by that," Griffin said dryly, pulling me in for a hug before I could offer a complaint. "Are you okay?" His hands were gentle as they roamed my back, and his tenderness nudged out a sigh. "You're not hurt, are you?"

"No." I tilted my head so I could stare into his eyes. "Let me guess, Aidan called you, right?"

"Aidan called your father. I was sharing a cart with him when the call came. Luckily the golf course is only a few miles away. We all knew where you were going."

"And my father let you come here alone? That doesn't sound like him."

"Someone had to stay with my family."

"I would think he'd force you to do that."

"I played the husband card." Griffin's lips curved. "Apparently there's no defense for that. I was already excited about marrying you. This is icing on the cake. A surefire way to win an argument with your father is always welcome in my world."

Hmm. Cake sounded good. "I'm glad you're enjoying yourself."

"And you're not."

"I would be if wraiths stopped popping out of dark corners and trying to kill me."

"Yeah, I'm not happy about that either." He pulled me flush against his chest, ignoring the fact that I put up a fight and stared hard into my eyes. "I hear you took out a wraith in front of my mother. I expect that to be a truly terrifying tale later."

"I'm sure from her perspective it looked worse than it really was." I licked my lips, uncomfortable. "I made sure she wasn't in danger. It was quick work, although I did make her help me sweep up the wraith after to make sure the spa owners were none the wiser. I didn't have a choice about that."

Griffin eyed me speculatively. "Do you think I'm angry with you?"

I shrugged. "Why else are you here?"

"Because I love you."

"I know that." I honestly never doubted his feelings. I could see it when he looked at me. After my initial disbelief that anyone would be able to put up with my father and brothers, I opted to embrace what Griffin had to offer. I never looked back. "But she's your mother"

"And you're my wife."

"Not yet."

"Close enough. Truth be told, I've thought of you as my wife since the moment I decided to propose. It wasn't a gradual thing I had to work up to. It was simply my new reality."

"That's nice."

"And you're not in the mood to talk about our relationship and gush about how happy you are to have landed me," Griffin surmised. "What's on your mind? Why did you decide to come here instead of Grimlock Manor after the attack? Keep in mind, before you answer, the correct response was to return to your father's house. This shouldn't have been your destination."

I managed to keep from exploding, but just barely. "I made a choice to come here because I need to get back inside."

"Why?"

"Because it was dark last night and I didn't get a chance to search as much as I wanted to. Things are going to be different today ... no matter what you have to say about it."

Griffin narrowed his eyes. "I see."

"Yeah." I had no intention of backing down. "I need to look."

"Then we'll look together." Griffin was matter-of-fact. "You are not, however, going inside until you tell me exactly why you've decided this is the place to look. I have no problem getting arrested with you — even though that means I'll probably lose my job — but I want to know why I'm risking everything before I do it."

That seemed fair. "I saw my mother again. I mean ... my other mother. The younger one. She was outside the spa."

"Did you talk to her?"

"No. I was in the lobby. I was heading outside when my real mother caught me."

"Huh." Griffin tilted his head to the side, considering. "What did Lily say when she saw the younger version of herself?"

"She didn't see her." I wasn't sure I should admit that, but we'd come this far and lying when I was in the middle of a nervous break-down was clearly the wrong way to go. "The younger Mom flipped off the older Mom and made a bunch of weird gestures. She also did the 'shh' thing when I realized they were close. It was as if she didn't want me to tell my mother about seeing her."

"Did you say anything?"

"No. I don't trust my mother. I told you what she said about the disc last night. She's lying. I know she is. I can't trust her with something like this."

"That was smart." Griffin moved his hand to the base of my neck to attack some of the tension pooling there. "I hoped visiting the spa would relax you. It seems to have had the opposite effect."

"It was a stupid idea," I agreed.

"I don't know that I would go that far, but I am troubled about a few things," he said. "For starters, how did the wraith get into the spa?"

"I've been asking myself that very question. There is a back door, but it somehow made its way through the entire building without anyone seeing it. Then it wandered into the room where I was sched-uled to get a massage. That can't be a coincidence."

"How many massage rooms are there?"

I searched my memory. "I think six, although it might only be four. There are six rooms along that hallway."

"Six or four doesn't really matter. The wraith knew which room you would be in. That means someone told it where to look."

"And I'm narrowing my list of suspects to one – my mother."

"She makes the most sense," Griffin conceded. "I don't want you jumping to conclusions, though. There's always a chance your mother didn't know what was about to happen."

"How?"

"I don't know. Maybe your father has a leak in the household staff. Have you considered that?"

"That would explain how the wraith knew to go to the spa in the first place," I countered. "That doesn't explain how the wraith ended up in the correct room. Someone at the spa had to tell it where to go ... and I'm pretty sure it wasn't a member of your family. Jerry and Aidan clearly wouldn't do it. Who does that leave?"

Griffin exhaled heavily. "Your mother. It seems to make sense."

"Oh, you think?"

Griffin tweaked my nose. "I don't need the sarcasm."

"Everyone needs a good dose of sarcasm in their daily life."

"You give me more than a good dose."

"I do my best."

Despite the serious circumstances, Griffin grinned. "I love you so much. Sometimes I think it should be criminal to love someone as much as I love you."

Even though my reaction mortified me, I went all warm and gooey. "Even though I'm clearly going insane?"

"I wish you would stop saying things like that."

"It's probably true."

"I know, but that doesn't change the fact that you happen to be talking about my wife."

"Soon-to-be wife."

"It's the same thing."

"Not yet."

"Stop being such a Debbie Downer," Griffin ordered. "I don't think you're insane. It would be great if you could start believing that, too."

"How else do you explain it?" My temper was on full display as I planted my hands on my hips. "No one else has seen her. She showed up while I was in the spa lobby by myself, and when my mother joined me she didn't see her."

"You didn't ask her if she saw her, did you?"

I shook my head. "No. I didn't want to point her out in case she was invisible. She was putting on a show in front of the window, though. If Mom saw her, she would've commented. It was impossible to miss her."

"I guess that means our hunch that someone either used magic or plastic surgery to make a human look like your mother probably doesn't fit," Griffin mused.

"I'm the only one who can see her," I persisted. "Mom looked right through her. That means she's not there."

"You don't know that."

Griffin's loyalty was one of the things I loved most about him. That didn't mean he wasn't being a ninny. "If you had someone walk in off the street and claim he or she was the only one who could see a person who supposedly disappeared eleven years ago, what would you think?"

I expected Griffin to stumble over an answer. He didn't. "If that person was you and was surrounded by surreal and magical things, I would think it sounded like the truth."

"I think you're just saying that to make me feel better."

"And I think we're going to figure this out." Griffin was firm as he rested his hands on my shoulders. "You need to have faith in me. Have I ever failed you?"

I was taken aback. "No."

"There's an answer out there. I promise we'll uncover it. You don't have to do it alone. You can rely on me. It's okay."

I didn't want to cry. I hated how weak I felt during the act. In my world, tears were only useful as a last resort or if I wanted to manipulate my father into doing something he was against. I couldn't stop them now. "I know. It's just ... I don't want to drag you into my madness."

"You're not mad, baby." Griffin gave me a hard kiss. "Someone is messing with you. I feel that in my bones. Don't let them get a foothold. It will only make matters worse."

I pressed my lips together and nodded.

Griffin gave me another kiss before turning serious. "Now, we need to get back inside. It's important we act nonchalant about what we're doing."

I swiped at the errant tears. "You're going inside with me?"

"Of course I am." Griffin wiped away a final tear. "It's you and me forever. I promised you that a long time ago. That's never going to change."

"Thank you."

"It goes with the husband package."

"You just like saying 'husband,' don't you?"

"It's just as much fun as referring to you as my wife."

"I'll have to take your word for it."

GRIFFIN WAS QUICK AND EFFICIENT when he picked the padlock a second time. He shoved me inside with little preamble, and the gentleness he displayed on the street had evaporated. Thankfully, the windows offered more light than the other night and the fact that neither of us had a flashlight wasn't a detriment.

"This lobby doesn't look as run down as the rest of the building," Griffin noted as we walked through the first room. "The carpet looks relatively unscathed and the furniture is intact."

I wasn't sure what he was getting at. "What does that mean?"

"That someone has been taking care of this room."

Hmm. I took the hint and started prowling. "There are shelves down here." I pointed for emphasis. We didn't see these the other night."

"Let's take a look." Griffin linked his fingers with mine, more out of companionship than romance, and walked with me to the shelves. There were a number of scattered odd items. I couldn't decide if there was any rhyme or reason for the placement.

"This is weird, right? What is that thing?"

"It's a film cell," Griffin replied as he lifted the item in question. "It looks to belong to one of the *Star Wars* movies."

"Why would that be here?"

Griffin shrugged. "It could've been a decoration. You said the theater was up and running five years ago, although I have my doubts given what we saw inside. I can't believe anyone would want to see a film in this place."

"It was warm and cozy before. The bank shouldn't have let this happen. It's a travesty."

"I prefer newer theaters, the ones with those reclining chairs."

"Yes, well, there's something to be said for the classics."

"I guess." Griffin's eyes returned to the shelf, his forehead wrinkling when he found something of interest. "What's this?" He plucked a small metal object from the shelf. "It looks newer than everything else. There's no dust."

"Let me see." I took the item from him, my lips curving down when I recognized it. "Oh, my ... ."

Griffin read the change in my demeanor and was instantly alert. "What is it?"

"It's a compact. Er, a mirror. There was never any makeup in it."

"Is it yours?"

"No." My heart pounded as I flipped it over and showed him the engraving on the back.

"L. A. G." Griffin read the letters aloud. "What is that?"

"Lily Anne Grimlock."

"Oh." Realization dawned on Griffin. "This belonged to your mother. Maybe she's been hanging out here."

I swallowed hard as my heart pounded. "I gave this to my mother about two weeks before she died. I mean ... two weeks before she was in the fire and didn't die but we thought she did. You know what I mean."

"I do."

"It was a gift. I'd been a real jerk to her a few days before — I blame teenage hormones — and I got her the mirror to say I was sorry. She loved it. For those last two weeks she carried it in her pocket constantly."

"That's nice. Not the part about you being a jerk, but everything else."

"Yeah." I fumbled with the clasp and opened the compact. It was intact. The only thing out of the ordinary was a small slip of paper folded inside. I grabbed it without thinking. "I haven't seen my mother carrying it around since she got back. It was with her during the fire."

"Maybe she had it with her the entire time and didn't bring it up because she forgot."

"Why leave it here?"

"I don't know."

"As far as I can tell, my real mother has never been here," I argued. "I only saw my other mother come here."

"What are you saying?"

"I have no idea." That was the truth. "I don't understand any of it."

"What does the paper say?" Griffin's eyes roamed my face as I studied the single word on the sheet of paper.

I handed it to him and rubbed my forehead.

"'Remember,'" Griffin read aloud. "What does that mean?"

"Your guess is as good as mine, but I think it's a message meant for me."

"From your mother or your ... other mother?"

That was the question of the day. "I don't know. I don't know what to think."

"Well, we'll figure it out together." Griffin folded the note and returned it to the compact. "You won't be going through any of this alone. We're a team."

"Good. I don't think I could do this without you."

"Thankfully for both of us, you'll never have to find out."

I was thankful. I needed him. It was hard to admit, but this was too much for me to deal with alone.

I found my voice. "We should head back and show this to my father."

"We should head back and take some time alone," Griffin corrected. "Your father won't be back until this afternoon."

"That's fine. I need some time to think."

"We both do. Come on."

Eighteen

Once back at Grimlock Manor, I spent the better part of the afternoon pacing. I mumbled a bit to myself, too. Griffin watched the phenomenon for an hour before giving up and heading downstairs. It was a relief when he left, because it allowed me to fixate on my problem without having to listen to him rationalize what was happening. I was in no mood for being rational.

Thirty minutes after Griffin left, Dad appeared in my doorway. He looked thoughtful.

"Griffin made you come up here, didn't he?"

"No." Dad shook his head and stepped into the room. "He is worried about you, though."

"That means he sent you up here."

"That means we're a tag team and he tagged me to see if I could help," Dad countered, his eyes shifting to my dresser where the small mirror sat. "Is that it?"

I swallowed hard and nodded as he palmed the compact and flipped it over. "I remember when you got this for her. She cried."

"I was trying to butter her up, not make her cry."

Dad smirked. "You looked for it after the fire. I remember. You had a panic attack one day when you couldn't find it."

"You suggested she had it with her during the fire."

"I did."

"I thought it was long gone."

"I did, too." Dad opened the compact and pulled out the sheet of paper, a muscle working in his jaw as he read. "This is her handwriting."

"It is?" I raised my eyebrows. "I wasn't sure. I can't remember. I didn't keep anything she wrote. I threw it all away when I was angry one day."

"I know." Dad shut the mirror. "I saved it from the garbage. It's in a storage room on the third floor if you want it."

The temper I'd been hoarding like gold diminished. "You saved it?"

"I knew you would regret your decision."

"That was years ago."

"It was," Dad agreed. "Everything is still there, in the same box and everything."

I wanted to cry. I had no idea why, but tears flooded my eyes. "I can't believe you did that."

"Kid, there isn't anything I wouldn't do for you guys." Dad slid an arm around my shoulders as he sat on the bed next to me. "I love you."

"I love you, too."

"So ... tell me what you're thinking."

"I don't know. I'm either crazy or there's some weird ghost haunting me."

"You're not crazy."

"You're going with the ghost theory? That does seem to be the lesser of two evils."

Dad's chuckle was warm and throaty. "I don't know what is happening, but I know I'm not going to allow you to retreat inside and push everyone away while you try to figure it out. We're going to work together."

I swallowed hard. "Does that mean you want me to tell my brothers what I've been seeing?"

Dad was taken aback as he tilted his head to the side, considering. "I don't know," he answered finally, his voice soft. "I'm torn on how to answer that. On one hand, I always want you to confide in your brothers. You guys are close. I don't want that to change."

"But on the other hand?" I prodded.

"On the other hand, the meltdowns when you explain what you've been seeing will be profound," Dad acknowledged. "Cillian will try to find a scientific answer and will disappear into his books. Aidan will go quiet, because that's his way, but he'll start hovering to make sure you're safe."

"Aidan already knows," I offered. "I told him and Jerry because they walked in on Griffin and me talking. I didn't have a choice."

Dad turned philosophic. "Well, at least he didn't tell anyone else yet," he muttered. "As for your other two brothers, Redmond will start stalking the house, checking every door and window to make sure they're secure while staring outside. Then, after six or seven hours of that, he'll take off on a whim to check out the theater because he won't be able to stop himself. That's where he'll run into Braden, who will be so excited at the prospect of two mothers that he'll throw a tea party and invite every ghost in the neighborhood."

His response wasn't funny, but I couldn't stop myself from laughing. "That's the family in a nutshell."

Dad returned my smile. "Kid, I don't know what to tell you. I don't want to cut your brothers out, but I don't know how to explain this either. If I had my druthers I would want you to hold back for a bit longer. It's your choice, though."

"Are you saying that because I'm going to be married in a few days and you want to spoil me rotten?"

"I'm saying that because I don't have an answer. This might come as a surprise to you, but I don't always have an answer that will satisfy you."

"Fair enough." I rolled my neck. "Just for the record, if you want to keep spoiling me until the wedding, I'm fine with it."

Dad's lips quirked. "I'm shocked you would say anything of the sort."

"I know. I'm a constant surprise."

"Actually, you are, kid." Dad pressed a quick kiss to the top of my head. "I don't know what to tell you. I've asked a researcher at the main office to see if he can come up with an explanation for what you're seeing.

"Before you fly off the handle, you should know that I didn't give him your name when I explained what was happening," he continued. "I kept it vague. I would like to turn Cillian loose on the problem, but … ."

"We might never see him again," I finished. "I get it."

"Yes." Dad ruffled my hair. "For now, I think we should keep it under wraps. Just you, me, Aidan, Jerry and Griffin."

"Okay." I readily agreed, mostly because I didn't have an argument to mount. "I'll do whatever you want. I'm crazy, so my judgment can't be trusted."

"Ugh." Dad made a disgusted sound in the back of his throat. "Must you keep saying that?"

"It's true."

"You're not crazy."

"I feel crazy."

"Crazy people don't know they're crazy."

"You sound like Griffin."

"Despite that, you're not crazy."

I heaved a sigh. "Great. I'm not crazy. I'm simply seeing a ghost no one else can see."

"I don't understand why you think that makes you crazy."

"You wouldn't."

"You're not crazy."

"Great. I'll alert the media."

Dad grimaced. "I don't like your attitude, but I think I have a way to fix it."

I was intrigued. "And what way is that?"

"It's a surprise until after dinner."

"You know I hate surprises."

"You'll like this one."

I hoped that was true.

IT TURNED OUT, AS far as ideas go, Dad's wasn't terrible. Once dinner was finished and the Taylors headed upstairs to enjoy the game room and small theater, Dad insisted we needed some bonding time at the neighborhood bar.

Woody's Bar was a staple in Grosse Pointe. Conveniently, it was within walking distance of Grimlock Manor. Most families didn't go to the bar together, but the Grimlocks weren't like most families.

The owner of the establishment, Woody, was behind the bar when we walked through the door, He broke out into a wide grin when he recognized our group.

"There she is." He wiped his hands on his apron as he came out to greet us, heading straight for me. "I wasn't sure if I was going to see you before the big day. I'm so glad you decided to drop in."

He wasn't the only one. "I want the biggest glass of whiskey you have."

Woody snorted. "I take it the wedding nerves are hitting you hard, huh? I can't say I'm surprised. I never saw you as the settling down type. Are you considering leaving your groom at the altar and making a break for it?"

"No, she's not," Griffin automatically answered. He could've stayed back and enjoyed some quiet time with his family, but he opted to glue himself to me. I chose not to comment on it because it would ultimately lead to an argument and I wasn't in the mood to deal with that ... although making up didn't sound so bad.

"I'm not," I agreed. "I'm not really worried about the wedding. Jerry is doing all the worrying for me. He's an awesome wedding coordinator."

"I am." Jerry preened at the compliment. "I want a Pink Squirrel with extra cherries."

Griffin furrowed his brow. "What is a Pink Squirrel?"

"Nothing you're going to drink," I answered. "I want a Jack and Diet Coke. Make sure it's Diet because I've been stress eating and want to make sure I fit into my dress. Griffin doesn't want a fat bride."

Instead of agreeing, my husband-to-be extended a warning finger. "Don't put that on me," Griffin groused. "I like you just the way you are."

"It was a joke."

"No, it was something you said that you expected me to agree with so you could use it against me at a later date."

"You have marvelous deduction skills." Dad's grin was wide as he directed us toward the large booth at the center of the bar. "That was exactly what she was doing. You're smarter than I ever gave you credit for."

"Yes, I'm a veritable genius," Griffin agreed. "That's why I'm marrying your daughter."

"Awwwww!" Redmond, Braden and Cillian made exaggerated sounds as they bumped their heads together and snickered.

"He's so cute," Cillian cooed, grabbing Griffin's cheek and giving it a good shake. "He's a big marshmallow before the big day."

Griffin slapped away the hand and glared. "Don't push me."

"Oh, good." Cillian sobered. "I worried you'd been taken over by a droid. It worried me so much I thought maybe we were in a bad science fiction movie and nobody told me. Whew!" He mocked wiping his brow. "The last thing we need is the plot of some B-movie throwing us off schedule."

I exchanged a quick look with Dad. That was exactly what we were dealing with. Mom's ghost was a plot twist from a bad movie. That didn't mean we could escape it.

"Let's sit," Dad prodded. "This is essentially your last night to drink with your sister as a single woman. You should enjoy it."

"I'm actually looking forward to giving her away to Griffin," Braden supplied. "I'm going to enjoy that."

Dad cuffed him. "Don't ruin this night." The warning was akin to a growl. "If you ruin this night I'll ruin your work schedule."

Braden immediately changed his demeanor. "It was a joke."

"Well, you're not funny."

"I'll work on it."

"You do that."

A LOW-KEY NIGHT WITH my family was exactly what I needed. The Grimlocks weren't exactly quiet, but that was okay. There was something comforting about the noise.

"I need a fresh drink, Woody," I said as I hopped on a stool at the bar about an hour after we'd arrived. "I forgot about mine and it's all watery now."

Woody accepted the glass I handed him with narrowed eyes. "This is the second time you've said that. Are you feeling sick?"

"No. I'm fine. I simply keep forgetting to drink."

"I think you're excited about your wedding," Woody teased, dumping the contents of my glass into the sink before adding ice to start over again. "Do you have butterflies in your stomach?"

I found the question insulting. "I most certainly do not. I'm not a girl."

"She's definitely not a girl," a familiar voice offered from behind me, causing the hair on the back of my neck to stand on end. "There was a rumor when we were in high school that she had a penis, but her parents had it removed because they were desperate for a girl. That's why she's such a freak. She's a genetic experiment gone awry."

I narrowed my eyes as I swiveled slowly on the stool and came face to face with Angelina. She was dressed up — which seemed to signify she was staying and on the prowl — and she had a triumphant air about her as she tossed her purse on the bar and picked a seat one away from mine. The buffer was purposeful ... and probably a good idea because I'd been known to get violent a time or two when we were near each other.

"Angelina." Her name came out as a hiss. "I didn't know it was Skank Night. Do you have to pay double for Woody to allow you in?"

"I think you're confusing me with you."

"Oh, geez." Woody made a tsking sound with his tongue and shook his head. "Are you two still going at it? I thought you would've outgrown this when you hit adulthood. I guess I was wrong."

"Very wrong," I agreed. "My parents taught me at a young age that I was supposed to fight evil. I can't simply ignore that edict now that I'm an adult."

"Didn't your parents tell you to shower daily?" Angelina asked sweetly. "You've been ignoring that edict if the smell is any indication."

Hmm. I had to hand it to her. She was picking up her game. That must mean she was feeling better after the death of her mother. "Speaking of smells, have you ever considered bathing in douche?"

Griffin, who had moved up beside me to order a drink, raised his eyebrows and glanced around. "Wow. You're feeling better." He rubbed the back of my neck as he slid a sidelong look to Angelina. "I guess I know what — or rather who — fired you up."

"She smells like the catch of the day," I complained.

"Uh-huh." Griffin was used to my shenanigans when it came to Angelina, so he merely nodded as he focused on my nemesis, his expression hard to read. "I want to offer you my condolences, Angelina. I'm sorry you lost your mother."

Angelina widened her eyes, surprise evident. "Oh, well, thank you."

"I lost my father when I was a kid. My mother was still there, but you can't always shake the hole of a doomed parent. You and Aisling have that in common, too."

I knew exactly what he was doing ... and I didn't like it. "I have this conversation under control," I said. "Why don't you head back to the pool table so you can posture with my brothers?"

"I would rather watch you to make sure there's no hair pulling. We're getting married in a few days and I'm still determined to make sure it happens without you getting any bruises."

"You should try to make her do it with a bag over her head," Angelina suggested. "That would make things even better."

Griffin's sigh was heavy. "Yeah, well, I just wanted you to know that I'm sorry about your mother."

Angelina stared at him for a long beat, her tongue moving over her lips. I could practically read the debate raging behind her eyes. She wanted to say something snarky, but Griffin's condolences were heartfelt.

"Thank you," Angelina said finally. "My mother's death wasn't unexpected. I've been getting along."

"That's because your mother was bitchy and it's a relief not to have her picking at you every five seconds," I noted.

Angelina's eyes flashed with fury. "You take that back. My mother was a good woman. You shouldn't be making fun of the dead."

The misery on her face was enough to give me a hard jolt. I didn't often feel guilt, but I couldn't get past it this time. "I'm sorry. I shouldn't have said that."

Griffin's eyes widened. "Did you just apologize to her?"

"No."

"You did."

"I did not." I made small shooing motions with my hands. "Go over there and ooze testosterone with the other fools at the pool table. This is my show."

Griffin didn't look convinced. "I think you should come with me."

"Why?"

"Because fighting with Angelina is a surefire way to get hurt."

"We're not going to fight." I was mostly certain of that. "We'll hurl some insults, but nobody has the energy to pull hair or start throwing boob punches."

Griffin's expression turned horrified. "Do I want to know what that is?"

"No. It's fine."

Griffin spared a moment to look between us again before finally shaking his head and claiming his drink. "No fights. If you disappear outside we're going to have a huge argument and I'm going to ground you until the wedding."

"Yeah, yeah." I waved him off, keeping my eyes on Angelina. "Don't worry about me. I've got everything under control."

Angelina watched Griffin saunter off, her gaze turning wistful. "You're lucky to have him."

"I know."

"He must be stupid to be with you, though."

"I agree." Something occurred to me as I regarded her. "You know I hate you, right?"

"I'm well aware. I hate you, too."

"Good. That means I can offer to pay you to do something without you having to take offense."

Angelina knit her eyebrows, surprise obvious. "You're going to pay me to do something?"

"Don't worry. It's nothing your pimp will get upset about. And, hey, you might even make enough money to get a round of antibiotics and knock that chlamydia right out."

Angelina's lips tipped down. "Why do you always take things too far?"

"I have no idea. I've been asking myself that question since I learned how to talk."

"Whatever. Just tell me what you want. Then I'll decide how much to charge you."

"So ... it's like prom night with Donnie Dickerson, huh? Isn't that how things went with you guys?"

"Yup. You're still an ass."

"That's never going to change."

Nineteen

I woke the next morning with Griffin wrapped around me. He slept hard, the drinks he had at the bar making for a restful slumber. I slept, too, but I never finished a drink, and I woke several times during the night. My mind was too busy to allow for uninterrupted slumber.

"What are you thinking?" Griffin shifted so I could roll to face him, his eyes sleepy. "Why aren't you hung over?"

"Because I didn't get drunk."

"You also didn't get in a fight with Angelina. I'm proud of you."

"Yeah, well, don't let your chest puff out too much." I poked his side. "I can't pull her hair when she's in mourning. I have to wait another few weeks. Otherwise it's just mean."

"At least you've given it some thought." Griffin combed his fingers through his hair. "Why didn't you drink? You would've slept better if you'd allowed yourself to relax."

"I was relaxed."

"Only after you started throwing verbal jabs at Angelina. Are you replacing alcohol with insults?"

That was an idea I'd never considered. "No. I just ... wanted to keep my wits about me."

Griffin's gaze was steady. "Because you were afraid wraiths would attack?"

That was only part of it. "Because I've got a lot on my mind. And, before you get all freaky, you should know that I'm not worried about the wedding or having second thoughts. I know people keep teasing you about that, but it's not going to happen."

"I never doubted you for a second."

I studied the sharp angles of his face for signs he was lying. Satisfied he was telling the truth, I pushed forward. "I have an idea."

"Oh, you have no idea how much terror those words fill me with."

"No. It's a good idea."

"You always think your ideas are good. That very rarely turns out to be true."

"Fine." I was in the mood to be petulant, so I folded my arms over my chest. "I'm not going to tell you my idea."

"I didn't say I didn't want to hear about it."

"It's too late for that."

Griffin's eyes gleamed when I jutted out my lower lip. "I love it when you pout. It's like a challenge."

"It's not a challenge."

"Oh, but it is." Griffin rolled on top of me, his fingers digging into my sides as he tickled, causing me to gasp. "How am I supposed to make you stop pouting this morning?"

"I'm not pouting." I squealed when he found my secret tickle spot and made my eyes water as I fought off laughter. "Stop that!"

"No way. It's my job as your husband to make sure you start the day in the right frame of mind."

I had a feeling I knew what he meant by that. "I'm happy. You don't need to worry."

"I simply want to make sure that's true."

THIRTY MINUTES LATER, I LEFT the shower with a smile on my face, stopping in front of the bed to make sure Griffin hadn't fallen back asleep. He was on his stomach, his face buried in the covers, and he looked comfortable.

Unfortunately for him, I couldn't allow things to stay that way. "You need to get up."

"I'm up." Griffin's words were muffled into the sheets.

"You don't look up."

"Shh. I'm merely resting my eyes."

He was utterly adorable when he wanted to be. That didn't mean I could allow him to stay in bed all day. "You need to get dressed. I'm taking over the room for a bit and you can't be here when I do."

For the first time since waking, Griffin showed genuine interest as he rolled and fixed me with an unreadable look. "You showered."

"Oh, really?" I deadpanned. "Is that what happens in that little room with the fancy water machine? Good to know."

Griffin ignored the sarcasm. "You immediately got up after I wowed you — and if I didn't wow you, I don't want to hear about it because my ego can't take it this morning — and showered. You're never the first one up."

He wasn't wrong. I was a bit of a slug in the morning. The only reason I was up today was because I had an appointment scheduled. "Perhaps I'm turning over a new leaf."

"Or perhaps you're up to something." Griffin propped himself on his elbow and gave me an extended once over. "Why don't you come over here and let me dry you with that towel you're wearing? I don't want you taxing yourself with the wedding so close."

He was in a mood. On most days I would take advantage of it because it was rare that we had time to play together on a workday. "I can't. I already have plans."

Griffin struggled to a sitting position. "You have plans?"

"That's what I said."

"What plans?"

Hmm. How to explain myself? "It doesn't matter. It's private."

"Wedding stuff?"

I could've lied. He would've backed off if I claimed it was wedding stuff. He knew brides had secrets — like dresses and undergarments (Jerry explained that in great detail over breakfast one morning) — but lying wasn't my first choice. "Girl stuff."

"Girl stuff?" Griffin cocked an eyebrow. "Do you want to expound on that?"

"I have girl stuff to do this morning."

"Like ... what?"

"It doesn't matter."

"It matters to me."

"I'm not leaving the house if that's what you're worried about. My appointment is scheduled for right here."

"You have an appointment?" Griffin was slower than normal this morning thanks to the alcohol burning its way through his system. He wasn't exactly hungover, but he wouldn't be sharp until he mainlined some coffee and inhaled the stack of pancakes I'm sure my father would offer at the breakfast bar. "Who do you have an appointment with? Is it the wedding coordinator?"

That would've been another convenient lie. "No. It doesn't matter. Worry about yourself. I'm fine and I won't be long. I promise."

Griffin didn't look convinced. "I'm going to figure out what you're up to."

"I can't wait."

I WAITED IN THE FOYER until I saw Angelina park, opening the door to allow her entrance before she could ring the doorbell and alert the entire house she was visiting. If anyone saw her with me it would be over. I would never live it down.

"Upstairs." I pointed toward the staircase that led to my wing of the house.

"Well, good morning to you, too," Angelina drawled. "It's a fine day, isn't it?"

I hadn't been able to suck down any caffeine because I didn't want to risk running into my brothers or father, so my patience was at a minimum. "Do you want me to pull your hair?"

"Not last time I checked." Angelina lifted her nose into the air. "What is that smell? Is your father serving pancakes? I haven't had carbs in two weeks."

"That's nothing to brag about." I gave Angelina a hard shove toward the stairs. "You're not invited for breakfast. I'm paying you to run a search for me. That's it."

"Yes, but a good hostess offers breakfast to her business associates."

"I'm not a hostess and you're not my business associate."

"What am I?"

"The neighborhood bicycle ... because everyone gets a ride!" I offered her a demented smile as she scowled.

"I don't even know why I'm helping you," Angelina complained as she trudged up the stairs. "You're a horrible person. You don't deserve help."

"I'm paying you. It's the same reason you help your pimp."

"That joke is getting old."

"It's still funny."

"Only in your head."

I assumed Griffin had finished with his shower and was conversing with family members, so I shut my bedroom door after dragging Angelina inside. I widened my eyes when I realized he was standing at the foot of the bed, nothing but a towel wrapped around his waist.

"Hello!" Angelina's eyes practically bugged out of her head. "I see someone takes manscaping to heart."

Griffin wasn't a fan of the word "manscaping," but he primped and preened as much as Jerry, so he couldn't exactly deny it. The look on his face when he saw Angelina in my childhood bedroom, though, served as a distraction from the water beading on his muscled chest.

"What the ... ? Am I dreaming? Is this a nightmare?"

"I think I might be dreaming." Angelina gave Griffin a long once-over. "What do you have underneath that towel?"

"Don't make me hurt you," I threatened, giving Angelina's shoulder a hard pinch. "I'll still rip your hair out if you're not careful."

"It was simply a question."

"I'm confused," Griffin snapped. "What is going on? Why is Angelina in our bedroom?"

"I thought you guys had a townhouse," Angelina said, wrinkling her nose. "Did you move in here again? I can't say I'm surprised. Aisling needs her brothers to keep her alive because with that mouth, seventy-five percent of the world wants her dead."

"I think the same can be said about you," Griffin said dryly. "That doesn't explain what you're doing here. I mean ... why are you guys together? It's not the end of the world, is it?"

"Ha, ha." I openly glared at him as my cheeks burned. "I thought you were downstairs eating pancakes."

"Obviously." Griffin crossed his arms over his chest. "I thought you were doing girl stuff."

"This is girl stuff."

"That's Angelina."

"She's a girl," I argued. "Her pimp makes a big show of telling people that so there's no confusion on the street."

"I will smack you silly," Angelina threatened. "I mean it. I've been working out. I can take you."

Griffin and I snorted in unison, never moving our eyes from one another.

"Aisling wouldn't even break a sweat if it came down to a fight between you two," Griffin countered. "Get real."

"I've been working out." Angelina turned screechy. "I don't have to take this abuse. I'm here to do her a favor."

"You're here to earn a couple hundred bucks," I countered. "You're not doing me a favor."

"I could be doing you a favor," Angelina grumbled as she pulled a laptop out of the bag she carried. "If you were a nicer person I might do you a favor."

"And if you didn't accept money for sex you wouldn't be the neighborhood pro," I said sweetly. "Let's get this over with. I don't want you in here contaminating my room with fleas if I can help it."

"I'm going to get dressed in the bathroom." Griffin grabbed a pair of jeans and a shirt from the bureau and cast me a considering look. "Please don't fight. I don't want my bride bruised."

"Do you have any idea how many times you've said that to me over the last few weeks?" I challenged. "It's starting to get annoying."

"Nowhere near annoying as a bruised bride."

"Yeah, yeah."

Griffin carried his clothes into the bathroom and shut the door, leaving Angelina and me to snipe to our hearts' content.

"It will take me a minute to boot the computer." Angelina sat on the bed, her eyes busy as they roamed my childhood room. "I always wondered what your bedroom looked like. I pictured skulls as decorations and Kleenex next to the bed."

I rolled my eyes. "I hear you have Kleenex next to your bed. Your pimp insists on it to cut down on the herpes outbreaks, right?"

"Knock it off." Angelina was firm as she rubbed her forehead. "You don't always have to make things so uncomfortable. Every once in a while it's okay to simply sit in silence."

"Not when you're in my house."

"Fair enough." Angelina shifted, discomfort obvious. "I wanted to ... um ... thank you."

The conversational shift threw me for a loop. "For what?"

"For collecting my mother's soul and making sure she went on to a better place."

Uh-oh. This was the last thing I wanted to talk about with Angelina. "I didn't do that. I have no idea what you're talking about."

"I know what you are. You told me."

"I don't remember that."

"I put the rest together myself," Angelina added. "I know about the monsters that attack ... and the fact that your mother came back from the dead and you still don't quite understand how. You told me some of it, even though you want to deny it now, but I get the rest of it. I know you're the one who collected my mother's soul."

"How?" There was no sense in keeping up the denials. "How do you know it was me?"

"I asked your father."

My stomach twisted and, for a moment, I thought I was going to lose the breakfast I hadn't yet eaten. I sensed Angelina recognized when I was there to take her mother's soul the day it happened. "You talked to my father about this?"

"I came to visit right after," Angelina explained. "I was upset ... questioning death. You're the only people I know who can answer questions about the afterlife."

"My father let you in this house and answered your questions?" I was flabbergasted. "Why? He's against fleas, too."

Angelina ignored the dig. "Because he knew I was struggling and he seemed ... sympathetic. I never thought of your father that way before. I actually stopped by hoping that Cillian could help, but your father insisted I join him in his office."

"He didn't tell me."

"I asked him not to."

"What did he say to you?"

"That my mother was gone and in a better place. That you volunteered to take the soul even though you were exhausted and needed a break. He kept harping on that, saying you didn't have to do it but wanted to. I didn't understand what he was saying at the time, but I think I do now."

"What was he saying?"

"That you thought it was important to be the one to take her from me," Angelina answered without hesitation. "That you were doing me a kindness and you had no control over life and death, just the ride to the hereafter."

"That sounds much more poetic than how I would've referred to it," I admitted, watching as Angelina pulled up a search engine on her computer. "It's the old theater on Main Street, the one that's practically falling apart. I want to know who owns it."

"I know." Angelina's eyes flashed with impatience. "I'm not an idiot. I remember what you said."

"You could've run the search and simply texted me the results," I pointed out. "You were the one who insisted on coming here."

"I was hoping to see Cillian."

Even though I was sympathetic regarding Angelina's current state of mind, I could put up with only so much. "We've had this discussion. He's moved on. He's even talking about getting a new place with Maya so they can move in together."

Angelina was stoic. "Oh. I guess I screwed that up forever."

"You really did," I agreed. "It wasn't going to last anyway. You're not compatible."

"He's a good guy."

"He is. You need someone with an edge, though. You need someone who wants to fight and argue. Cillian isn't that guy."

"Do you fight and argue with Griffin?"

"All the time."

"If I had a guy who looked that good without a shirt I wouldn't ever argue with him," Angelina supplied. "I wouldn't want to risk losing him."

"That's not how a relationship works." I had no idea why I was explaining this to her. "You can't go through life worrying about losing someone. If that person is worth keeping, he'll put up a fight simply because it's the right thing to do for you. Nobody gets along twenty-four hours a day, seven days a week. It's impossible."

"But ... you seem happy."

"I am, for the most part. But life isn't a bed of roses. I have other things going on."

"Like the fact that your mother is back from the dead and you don't want to talk about it."

"That and a few other things." I flicked my eyes to the compact on my dresser. "Nothing is ever perfect. Relationships — all of them — are constant work. You have to put in the work."

"Wow! You really know how to suck the fun out of a conversation, don't you?"

"That's better than the things you suck for your pimp."

Angelina's expression was so dark I thought her eyes were going to turn black. "I really hate you."

"I know. That's what will keep us young. Fighting erases fine lines." I tapped the computer screen. "Give me what you have. I need to know who owns that building and where I can find him or her."

"And you're not going to tell me why, right?"

"Not even a little."

"I figured." Angeline tapped on her keyboard. "I'll want breakfast after this."

"Not in this house."

"Do you want to place a bet?"

"You're on."

Twenty

reakfast was tense thanks to Angelina's insistence on joining us. She wouldn't leave quietly — oh, no — and made a huge stink in the foyer until Dad came out and invited her to stay. The only reason he did was because the Taylors were intrigued by the turn of events and kicking her out would've invited questions no one wanted to answer.

Once the dishes were cleared, Angelina willingly exited. She tried talking to Cillian during the meal, but he refused to make eye contact and instead spent all his time talking to Maya. It was a clear indication that he was done playing games. I could only hope Angelina would readjust her thinking and let him go.

I planned to head to Detroit on my own. I had the information I needed to start digging, after all, but Griffin hid my keys and forced the situation, so I had no choice but to ride with him or steal a vehicle from my father. I wasn't above theft. My father also wasn't above having me arrested for said theft. It seemed easier to go with Griffin.

"Do you want to tell me about what went down with you two?" Griffin asked as he navigated from one freeway to another. "I heard some of it through the door. It was almost a nice conversation, all the pimp talk notwithstanding."

"If I don't mention her pimp she gets upset. She has a minimum number of mentions she has to get through on any given day. I was doing her a favor."

"Uh-huh."

"It's the truth."

"Spill," Griffin ordered, refusing to back down. "I want to know what's going on with you."

Ugh. Sometimes you had to compromise with an enemy because it was the quickest way to information. "She has software on her computer and can find out who owns a business."

"I can do that."

"You're on vacation."

"You mean that you thought there was a chance you could get the information and sneak out to investigate on your own," Griffin corrected. "Don't bother denying it. I know the way your mind works."

"Maybe I simply didn't want to involve you because I don't want you to have to take time away from your family. Have you considered that?"

"No."

I scratched an itch on the side of my nose and stared out the window. "I can't let it go. You know that. I don't understand why you're giving me grief."

"You're right. You can't let it go. I get it. What I don't understand is why you feel the need to investigate without backup. That's not safe."

"It's just a business. Nothing is going to happen at a construction office."

"Well, if nothing is going to happen it's going to be a quick trip." Griffin was unusually chipper as he exited the freeway. "What are you going to ask this guy about the theater? How do you think he can help you?"

I shrugged. That was a good question. "He must realize people are going in and out of that place. He would be a negligent property owner otherwise."

"He might own many properties. Maybe he can't check each address more than monthly."

"Or maybe he leased the property to someone."

Griffin was quiet for a beat. "I didn't consider that. Do you think that's likely?"

"Probably not, but it can't hurt to check."

"You could've called."

"My charm works better in person."

Instead of arguing, Griffin chuckled. "I can attest to that." He reached over the console and squeezed my hand. "I would still prefer you didn't wander around on your own right now. This situation is tense. You don't have to spend all your time with me — I'm not sure our relationship can take that — but you have four brothers and a father to choose from, too."

"And Jerry."

"I think it would be better if you added another person to the mix if you plan on taking off with Jerry."

I was affronted on my best friend's behalf. "Are you saying you don't trust us?"

"I'm saying that I want you safe. Don't turn this into an argument."

"Fine." I exhaled heavily and tapped my fingers on my knee. "Jerry is a great babysitter. Dad used to leave him in charge all the time when we were kids. I couldn't get away with anything when Jerry was around."

"I'll keep that in mind. Until then ... get used to me. I'm going to make sure you're always protected."

"I can't wait."

THE CONSTRUCTION OFFICE was dark.

It was more like a small ranch house located on what used to be a busy road. Most of the houses in the immediate area looked to be condemned, which wasn't a ringing endorsement for Happy Faces Construction.

"It's a stupid name for a business," I said as I tried the front door and found it locked. "Is anyone ever happy with construction?"

"Who isn't happy with home improvements?" Griffin shielded his eyes and peered through the window. "It's dark."

"Maybe they went out of business."

"That's a possibility." He shifted from one foot to the other as he regarded the lot. "This place looks empty. I guess I could pick the lock and we could check inside."

The offer caught me off guard. "Seriously?"

"Yes, but you have to keep it to yourself. I don't want your father to know I'm helping you break the law. I think he'll frown upon that."

"He frowns upon a lot of things. It's fine. The more his blood pumps, the better it is for his heart."

"You just make stuff up as you go along, don't you?"

"Pretty much."

I kept watch as Griffin worked his magic on the lock, making sure to study each house in turn. There wasn't as much as a hint of movement in any of the windows, some of which were broken. "Do you think it's weird that no one is around? It's the middle of the day. I get people are at work, but this is ridiculous. It's like a zombie apocalypse whipped through here and nobody noticed."

"Oh, don't start with the zombies again." Griffin's forehead wrinkled as he toiled over the lock. "That was a fluke thing. I can almost guarantee we won't see zombies a second time."

"Once was definitely enough," I agreed. "How are you coming with that lock? Do you want me to try?"

"I've got it." Griffin made a face as he concentrated, the lines around his eyes easing when he heard the lock tumble. "Ha! And you thought I couldn't do it."

"I said nothing of the sort." I brushed past him to enter first, the reassuring weight of the letter opener in my pocket giving me courage. "I merely meant that I could probably do it faster."

"Faster isn't always better."

"That's not what you said this morning."

Griffin's scowl was on full display when I risked a glance in his direction. "That's it. As soon as we're done here I'm taking you back to Grimlock Manor and I'm going to wow you appropriately. I knew I fell down on the job earlier."

"Oh, you were fine." I patted his chest and scanned the office. A desk remained in the front room, which featured several chairs and a couch. There was a thin layer of dust on the desk, and it gave me pause. "If you want to improve on your effort after lunch, though, I won't put up a fight."

"You can put up a tiny fight," Griffin offered, his eyes busy as he knelt to look over a few sheets of paper scattered on the floor. "That sometimes makes things more fun."

"Only when we're playing certain games."

"I have no problem with games." Griffin rolled his neck as he chewed his bottom lip. "It almost looks as if there was a struggle in here, doesn't it?"

I was glad he made the observation because I was worried about looking like a nervous idiot. "It does," I agreed. "That chair is turned over. There are papers scattered around. There's a broken mug next to the desk."

"Yeah." Griffin was in full concentration as he strode to the filing cabinet against the far wall. He used the sleeve of his shirt to cover his hand as he opened the top drawer. "Files are still here. I don't care who you are, if a company goes out of business it doesn't leave the files behind for anyone to stumble over ... especially when financial information is involved."

"Is there a file on the theater in there?"

Griffin thumbed through the vertical files and nodded. "Yeah."

"Take it."

"Why?"

"Just because. There might be something of interest."

"Don't you think I should call this in?"

"Do you want to explain what we were doing here?"

"Not particularly."

"Then I'm thinking that calling it in is probably a mistake."

"I guess." Griffin heaved out a sigh and removed the theater file. "Let's get out of here. I don't see any bodies — which I'm thankful for — but this place gives me the willies."

He wasn't the only one. "Do you want to stop at that Middle Eastern place around the corner on our way home?"

"You just ate."

"I know, but they've got awesome garlic sauce and I'm craving it."

"Fine. But you need to brush your teeth before we start playing again this afternoon. That garlic sauce might taste amazing, but it's enough to knock me over when you eat a vat of it."

"Deal."

MY BELLY WAS FULL AND I was in a good mood when we returned to Grimlock Manor. Griffin splurged on a huge container of takeout garlic sauce, and I had grand plans for eating in bed later that night. The fact that I was looking forward to that rather than going out was mildly depressing, but I opted not to dwell on it.

"Where have you been?" Dad asked when we walked into his office.

"Eating the best garlic sauce ever," I answered.

Dad gave me a hard look. "What were you really doing?"

"I left a note," Griffin answered, sighing as he sat in one of the open chairs. Cillian was also in the room, huge magic encyclopedias and notebooks spread around him as he reclined on the floor. "I said we wouldn't be gone long."

"Yes, but you didn't tell me where you were going."

"I didn't realize that you wanted to know. I'll think better next time."

"Thank you."

The forced politeness was grating. "Angelina ran the theater for me. I needed the owner's name, which she provided ... for a price."

"That's why I was looking for you," Dad said. "I couldn't figure out why she was in this house. You made things unnecessarily awkward during breakfast."

"Things are always awkward when Angelina is around. It's beyond my control."

"Right." Dad rolled his eyes. "I'm done talking to you for now. I'm going to focus on Griffin."

"Great. We just finished a big meal. I need to let it digest."

"You ate here three hours ago," Dad snapped. "Why did you need another meal?"

"That's like asking why you need a bag of potato chips instead of a handful. The answer is in the question."

"Whatever." Dad held up a hand. "Be quiet while I'm talking to Griffin."

I graced him with a saucy salute. "Yes, sir."

The growling emanating from his throat reminded me of my childhood, which caused me to turn nostalgic.

"Where were you, Griffin?" Dad repeated.

"We went to the address listed for the construction company that owns the theater," Griffin replied. "It was empty, but if you ask me it looked as if there had been a struggle inside."

"What kind of struggle?"

"There wasn't any blood or anything. It didn't feel right, though. We grabbed the file for the theater and skedaddled."

"Well, that was probably smart." Dad rubbed his chin with one hand and extended the other. "Let me see the file."

Griffin wordlessly handed it over as I studied Cillian. My brother was intent on his work, so intent that he didn't bother looking in our direction.

"I think that someone killed the construction company people so they could have free rein over the theater," I said after a beat. "That way they wouldn't have to worry about anyone discovering them — at least for the time being — and they had a home base that was close to my townhouse."

For the first time since we entered the office, Cillian stirred. "Wait ... what theater are you talking about?"

"That abandoned one on Main Street."

"And why do we care about that place?"

Uh-oh. I hadn't fully considered the ramifications of running my mouth. Per usual, it was already too late when my brain managed to catch stride with my tongue. "Um ... ."

"We're simply covering our bases because some things have been going on," Griffin answered smoothly. "Between the wraith attacks and the upcoming wedding, we want to be proactive."

"Wraith attacks? Plural?"

"Oh, well ... ." Griffin shifted in his chair.

"Is it wrong that I'm happy about not being the only one who says stupid things?" I asked.

"Aisling was attacked by a wraith at the spa yesterday, too," Dad offered. "We're not sure why it was there. Your sister fought it off and managed to keep things from imploding."

"Why didn't you tell me this?" Cillian's anger was palpable. "We would all be paying more attention to her if we knew she was in danger."

"That's why I didn't tell you." Dad's tone was practical. "She chafes under constant supervision, and the world is a worse place when she's in the mood to punish those who irritate her."

"You don't generally care about that," Cillian pressed.

"No, but ... ." Dad broke off, uncertain.

I decided to take the onus of the conversation off him. It was time. "I've been seeing a ghost that looks a lot like Mom — only the Mom of eleven years ago — and she's the one who led me to the theater. We broke in and looked around. I found a compact that we thought burned with Mom, so now we're scrambling to figure out if I'm crazy or something else is going on."

Cillian's mouth dropped open. "What?"

"I can't believe you just blurted it out that way," Dad complained.

"I feel better." I patted my stomach. "I think I'm up for some wowing, Griffin. Do you want to head upstairs?"

"Absolutely not." Dad's eyes flashed as he pinned Griffin with a warning look. "You will not drop that bomb and take off. I'm putting my foot down."

Despite myself, mirth bubbled up. "I love it when you put your foot down."

Cillian was in no mood for games. "Why have you been keeping this a secret? Didn't you think that additional information might help with my research?"

"It was my decision to keep it quiet," Dad interjected. "I didn't want things to turn ugly before the wedding, and that's exactly what's going to happen if Braden finds out. He won't take it well."

"No, he won't," Cillian agreed. "That doesn't change the fact that we don't keep secrets in this family."

"Every family has secrets," Dad countered. "As for this one ... well ... I don't know if it was the right decision. Your sister was freaking out about being crazy. That's on top of her being attacked twice by wraiths. I can take only one crisis at a time. If Braden finds out that Aisling has been seeing images of your mother he's going to lose it. That's one crisis too many in my book."

Cillian pressed the heel of his hand to his forehead as he absorbed the words. "I can't believe this."

"Well, now you know everything." Dad folded his arms over his chest. "You can research to your heart's content now that you have all the information."

"What about the others?" Cillian persisted. "They have a right to know, too."

"Jerry and Aidan know because they went with us to the theater the other night," I volunteered. "Redmond and Braden do not."

"Redmond isn't my worry," Dad explained. "He'll go into protective mode, but it won't be the end of the world. Braden is another story. He'll force a choice if he thinks we don't trust your mother."

Cillian nodded, his expression thoughtful. "He will do that."

"I want to wait."

"For how long?" Cillian asked. "You can't hide this forever."

"I know that." Dad leaned back in his chair and rubbed his forehead. "We need more information. It will be easier when I have actual facts to back up my assertions."

"He's going to melt down regardless."

"I know. I need to be able to protect him when the time comes, though, and we're not there yet."

"Fine." Cillian threw up his hands in defeat. "I'll help. But I'm not happy about being kept in the dark."

"We'll make it up to you."

"We will," I agreed. "Griffin bought garlic dip from the Middle Eastern place. You can have some if you keep your mouth shut."

"Good grief." Cillian made a distressed sound as he sank lower on the floor. "You're completely losing your mind. I'm starting to lean toward the 'you're crazy' scenario."

"That's good. That's the one I'm leaning toward, too."

Twenty-One

O nly two of my brothers were in the dark, and despite what Dad said about Braden, it wasn't sitting well.

"Maybe I should tell them."

Griffin and I had retired to my room for a nap — something his family waggled their eyebrows at as they issued catcalls and noises that strangely enough sounded like a dying duck — and spent the entire afternoon holed up there. I didn't miss the look on my father's face when Clint told his grandson to give it to me good, but otherwise things had been quiet and restful.

"Tell who?" Griffin asked, shirtless as he rolled onto his back and stared at the ceiling.

"Redmond and Braden."

"Oh. You want to know what I think?"

"No, I just like looking at you shirtless."

Griffin arched an eyebrow. "Why are you in a bad mood? I totally wowed you that second time. I know I did."

He was so earnest I couldn't hold out. "You did." I flashed two exaggerated thumbs-up for his benefit. "I'll be telling the story of our afternoon romp for the rest of our lives. When our children need to be embarrassed, that's the story I'll whip out."

His motions exaggerated, Griffin scratched his cheek and winked. "I know you mean that as an insult, but I'm totally up for it."

I wanted to give him a good shake, but it seemed counterproductive in case the movement forced him to prove himself a third time. "I'm serious."

"I don't know what to tell you." Griffin sobered as he stretched. "Maybe you can just tell Redmond. He seems to be the one you're most agitated about not being on your side. If you tell him, he's likely to form ranks around you, and that's what you really want."

My jaw flapped as I considered the statement. Ultimately, I decided it was an insult. "I don't need my brothers to take care of me. I don't need you to do it either. I'm not helpless."

"Calm down, tiger." Griffin mock growled, clearly enjoying himself. "You don't need to take it to a personal level. It was merely an observation ... and not one that conveyed the opinion you thought I just did."

I dialed back my anger, but just barely. "I don't like keeping secrets from Redmond. He was always the one who beat up all the boys who broke my heart when I was in middle school. He didn't care if he was older than them. He developed quite the reputation."

Griffin chuckled, clearly amused. "He would've been in high school at that point, right?"

"Yes."

"So he was eighteen and beating up thirteen-year-olds?"

"Seventeen. My father warned him what would happen once he was legal, that he could be tried as an adult."

"Much better." Griffin held out his hand and drew me to him, making sure I slid under the covers and rested my head on his shoulder before continuing. "If you want to tell them I'll stand by you even though I know that's going to turn into a huge argument thanks to Braden."

"You don't know." For some reason I decided to be optimistic. "Braden could be fine with it. He could accept what I'm saying as fact and look at it as a good thing, like maybe our real mother is a ghost and she's trying to warn us that the half-wraith who came back isn't legit."

His big hands were soft on my back as he rubbed, immediately going to the nape of my neck, where I carried the bulk of my tension. "Would you act that way in his position?"

It seemed a simple question on the surface, but I recognized it as a trap. "Yes."

"I think you're lying."

I knew I was lying. "I'd be upset," I admitted, heaving a sigh as my stomach picked that moment to flip. "Ugh. You shouldn't have let me eat my weight in garlic dip this afternoon. I think I'm going to be sick."

"Like I had a chance of stopping you," Griffin deadpanned. "You almost bit my hand off when I took a carrot stick."

"That's a gross lie. I'm not territorial about the carrots, just the cucumbers ... and tomatoes ... and that warm bread they serve that smells like a little slice of heaven."

"Right. I forgot. How silly of me."

"I'm not joking about being sick." I rolled to a sitting position and put my head between my knees to cut down on the internal churn that made me feel as if I was about to lose five pounds of lunch. "I was fine a few minutes ago. Why am I sick now?"

"You're working yourself up." Griffin went back to gently rubbing my back. "Your health is tied to your emotions more than anyone I know. When you get upset, or angry with someone, you often throw up. It's an interesting phenomenon."

He said it in such a reasonable manner I couldn't stop myself from chuckling. "You have watched me throw up a time or two. You're stronger than my brothers in that respect. They're all sympathetic pukers. My mom was that way, too. When we all got the flu as kids, there was a mad run on bathrooms so people could claim a convenient one. My mother could never check on us because if she was there when someone threw up she'd end up sick, too."

"Does that mean your father had to check on all of you?"

I nodded, smiling at the memory. "He carried around a six-pack of ginger ale and a bucket of ice so he could keep cold cloths in it. The final ginger ale was for him, and he drank part of it while spending time with all of us."

"That sounds nice."

"He was a big marshmallow. I didn't see it at the time because he always did that yelling thing that he thought terrified us, but he bent over backward for us."

Griffin adjusted his tone as he leaned forward. "That won't change. Why do you sound as if you're worried that it might?"

"I've been thinking." I licked my lips. "You're the only one who knows about the disc. I didn't tell anyone else. Maybe I should have."

"I told you to tell the others from the start."

"Nobody likes a guy who walks around saying 'I told you so' all day long."

"What about a girl who says it? Like, maybe one with black hair with white streaks?"

"She's an absolute delight."

"Good to know." His lips brushed against my ear as he slowly caressed my shoulders. "If you're going to tell Braden and Redmond, you should tell them everything. Your father would want to know what you saw that day."

"What if I'm wrong?" I sounded petulant, but I couldn't shake the whininess causing my voice to crack. "What if she has a legitimate reason and I blow up things for nothing?"

"You don't believe that. Not in your gut."

"No. I think she's evil."

"Then it's time to tell them."

"Maybe." I rested my cheek on my knee as Griffin pressed his forehead against mine. It probably looked like a strange mating ritual to anyone outside the bedroom, but it was comforting and normal for us. "I love you." I almost choked on the words as tears threatened.

"I love you, too. That won't change. And I'll stand with you if you want to tell your family everything. It might be time."

"I need to think about it."

"Okay."

I pressed my eyes shut, but he didn't move his forehead.

"Aisling?"

"Hmm."

"You need to brush your teeth because the garlic dip has taken on a life of its own."

My eyes flew open as he started laughing. "I was just thinking about how charming you are, too. No more, though. You're a pain in the butt."

"We have that in common."

MY FATHER WAS A MAN who liked his theme dinners. With Griffin's family on the premises, he could show off. That was firmly on display when I hit the main floor of Grimlock Manor and found a strange scent assailing my olfactory senses.

"What is that?" I wrinkled my nose as Braden slid by on stocking-clad feet.

"Dad is serving Indian food," he announced, holding out his elbow when Redmond got in his way and throwing a bit of extra "oomph" behind his shoulder when he barreled into our older brother. "Apparently he's hoping we all get the runs or something."

I widened my eyes when I realized Aidan and Cillian were on hand to play, too. "You're playing sock hockey without me?" I narrowed my eyes. "That's not fair. I'm supposed to be able to pick teams the next time we play. We all agreed."

"Yes, but your future husband says that if you have bruises on your arms or face — especially your face — the day of the wedding and we're to blame he'll arrest us and forget to tell anyone until after you're back from your honeymoon."

My mouth dropped open as I shot an accusatory look toward Griffin. "How could you?"

"Yes, how silly of me." Griffin rolled his eyes as he moved through the room, skillfully avoiding my brothers as they slid across the floor. "I want an unbruised wife. Clearly I should be flogged."

"Definitely," I agreed without hesitation. "I also wish I hadn't brushed my teeth. You deserve the garlic smell."

"Oh, don't worry," Redmond intoned. "We're all going to have bad breath by the time Dad is done with us tonight. That curry smell is going to linger until long after you're gone on your honeymoon."

He wasn't wrong. "I don't understand why he picked Indian food. We don't even like Indian food."

"My mother does," Griffin volunteered. "He's probably trying to appease her."

"But I'm the bride. He should be worried about making me happy. I wanted prime rib."

"I believe that's tomorrow ... or, wait, that's for the day before the wedding," Aidan offered. "Don't worry. Dad's world still revolves around you this week. The rest of us are merely afterthoughts."

"That's how it should be every day."

"Ha, ha." Redmond tweaked my nose as he skirted around me. "Dinner is still thirty minutes away. If we promise not to damage her, can she play, Griffin?"

I was appalled. "He's not the boss of me. He doesn't get to decide." Despite my bold words, I slid a pleading look toward my future husband. "I really want to play."

Griffin merely shook his head, his lips twitching. "Fine. Play. But don't hurt her. If she ends up with a broken bone I'll make sure all four of you have one to match."

"Yes, sir." Braden clicked his heels together and saluted. "We promise to keep her from being seriously injured."

"No bruises on her face," Griffin ordered as he headed toward the parlor. "Let her win, too. If she loses, she'll be a bear, and I have plans for her later."

"Oh, gross!" My brothers made quadruple faces illuminating their disgust.

"You're lucky we don't kill you right here." Redmond, in full big brother mode, puffed out his chest. "That might be fun for old time's sake. We'll wrestle Detective Dinglefritz to the ground and make him cry. Maybe you should play with us."

"I'll pass." Griffin ruffled my hair. "I think this should be a Grimlock bonding experience."

I knew what he was doing. He was giving me the opening I needed to tell them the truth. The problem was I hadn't yet decided if telling the truth was prudent. Still, I had a chance if I wanted to take advantage of it.

"Thanks for your permission, stick in the mud," Aidan offered, grinning when Griffin scorched him with a dark look. "We'll take care of her. I promise you'll get her back in one piece."

"That's all I ask."

GRIFFIN'S FAMILY CONVENIENTLY left us alone for the duration of the game. We had uneven teams because Griffin and Jerry refused to play, but the game wasn't for pride as much as fun. That rarely happened in the Grimlock house, so I took advantage of the situation and enjoyed it.

"So, the big day is soon." Redmond slung an arm over my shoulders as we took a few minutes to catch our breath. "Tomorrow is the night of the dual bachelorette and bachelor parties. I'm looking forward to that more than the wedding."

"That's because you want to see strippers, and I don't have any bridesmaids for you to mack on at the reception." I brushed the sweat from my forehead and leaned into him. "I guess I should've tried to make more female friends over the years. I didn't realize it would be a thing until Griffin had to cut down on the people he wanted to stand up for him."

"Yes, well, you don't play nicely with others wearing skirts."

"Definitely not."

"You have Jerry. He's the one you want standing with you."

In truth, I wanted all my brothers, too. Even Braden, who spent most of his time being a butthead. "I tried to talk Griffin into letting all of you stand with me, but he didn't think it was a good idea."

"Why not?"

"Because most of his groomsmen are police officers and they don't want to walk down the aisle with other men."

"That just shows they're uncomfortable with their sexuality." Redmond's grin was impish. "That reflects poorly on them."

"Yeah." I heaved out a sigh as I sat at the foot of the staircase that led to my wing of the house. Griffin's family seemed to be having a good time in the parlor, Clint apparently holding court, and no one had bothered us in a long time. I had my opening. It was time to take it. "So, I have a few things I should tell you guys."

Aidan widened his eyes to comical proportions as his cheeks flooded with color. "Now? You're going to tell them now? That's a bad idea."

I tended to agree, but this might be the only opening I got. "Cillian found out this afternoon. I think it's time."

"Time for what?" Braden asked as he leaned against one of my father's ornate statues. "I knew you were hiding something. I told Redmond. Didn't I tell you?"

"Yes, you opened your big mouth and told me multiple times," Redmond drawled. "This conversation isn't about you. It's about Aisling. What's going on, kid?"

I swallowed hard. "Well, the thing is, I've been seeing Mom."

The truth bomb didn't land as hard as I'd expected.

"We've all been seeing Mom," Braden noted. "She's part of the family again."

That was precisely the problem. "I guess I should clarify." I chewed my bottom lip and looked to Cillian for help. Sensing my distress, Aidan came to my aid.

"She's been seeing two moms," Aidan volunteered. "One of them looks young, like our mother did right before she supposedly died in that fire. She warned Aisling about the wraith that attacked in the alley and she led her to an abandoned theater in Royal Oak a few days ago. She might be invisible, because only Aisling can see her. So, either Aisling is crazy or something else is going on."

The silence that swept over the room was profound ... and uncomfortable.

"What?" Redmond drew his eyebrows together as he tried to sort through Aidan's story. "You've been seeing another mother?"

I nodded, miserable. "Yeah. I think she's trying to warn me that our real mother — the one we've been dealing with — is evil."

"Oh, not this again." Braden's temper was on full display as he clenched his fists on his hips. "We've been over this. She's not evil. She saved you a few weeks ago when that cop wanted to kill you."

"She didn't save me," I clarified. "She ultimately fought on our side. Kind of. I saved myself. And quite frankly, Griffin was the real hero that day. He managed to fight against the storm. That took strength that I'm not sure the rest of us have."

"He was unbelievable," Redmond agreed, holding up his hand to silence Braden before my brother got too far down the track. "That doesn't change the fact that you're seeing someone who might not be there."

"I know." I dropped my forehead into my hands, miserable. "I wanted to keep it to myself at first because I thought I was going crazy. I had to tell Griffin. Then Aidan and Jerry overheard. I told Dad, too, because I didn't know what else to do. Cillian found out today. I didn't think it was right to leave the rest of you in the dark."

"She's not evil." Braden refused to back down, although at the same time he said the words the chandelier in the foyer flickered. "You're making things up in your head. Our mother isn't evil."

I opened my mouth to argue but forgot what I was going to say when the light flickered again. "Is it storming out?" I slowly got to my feet.

"Not that I know of," Redmond replied. "You need to sit down. We're not done talking about this."

I ignored the order and moved to the window next to the door and looked out at the driveway. Grimlock Manor was surrounded by a fence. The only way in was through the back alley, which almost nobody knew about, and the front gate.

"I'm not having this conversation with her again," Braden argued. "She wants to hate Mom because ... well, I don't know why. I'm not playing that game."

I ignored his petulant tone and stared at two figures moving across the driveway. The mere sight of them was enough to make my blood run cold.

"I think we should hear her out," Aidan argued. "It's not as if she's making it up to get attention. She's getting married. She already has all the attention."

"That doesn't mean she doesn't want more," Braden sneered. "She always wants more attention."

"I do," I agreed, my mind busy as I stared back at my brothers.

"With that in mind, I want you to realize I'm not making up what I'm about to tell you. It's not a game. It's totally true."

"And what's that?" Braden demanded, clearly spoiling for a fight.

"There are two wraiths in the driveway and they're staring at the house."

Whatever he was about to say died on Braden's lips as he hurried to my side. He looked over my shoulder and out the window before viciously swearing under his breath. "Well, great. There are wraiths outside and Indian food in the dining room. Which horror do you want to deal with first?"

Twenty-Two

I remained frozen at the window as the wraiths walked across the cobblestone parking expanse. I didn't know if they could speak, other than a few odd words here and there, but they looked as if they were communicating as they tilted their heads to the side.

"What are we supposed to do?" I kept my voice low and gripped my hands together. "If the Taylors see them, we'll have a lot of explaining to do."

Braden shifted to look over his shoulder and stare at the open parlor door. "Then I guess we'll have to keep the Taylors from finding out."

"How do you suggest we do that?"

"By being really quiet."

Oh, right. Like the Grimlocks could be quiet. "And when that fails?"

"We can only do what we can do," Redmond said. "We need weapons."

"I say we get them from upstairs, use the back door to escape, and take out whatever we find in the yard," Cillian suggested. "There are five of us. We can split into teams."

I didn't like the sound of that one bit. "Maybe I should get Griffin."

Redmond made an exaggerated face. "We don't need Griffin. We're Grimlocks. We can protect ourselves."

He had a point. "Fine. Griffin won't be happy, though."

"He'll live."

WE DIDN'T BOTHER TO change our clothes, instead heading straight outside with daggers and swords clutched in our hands. I opted for my new *Game of Thrones* sword, which Aidan and Redmond appropriately "oohed" and "aahed" over as we walked down the back stairs.

"That's kind of cool." Aidan reverently touched the hilt. "Poor Ned Stark."

"If Ned Stark didn't die, *Game of Thrones* would've been a completely different show," Braden argued.

"Books," Cillian corrected. "They were books first."

"Thank you, nerd," Braden drawled. "I think this situation calls for a huge argument about the merits of reading. That will make things better."

"Whatever." Cillian paused by the back door, ignoring the way the kitchen staff stared at us. "We need to come up with a plan. I suggest that Redmond, Aidan and Aisling go right. Braden and I will go left."

"Maybe we shouldn't split up," I suggested, my heart giving a little lurch. "Maybe we should stick together."

"Or maybe we can take them out quickly and efficiently if we're quiet and in smaller groups," Cillian shot back. "I don't see where we have a choice. We can't be loud and rowdy on this one."

He wasn't wrong. "Fine." I blew out a sigh and gripped my sword tighter. "Don't screw around. Work your way through them fast. We'll meet at the front of the house."

"That sounds like a plan."

Redmond and Aidan kept me between them as we began slowly circling the house. The backyard was empty, which made sense because the windows on that side of the house were the easiest to spy from. Once we hit the east side of the manor, the movement near Dad's office window was obvious.

Redmond held up two fingers as he brandished his sword. Aidan nodded and moved ahead of me. My brothers were already halfway down the yard before I realized they were going to cut me out of the fight.

I wanted to yell at them, come up with a few inventive curses, but I wasn't dumb enough to scream and draw attention from our enemies.

Redmond's wraith was already turning to dust when I caught up, and Aidan had his creature in a panicked state as it tried to escape. Instead of allowing it to slip away, Aidan sliced hard at the creature's neck — causing the wraith to drop its weapon and clutch its fingers around the wound — while Redmond slammed his sword into the creature's chest.

"That's two," Redmond whispered as the wraith ashes blew into a nearby bush. "I'm guessing there's more out front."

"I want to kill one." I knew I sounded like a whiny brat, but I didn't care. "I'm the one who saw them first. I should get to take one of them out."

"Then you'll have to be quicker next time," Redmond said simply. "If you want to win the game of Grimlocks, you have to swing first and ask questions later."

I rolled my eyes. "How long did it take you to come up with that?"

"Not nearly as long as you'd imagine. It just came to me."

"Good grief. This whole family is nerds."

"And you're the biggest nerd of all."

We resumed our trek around the house, being careful to stab any tall bushes that looked as if they might be capable of hiding wraiths. It was an underhanded way to fight, but we were more about winning than playing fair. That's why we almost always won ... and the other neighborhood kids fled in terror when we decided it was time to play an interactive game.

By the time we crossed to the front yard we were reasonably assured that the east side of the house was clear. The backyard was empty, too. If Cillian and Braden did their jobs, the west side of the house would be wraith-free in seconds. That left only the front.

Redmond didn't bother hiding this time, instead standing out in the open as we rounded the final corner. His eyes were keen as he stared hard into the approaching night. "Do you see anything?"

"There." Aidan pointed toward a spot behind Redmond's truck. "There's one between your truck and Braden's Explorer."

Redmond scowled. "Filthy little beasts. They're trying to get our rides dirty."

"Yes, that's obviously why they're here," I said dryly. "Can I kill it?"

"No. It's my truck."

"I want to kill it."

"Well, that's too bad."

I tried to slide in front of Redmond so I could beat him to our quarry, but he had longer legs and easily pushed me to the side. I was frustrated when Aidan strode in the opposite direction, heading straight toward the topiary that served as a decoration for my father's favorite cement bench.

"Do you see something?"

"I'm not sure."

"Let me kill it."

"You stay here." Aidan was firm. "If you end up with bruises Griffin will smack all four of us around ... and Dad will let him because he's worried you'll end up hurt. We should've left you inside. I don't know what we were thinking."

Annoyance, hot and quick, washed over me. "I'm part of this team."

"Not until after you're married. Then no one cares if you get beat up."

"Griffin will always care."

"Yeah, but he's extra prickly about it right now," Aidan noted. "Just ... wait here. I'll be back in a second."

That sounded like a terrible way to waste three minutes. "I hate all of you," I hissed.

"We love you, too," Redmond called out from behind his truck as he sparred with a wraith. "You're our favorite person in the world. We love to wait on you and do whatever you want."

I held up my hand. "I am done listening to you."

"Poor Aisling," Braden teased as he arrived in the front yard. He didn't bother to lower his voice. As long as the Taylors weren't by the front windows they would have no idea what was going on outside. "She doesn't like it when she's not the center of the universe." He narrowed his eyes as he searched for something to kill. "When others have an opinion, she makes sure that she talks so loudly hers is the only voice heard."

I narrowed my eyes. I knew exactly what he was doing ... and I didn't like it. "Listen here, Braden," I snapped, my temper on full display. "I know you're angry about what I said — about what I saw — but I can't change that. I saw what I saw."

"I think you're making it up." Braden lashed out viciously when a wraith detached from a nearby tree. "You don't want Mom to be welcomed into this house, so you're lying to make sure we shun her."

"Oh, that's the biggest load of crap I've ever heard." I abandoned looking for wraiths because my brothers were clearly going to suck the fun out of the evening and protect me at all costs. "I didn't want to see Mom. I mean ... going crazy right before my wedding isn't high on my list of things to do. Why would I possibly want that?"

"Because you're holding a grudge against Mom. Oomph." Braden made a strangled sound as a wraith barreled out from behind the limousine and plowed into him. "Son of a ... !"

My other brothers were busy, so I strode in Braden's direction and frowned when I realized the wraith was trying to wrestle him down, snapping as it attempted to bite my brother's neck. "What the ... ?"

"Are you just going to stand there like an idiot?" Braden complained, his voice going shrill. "This thing is trying to eat me."

"Maybe I should let it."

"And maybe I should let the one circling behind us eat you," Braden snapped.

I turned quickly, my eyes going wide when I registered the approaching wraith. "Oh, man!" I reacted out of instinct, hopping onto the small metal chair that belonged with a cutesy bistro set meant for looks rather than touching. It was located in one of the small gardens that offset the landscaping.

Once I had the high ground I gripped my sword tightly as the wraith approached, waiting until it was almost on top of me to jump high and slam the broadsword into the creature's chest. I dropped so fast and hard I glanced off the creature's shoulder at the same second it turned to dust, which essentially meant I felt through dust until I hit the ground.

"Oh, yuck!" I made a spitting sound when the ash touched my tongue. "I just ate dead wraith. I'm totally going to throw up. I can't fight it off this time. It's not like when I ate too much garlic dip."

"Aisling!" Braden was furious when he drew my attention away from my own predicament. He was still struggling with the wraith that wanted to eat his neck. "Do you think you can help me out here?"

"Yeah, yeah," I grunted as I swung to my feet. "You know, I don't see why you're trying to be so difficult. I don't want to hurt you. You might not believe it because we fight so much, but you're still my brother. I would give anything not to see what I'm seeing ... especially because I think it means I'm going crazy."

"You're not crazy," Braden grumbled as he struggled against the maniacal wraith. "If you're seeing something, there must be a reason."

"I feel crazy." I swung the sword high and brought it down in such a manner that I lopped off the wraith's head.

Braden's eyes went wide when the creature instantly turned into a puff of ash that exploded like a small bomb. "Oh, gross."

"That was kind of gross," I admitted, waving away the ash as I tried to keep from breathing in the noxious substance. "I didn't know they did that if you cut off their heads."

"Ugh." Braden sat up, an exaggerated shudder running through his body. "Now I've got wraith on my tongue. I hope you're happy."

"Oh, yes, it's the highlight of my day," I drawled. "Who doesn't want a side of wraith before they're forced to eat food that will set their tongues on fire?"

"Ahem."

I stilled when a familiar voice wafted from the front patio. "Uh-oh." My shoulders were stiff when I turned to find my father and Griffin watching the display with a mixture of fury and annoyance. "Hey. We were just coming in for dinner."

"Oh, really?" Dad didn't look convinced. "Is that why the kitchen staff informed me that the five of you snuck out through the back door with swords?"

"I think the kitchen staff needs a talking to." I straightened as I spit again to eradicate the taste of wraith. "They should mind their own business."

"You pains are my business," Dad snapped. "What are you even doing out here when we have guests in the house?"

Braden turned defensive. "Aisling saw wraiths in the driveway, so we thought it was best we take them out all quietly so Griffin's relatives didn't figure out what we were doing."

"I see." Dad's eyes traveled to the pile of ash at my feet. "How many wraiths are we talking about?"

"Oh, well ... ." Braden shifted his eyes to me for help.

"Aidan and Redmond killed two on the side of the house and a couple in the front yard," I offered.

"We killed two on the other side of the house, too," Cillian chimed in. "I would say there were about ten or so. There's no need to worry. They're all dead."

Dad rolled his eyes. "Good grief."

"Is there a reason you didn't tell us what you were doing?" Griffin asked as he broke from my father's side and made his way across the yard to check on me. He made a big show of looking me up and down. Apparently, whatever he found wasn't enough to cause him to melt down because he merely smiled as he wiped some ash from my cheek. "I would've liked to help you with this."

"I wanted to bring you," I protested. "They wouldn't let me. They said it was a Grimlock thing and you were better off staying inside with your relatives so they wouldn't get suspicious."

"Yes, that is true," Braden said dryly. "She whined like a baby when we said she couldn't fetch you."

"If you don't like the whining, perhaps you should listen to her next time," Griffin suggested, holding up a hand when I went to give him a hug. "No, you're dirty."

My mouth dropped open. "I was fighting for my life. I can't believe you're giving me crap about being dirty when I was fighting for my life."

"I don't want to change my clothes again." Griffin was all business. "I've already showered twice today because of your need to roll around before napping. I don't want to shower a third time."

Dad's expression was dark when his eyes caught mine. "She's still my baby," he barked at Griffin's back. "Watch what you say in front of me."

Griffin held up his hands in capitulation. "I'm sorry. I forgot you were there."

"That doesn't make what you just said acceptable."

"You're right." Griffin winked at me, clearly enjoying himself. "I shall punish myself later this evening. Better yet, I'll let Aisling punish me."

"I'm going to cut off your hands before the wedding," Dad groused, shaking his head. "I should've followed through on the initial threat when you first came sniffing around. I didn't because I thought there was a chance you would grow to fear me. Look how that turned out."

I grinned. "Yeah, well, it's too late for that now. You can't take his hands. That's how he does half the dirty stuff I've grown to love. I'll cry if he has no hands."

"Oh, you say the sweetest things, baby," Griffin crooned as he watched my father for signs he was going to implode.

"That did it." Dad had had enough. "I want everyone to put their swords away and get cleaned up. I don't want to have to explain this to the Taylors."

"Yes, sir." All five of us saluted in unison, something that obviously set my father's teeth on edge.

"I'll make all of you eat extra curry for this," he hissed.

My stomach flopped at the thought. "Can we order pizza instead? I don't think I'm up for Indian food tonight. It might make me sick."

"I thought it was the garlic dip making you sick," Griffin challenged.

"I got over that. Now it's the Indian food."

"You're feeling sick to your stomach quite a bit these days," he pointed out. "Maybe that's a sign that you shouldn't eat so much. I don't think all this stress eating is good for you."

"And here we go." Now it was my turn to be agitated. "You think I'm getting fat."

"I said nothing of the sort," Griffin protested. "Why do you always have to take it there?"

Dad grinned at our exchange. "Oh, see, this is nice. I don't have to cut off Griffin's hands because Aisling is going to punish him her own way. I taught her that. Me. What's not to love about that?"

Griffin scowled. "You get proud at the oddest times."

"I'm fine with that. It's a father's prerogative." Dad's smile remained in place for a moment before he straightened. "Now, get inside. We have guests, and you're all filthy. Change your clothes and find your manners. Understood?"

We all answered at the same time. "Yes, Dad."

"Good. Oh, and nice work. You took out a threat without breaking a sweat. I've taught you well."

Twenty-Three

The spicy food left me restless. Again.

Griffin fell asleep the moment his head hit the pillow, which only made me slightly bitter.

I headed toward the kitchen, leaving him to what I hoped were pleasant dreams, and grabbed a Vernors from the refrigerator before winding my way through the house. The light in my father's office was on. I paused in the doorway.

"You're up late."

Dad flicked his eyes to me. "Why are you up?"

I held up the Vernors. "I can't sleep. You shouldn't have gone with such spicy food."

"It didn't use to bother you."

"Yeah, well, apparently I'm getting old."

Dad chuckled as I sat in one of the chairs across from his desk and sipped my soda. "You still look pretty good for your age."

"I look awesome," I agreed, crossing my feet at the ankles and regarding him. "What are you doing?"

"Just some paperwork."

It was an evasive answer, and the fact that he couldn't make eye contact told me that he was lying. "What are you really doing?"

Dad heaved a sigh. "Research on soul walkers."

I shouldn't have been surprised. He was trying to downplay my worry, but that didn't mean he could ignore the little voice whispering in the back of his mind, the one that told him his children might be in trouble and he needed to protect them. "Anything good?"

"Nothing concrete. It seems that soul walkers were the secretive sort. They didn't want anyone else to have the key to everlasting life."

"It seems to me they had two keys," I pointed out. "One led to everlasting life and the other led to turning into a wraith. I'm not sure I would risk losing my soul just to have a shot at living forever."

"That's because you're more of a 'live-in-the-moment' girl. You always have been. You focus on the here and now instead of the future. It's both a blessing and a curse from what I can tell."

That was an interesting observation. "I think about the future more now. Like ... everyone keeps talking about kids. I never gave it much thought until Griffin. Now it seems that's all anyone wants to talk about."

Dad chuckled. "You'll get used to that. Once the 'when are you getting married' questions stop, the 'when are you having children' discussion begins. There's no hurry. You have plenty of time."

"I know. I can tell you one thing for sure: I'm not having five kids."

"No, I don't think you have the patience for that."

"I'm going to have just one, so it won't matter how much I spoil him or her."

"That sounds like a great way to ruin a kid."

"I'm fine with that." I took another drink of my Vernors to settle my nerves. "I told Redmond and Braden about seeing the other Mom. Redmond took it okay. Braden was a butthead."

"That's to be expected."

"He's not as angry as I thought he would be."

"Braden is ... you in a more masculine outfit," Dad said after a beat. "I know you don't want to hear or see it — it bothers you because you two fight so often — but you're very similar."

It wasn't the first time he'd said that to me and I knew it wouldn't be the last. He was constantly looking for common ground that Braden and I could share to cut down on the sniping. "You like me better, though, right?"

Dad's grin was back. "You're definitely my favorite."

"Good." I leaned back to rest my head on the leather-backed chair. "So, um, there's one more thing. I should've told you weeks ago, but I didn't know how to broach the subject. I thought maybe I was reading something into it that wasn't there, but ... now I don't think so. Now I think it plays into the bigger picture."

Dad's eyes, mirror images of my own, were keen. "I figured you were hiding something."

"How?"

"You're not a very good liar."

"I am an excellent liar. That's how I got away with so much stuff as a kid."

"You got away with 'stuff' because I'm indulgent and easily manipulated," Dad corrected. "You weren't fooling anyone."

"Whatever."

"Tell me what you've been hiding," Dad prodded. "It will make you feel better."

I wasn't sure that was true, but it was time. I was beaten down from keeping secrets and wanted everything out in the open. "The day we had the big fight at the cemetery, when the storm hit while we were there and Griffin almost ... well, you know."

Dad nodded, his expression dark. "I remember."

"I stayed up on the hill after, so I could be close to Griffin and keep him calm while you guys destroyed the discs and put an end to the storms."

Dad furrowed his brow. "I remember that, too. I thought it was a good idea for you guys to remain separate from the pack. Griffin was only calm because it was just the two of you."

"He fought hard that day."

"He did."

My eyes burned with unshed tears at the memory. "I thought something bad might happen even though I told you I never had a doubt. There was a moment when I thought he was going to hurt me, and I wasn't afraid for myself. I was afraid for him."

"You should've been afraid for him," Dad growled. "If he'd touched you I would've killed him."

"And he would've let you because the guilt would've been too much," I supplied. "He wouldn't have wanted to live after that, even though it wasn't his fault."

"Blame is a hard game to play," Dad offered. "In my head, I would've understood it wasn't his fault. My broken heart wouldn't have allowed me to see anything but retribution. Thankfully for both of us, you took care of yourself and weren't hurt. You took care of Griffin that day, too."

"I like to think we took care of each other."

"Fair enough."

I licked my lips as I gathered my courage. "While we were sitting on the hill we talked about inane stuff. Griffin didn't want to look at me in case the spell kicked back in, so I soothed him while watching you guys work, kept up a running commentary and stuff. It was actually sort of fun because I hate manual labor."

Dad's grin was quick. "I'm well aware."

"You guys were busy. We had bodies to deal with. There was a fire going. That's how you destroyed the discs so no one else could call the storms."

"I was there for all of this, kid. What's your point?"

"I'm getting to it."

"Get there faster. It'll be time for breakfast at the rate you're going."

He wasn't wrong. "Well, here's the thing. There were four discs. There was the one I found at the police chief's house. There was the one Mark Green carried. The rogue had another one, and we thought someone else had the fourth, but we had no idea who."

"That's right." Dad turned thoughtful. "We weren't all that worried about it because without all the discs no one could cast the storm spell. If even one of them was destroyed they all lost their power."

"Exactly. I watched you guys destroy them. You took the one Green had in his pocket. Redmond took the one from the rogue he killed. Cillian collected the one I had. All three of you threw discs in the fire."

"All right." Dad was clearly at a loss thanks to my roundabout story skills. "I don't understand what the problem is."

Here it comes.

I sucked in a calming breath. "I watched you guys destroy the discs. Then, when she thought no one was looking, Mom threw a fourth disc into the fire."

Dad moved to stand, but quickly returned to a sitting position as his face flooded with color. "Are you certain?"

"I've gone over it in my head a thousand times since it happened. I remember counting down in my head as you guys destroyed the discs. It was important to me because of Griffin. He was right there, wrapped around my legs to calm himself, and I counted each time one of them was destroyed because it made me feel better. Mom had the fourth disc."

Dad was flabbergasted. "Son of a ... !" He swore viciously as he gave up any semblance of calm and shoved away from his desk chair to pace. "Why didn't you tell me this sooner, Aisling? I could've questioned her."

"I did that myself."

"What did she say?"

"She said she got a disc from one of you guys, although she couldn't exactly remember who, and that's what she threw into the fire. She was lying. It was obvious. She didn't back down from the lie."

"I'll kill her." Dad gripped his hands together as he stood at the window and stared out at the darkness. "You should have told me. I would've kept her away from you."

That was exactly the reaction I was expecting. "What good would that have done?" I challenged. "It only would've made her more suspicious, more likely to turn on us in an overt way. At least now she's pretending to play the game."

"Yes, but it's a game." Dad was furious as his eyes tracked to the open door. "Good evening, Griffin."

I jolted at the greeting and swiveled quickly to find Griffin sheepishly walking into the office. He wore a T-shirt and boxer shorts, his hair mussed from sleep.

"I didn't mean to interrupt you," he offered. "I was worried about Aisling when I realized she wasn't in bed. After the wraith attack ... ."

Dad waved away the apology. "It's fine. You're part of this family. I have no intention of hiding from you what Aisling just told me."

I sank lower in my chair. "Oh, well ... ."

"I already know," Griffin said quietly. "She told me the next day. I think she wanted to do it when it happened, but she was afraid I couldn't take it. As it was, it took everything she had to stop me from tracking down Lily so I could kill her with my bare hands."

Dad nodded. "Of course she told you."

"I wasn't playing favorites," I argued as Griffin moved toward the chair, scooped me up and settled me on his lap. "I just ... didn't know what to do. If everyone started treating her with suspicion I worried she would move up whatever plan she has."

"Instead you played nice with her even though you clearly didn't want her around," Dad mused. "You still should have told me, kid. You shouldn't have gone through this alone."

"I wasn't alone." I rested my head against Griffin's shoulder. "I had backup."

"I didn't know what to do," Griffin admitted as he rubbed his hands over my shoulders. "Part of me thought you should know, but you're not exactly good at hiding your feelings. The way it worked out, Lily thinks everyone but Aisling trusts her. She's still trying to manipulate Aisling, but she's not going out of her way to do it."

"We need to come up with a plan." Weariness washed across my father's features as he sank into his chair. "We can't allow her free reign in this house. It's not smart to let her hear us plotting."

"She hasn't heard anything important. I've made sure of that."

"And yet you're in danger," Dad pointed out. "You've been attacked by wraiths several times the past few weeks, and that assault last night was clearly a coordinated effort. Your mother wasn't here, but she knew about the dinner. She begged off, saying she had other things she had to attend to."

"Do you think she was amassing a wraith attack?" Griffin asked.

Dad held his hands palms out and shrugged. "I have no idea. Someone let the wraith into that spa, though, and there are very few suspects. I'm going to guess your mother and sister didn't do it, Griffin. Your aunts and cousins would have no reason. Aidan, Jerry and Aisling aren't suspects. Who does that leave?"

"Lily," Griffin answered automatically. "She's the only suspect in that particular case. But she wasn't there when Aisling was attacked outside the Mexican restaurant. Nobody saw her last night."

"That doesn't mean she's not involved," Dad argued. "We also know she has ties to rogue reapers, including Duke Fontaine. She's tried to distance herself from his actions since coming back — and it's been easy because he's dead and can't defend himself — but Xavier's presence in town could easily be explained by a union with Lily."

"She could've told him anything," I mused. "We wondered why Xavier would get involved with this stuff, but the obvious answer is that Mom lied to him. He's motivated by the stories she's telling."

"That makes the most sense," Dad agreed. "The question is, what are we going to do about it? Your mother can explain away the disc. She'll say she picked it up in the mausoleum or something. That's her way."

"We have to figure out a way to get her to show her hand," I replied. "We can't understand why she's doing any of this until we know her end game."

"Whatever it is, it has something to do with you," Griffin noted. "You've been her primary focus since she came back. She feigns interest in the boys occasionally, but she's almost always more interested in what Aisling is doing."

"That's an interesting observation," Dad said. "It's been easier for you to watch her from afar because she dislikes you."

"She does," Griffin agreed. "She dislikes me because I'm standing between her and her end goal."

"Aisling."

"Yes." Griffin nodded. "She wants something from Aisling. She always has. We need to figure out what that something is and how ghost Lily fits into things. Why is she even here? What does she want? Why can only Aisling see her?"

"We don't know that only Aisling can see her," Dad cautioned. "We simply know that Lily can't see her. Maybe that's by design."

"Whose design?"

"Zake Zezo." The name came to me in a rush as I leaned forward excitedly. "I almost forgot about him because we've had so much going on, but the answer is right in front of us."

"The shaman?" Dad wrinkled his nose. "I thought you said he was dead."

"He is dead. He followed me to the airport the night we picked up Griffin's family. He said he wanted to talk and then he dropped in two seconds flat. He died at the hospital later." I faced Griffin. "Did you ever find out how he died?"

"No. I forgot to follow up because I was busy with other stuff. I can place a call tomorrow."

"Do you think Zake Zezo was the mastermind behind all of this?" Dad asked. "Do you think he fashioned the plan? If so, why kill him now? Why end him before he has a chance to see the plan come to fruition?"

"I didn't say I believed he was the one behind the plan," I cautioned. "He said weird things to me at his shop that day I stopped in with Redmond. He said that the enemy had been close the entire time, but he wouldn't go into details. I think he was trying to tell me then that Mom was the one working against us. I simply didn't see it."

"If someone killed him in that airport — which was quite the feat with that many people around, mind you — it could be that he had important information to share," Dad said. "We need to look at him tomorrow ... and hard. Do you remember where his shop is?"

"Yeah."

"I'll arrange for Redmond and Cillian to head over in the morning."

I balked. "I want to go. You can't keep me trapped in this house. I know you think you're protecting me, but what you're really doing is driving me crazy."

"Fine. We'll talk about it in the morning." Dad's eyes flashed. "Just for the record, though, I have no intention of letting you manipulate me on this. I'm putting my foot down."

"I'm looking forward to seeing that," I said dryly. "I love it when you put your foot down."

"I'm also having a waffle bar with that blueberry sauce you like so much."

I brightened considerably. "Score!"

Griffin tapped the side of the soda can. "I thought you were feeling sick."

"Things change."

"I guess so."

"We'll conduct research tomorrow," Dad said. "I want to hold off on telling your brothers until we know more about Zake Zezo. If I find your mother has been working against us this entire time, she will not be at your wedding. I can promise you that."

The wedding was the least of my worries. "If she has a specific plan, she's going to put it into motion either tomorrow or the next day. After that, Griffin and I will be out of town on the honeymoon you won't tell us anything about."

"Good point." Dad rolled his neck. "I'll call for more security in the morning. I have no doubt she's going to make a move. I only wish I knew what she wanted. That would help me think two steps ahead of her."

"Yeah." I finished my Vernors and eyed my father. "Where are you sending us on our honeymoon?"

Dad ignored the question. "It's time for bed. You need your sleep. You're almost a bride, after all. I don't want you looking tired on your wedding day."

"Oh, that's so much crap."

"Take her to bed, Griffin," Dad ordered. "She needs her rest."

Griffin smirked. "This family makes me laugh. You guys are such a trip."

"We definitely have our moments," Dad agreed. "She's exhausted, though. Sleep is the best thing for her."

"I'm on it."

Twenty-Four

I was ravenous when I woke, enough so that my hair was still wet from the shower when we made our way to the dining room. I could smell the waffles from ten rooms away and no one was going to deny me my blueberry goodness. Plans to take down my evil mother could wait. Even the fact that the wedding coordinator was already seated next to Jerry, their heads bent together, couldn't ruin my morning.

"Where are the sprinkles?"

Griffin shook his head as he added strawberries to his waffle pile. "Are you really going to eat four of those things?"

"Just watch me."

"You're going to get all sugared up and be a terror all day," he lamented. "I just know it."

"Hey, we only have two days left of being single. I want to party hard."

Griffin snorted as he moved to the table and sat. "How did everyone sleep last night?"

"This place is just like a hotel," Katherine replied, smiling fondly at her son. "There are maids and everything. What's not to love?"

"I can see why you like living here," Clint supplied as he cut into his own mound of waffles. "The food is pretty good, and the service is five stars."

Griffin's smile was tight as he regarded his grandfather. "We don't live here."

"You have been the past few days."

"That's because Aisling wants to be close to her family before the big day," Griffin said smoothly. "Her father likes to spoil her, and she likes to be spoiled. It's easier for everyone to be together right now."

"Yes, the day after tomorrow is the big day." Katherine's eyes sparkled. "You guys are getting married in a little over forty-eight hours. You must be excited."

"Definitely." Griffin flicked his eyes to me. "We're excited, right?"

"Oh, you have no idea. I love blueberries on my waffles."

"We're excited about the wedding," Griffin clarified pointedly. "That's what we're excited about."

"Oh, right. We're definitely excited about that, too," I agreed.

"What are the plans for today?" Katherine asked. "Do we have last-minute things that need to be taken care of?" Her question was aimed at Annabelle, so I let the wedding coordinator answer.

"We're on schedule," Annabelle replied. "I have a number of things to mark off my list for the day, but everything should be set by the time I leave this afternoon."

"And the bachelor party is tonight?" Clint asked. "That's what someone said."

"We're having joint bachelor and bachelorette parties at the same restaurant," Griffin answered. "Everyone will be partying together."

Since he had an expressive face, Clint's distaste for the party plans was obvious. "Wait ... everyone is partying together? Aren't the men supposed to be separate from the women?"

"There aren't a lot of women," Griffin pointed out. "Aisling's best friend is male ... and so are all her brothers. She wants to be with them. There's no point in separating."

The part he left out was that a joint party also allowed my family to keep a close watch so I wouldn't be attacked without back-up to fight off the growing wraith hordes. That was their primary concern.

"The point is that this is your last night for drunken debauchery,"

Clint replied without hesitation. "How are you going to hook up with the stripper if your fiancée is with you?"

Griffin worked his jaw. "Is that supposed to be a joke?"

"I'm pretty sure it's not a joke," I offered helpfully, holding out my canister of sprinkles. "Would you like some sugar?"

He ignored my attempt to smooth over the conversation. "I'm not hooking up with a stripper."

"Why not?" Clint was either being purposely obtuse or legitimately didn't understand the problem. I was leaning toward the latter. "You're not married yet. This is when you're supposed to cut loose. Otherwise you won't have a memory to sustain you when you're married."

Griffin made a face. "The only memory I want to sustain me is her." He jabbed his fork in my direction, his lips curving when he met my gaze. "I mean ... what's not to love about this memory?" He chuckled as he took his napkin and wiped the blueberry sauce from the corners of my mouth. "It doesn't get hotter than this."

"I know you're joking, but you're not wrong." I shook the sprinkles container enticingly. "Don't get worked up, Clint. There won't be strippers, but the bar we're going to has scantily-dressed women as servers. We rented the entire second floor. You'll have plenty of eye candy."

"That's not the point." Clint refused to let it go. "A bachelor party is supposed to feature strippers. I expected strippers."

"Don't worry about it," Jerry interjected, taking me by surprise with his vehemence. "I'll make sure you get a stripper. Just ... shut up. Nobody wants a side of strippers with their waffles."

Redmond cleared his throat. "Actually, that sounds like the perfect breakfast."

Braden chimed in. "Can we have strippers with our waffles, Dad? It would be a gift for all of us."

"Stop talking about strippers," Dad ordered, his temper flaring. "Strippers are not appropriate breakfast conversation."

"Definitely not," I agreed. "I'm feeling bloated this morning. Does anyone want to talk about that? I'm so bloated I'm worried my dress won't fit."

Dad scowled. "Really? Do you think it's appropriate to talk about that at the breakfast table?"

I shrugged. "If I'm bloated, everyone is going to feel the pain."

"I'll get some water tablets, Bug," Jerry offered. "It's probably because you have PMS."

"How do you know she has PMS?" Cillian asked.

"I keep track in my calendar. Even I can't put up with her on the first day of PMS."

I grinned when my father shot me a dirty look. "I'm a legend for a reason."

"Yes, I remember when Aisling was a teenager and had PMS," Redmond said, adopting a far-off expression. "She ate all the licorice in the house and threatened to castrate us if we didn't stop talking during her soap operas."

"She still does that," Griffin teased. "As for the water tablets, I don't think you're bloated because of PMS. I think it's because you've been eating two servings at every meal. You need to take a chill pill and calm down."

"Hey! I'll eat what I want." I waved a chunk of waffle in his face. "It's PMS. It will be fine, because the bloating should ease off tomorrow."

"I can't tell you how happy I am to hear that," Griffin drawled.

"And I can't believe we're having this conversation over what should be a civilized meal," Clint complained. "What is going on here?"

"For once, I agree with Clint," Dad said. "Kill the stripper and PMS talk. Let's focus on something more palatable for the entire group."

"Do you have any suggestions?" Braden asked. "Now that we've broken the seal on the PMS talk, I think it's going to be hard to top."

"I agree." I talked with my mouth full, which I knew drove my father batty. "Strippers and PMS would make a great television show. We should totally trademark the name and come up with a script."

"Ugh." Dad slapped his hand to his forehead. "This is going to overtake the entire day, isn't it?"

"Pretty much."

"I can't tell you how much I enjoy having children at this moment," Dad muttered. "You five sure know how to make a father proud."

I patted his hand. "We're nothing if not dedicated."

GRIFFIN AND I SLIPPED out of the house shortly after break-fast. His family was distracted in the game room, and my family had souls to collect. That left only Jerry to contend with, but he was busy talking to the wedding coordinator to make sure absolutely everything worked out perfectly. He barely looked up when we slipped out the front door.

Griffin drove, taking the freeway as far as he could before exiting onto the side streets, following the directions I provided. He parked a block from Zake Zezo's storefront so we could watch for an extended amount of time before approaching, and then he pulled his phone from his pocket and called his precinct.

I kept one ear on the conversation, although Griffin didn't share much, mostly grunting in response. When he was done, I watched him expectantly.

"It was poison," Griffin volunteered. "He had a mark on his neck, like from a dart, although no dart was found at the scene. That doesn't necessarily mean anything, because the dart could've been kicked away during the melee by the paramedics."

"Do you know what kind of poison it was?"

"Just that it was designed to knock him out almost immediately. They've been digging into his past for days, but they didn't mention his store. I'm guessing that's because they're not aware of it, which means his name is probably different on the lease."

"Yeah. I don't care how worldly you are. Renting to a dude named Zake Zezo is probably a fool's bet, even in this neighborhood."

"This neighborhood is bad." Griffin stretched as he studied the sidewalk. "Those guys over there are conducting a drug deal right out in the open."

"You're not here to arrest them," I reminded him.

"No, but they are idiots and I want to give them a good scare."

"That's a bad idea. We're about to break into a store. These people are trained to look the other way. They're going to feel differently if you give them a hard time before we break the law. They'll be less likely to cooperate if it comes to that."

"Fair point." Griffin snagged my hand and pressed it to his chest, his fingers roaming over mine as he watched the building. "I want to give it ten minutes, just to be on the safe side."

"He's dead. If someone decided to break in it probably happened days ago."

"I know. But what if someone is watching the building?"

"Then they probably won't stop in ten minutes."

"Can you just sit still for ten minutes?" Griffin's expression was rueful. "I know it's hard for you, but I'd feel better if we waited... just to make sure."

"Fine." I heaved out a sigh and shifted my attention to the Dairy Twist across the road. "Ooh, soft-serve ice cream. We should stop there on our way back."

Griffin made an exaggerated face. "You just spent half the morning complaining that you're bloated."

"I am bloated. That doesn't mean I don't want ice cream."

"Do you think the ice cream will help the bloating?"

"No, but it won't hurt it. Besides, you can't tell me that a twist cone dipped in chocolate doesn't sound heavenly."

"Aisling ... ."

"Come on. You know you want one."

"I don't know why I'm giving you grief," Griffin complained as he tapped his fingers on top of mine. "You're eating like a horse and are as thin as ever. I might not fit into my tux."

Warmth washed over me at his downtrodden expression. "Poor Griffin. Do you want me to give you a good workout when we get back to Grimlock Manor? We'll have plenty of time to burn before the big party."

"Sure." Griffin's smile was sly. "That will help me cool my urges for the stripper Jerry insists he's getting. Don't you think that's a mistake?"

I had a feeling I knew exactly which stripper Jerry was going to enlist for the night's festivities, so I merely shook my head. "It will be fine. Trust me."

"If you say so."

"I definitely say so, although ... where did we land on the ice cream?"

"If you're good while we're breaking and entering I'll buy you an ice cream cone. You have to shut up about it until then, though."

"Sounds like a plan."

"YOU'VE GOT TO be kidding me!" Redmond's eyes were wide when we walked back through the front door of Grimlock Manor, ice cream cones in hand. "Where's mine?"

"You should've gone with us," I answered as I licked my treat. "You snooze, you lose."

"Whatever." Redmond made a disgusted face. "If you keep eating like that you won't fit into your dress."

"It's two days away. I think I'll manage. Where's Dad?"

"Why?" Sensing a change in my demeanor, Redmond turned suspicious. "Where were you guys? You left without telling anyone where you were going."

"Dad knew," I said. "That's why I need to talk to him."

"Tell me where you were."

"We broke into Zake Zezo's store." I saw no reason to lie. The truth would come out in its entirety eventually. "Griffin found out he'd been poisoned, and because he was trying to talk to me right before it happened we figured there was a chance he left something for me in his store."

"And?"

"And we were too late." My stomach twisted at the memory of what we found inside his hole-in-the-wall space. "It was a mess. If he did leave something for me, it's long gone."

Redmond turned to Griffin for further explanation. "What does she mean by that?"

"Someone broke in between the day Zake Zezo died and now," Griffin replied, his expression serious. "The place had been torn to shreds. Aisling said that while it wasn't exactly clean when you guys were there, it was completely ransacked today in comparison."

"The place was torn apart," I said. "Papers were spread everywhere, although there was nothing worth reading. I did find out Zake Zezo's real name."

"Oh, are you saying his mother didn't toil through fifteen hours of labor to give him that name?" Redmond deadpanned. "I'm shocked. Shocked, I tell you!"

I snickered as I bit into my cone. "It's ... mmmph ... mmpf."

"So sexy," Griffin teased as I talked with my mouth full. "I can't believe that you're going to be completely mine in forty-eight hours. You really are the gift that keeps on giving, baby."

"Forget her," Redmond complained. "Tell me about Zake Zezo."

I held up a finger and swallowed. "While you fill in Redmond, I'm going to track down my dad. He'll want to hear what we found, too."

"Okay."

I left Griffin and Redmond to talk and wound my way through the house. The Taylors and my brothers who weren't out collecting souls were on the third floor, so that meant the main floor was quiet. That was exactly as I liked it.

"Dad?" I opened his office door, pulling up short when I found Annabelle standing behind the desk. Her face flushed guiltily, and she pulled her hand away from the book that was open in front of her. "What are you doing in here?"

"I was looking for your father." Annabelle straightened her shoulders. "I wanted to talk to him about the speech he has planned for the wedding. I thought he would be in here, but I was mistaken."

I took a long look around the office to see if anything was out of place. It looked normal, but I wasn't exactly known for my observational skills. "I don't think my father would like the idea of you being here."

"Of course not."

"Don't come in here again. This is his private space."

"I wasn't trying to invade his private space." Annabelle was apologetic as she held out her hands. "Honestly. It was simply an accident."

"Yeah, well, you should probably get out of here."

Annabelle didn't need to be told twice. She turned on her heel and strode through the open door, leaving me to survey the office without her prying eyes. I headed straight for my father's desk, the remainder of my ice cream cone forgotten as I stared at the book Annabelle had been looking at when I entered.

I had no idea if she was up to something. I probably would've stopped to look at the book, too, if our positions were reversed. The illustrations were quite graphic, and featured what looked to be a wraith and an ethereal figure that wasn't ravaged by a hard soul extraction. I figured that was what a soul walker was supposed to look like, although I didn't have time to dwell on that now.

I spent five minutes searching the office and came up empty. If Annabelle was snooping, she'd covered her tracks well. If she stole something, it wasn't an obvious trinket.

So, was she spying or simply doing her job?

Twenty-Five

I found Cillian in his bedroom, the door firmly shut. I barged in without alerting him that I was invading his personal space, which didn't make him happy.

"Don't you knock?"

"You don't knock on my bedroom door."

"First, your bedroom door is technically in the townhouse and I always knock on the external door. Second, since you started having Griffin over for sleepovers I have always knocked."

He was the polite one in the family, so that was probably true, but I was in no mood to capitulate. "Where's Dad?"

"He's not in here."

"Yeah, well, I just caught the wedding coordinator in his office and I can't decide if she was doing something suspicious or if I'm simply being cynical because that's how I roll."

"I'd go with the latter."

I pointed out the obvious. "Mom hired her."

Cillian stiffened as he tilted his head to the side. "I didn't think about that. What was she doing?"

"She claimed she was looking for Dad, but I found her standing behind his desk. He had a book open, one about wraiths and soul walkers. If she wasn't snooping, then she probably thinks we're into the occult or something."

"What did you say to her?"

"I told her to stay out of Dad's office. I gave it a good search, but nothing looked out of place."

"I don't think there's anything in there she could access that would hurt us, but it's probably best you tell Dad."

I graced him with the best "well, duh" look in my repertoire. "Why do you think I'm looking for him?"

"I thought maybe you wanted him to spoil you some more. He's been an indulgent daddy machine where you're concerned for weeks."

I hopped on the bed next to Cillian so I could see what he was working on. The text on his screen was in a language I didn't recognize. "You say that like it's a bad thing. I'll be a married woman in two days. He won't be able to spoil me after that. I deserve it."

Cillian choked out a harsh laugh. "Oh, puh-leez. That man is going to spoil you until the day he dies. You've trained him well."

"It honestly wasn't that much work." I sank lower on the pillows so I could get comfortable. "What are you working on?"

"Several things. The biggest is Zake Zezo."

"You mean Marvin Knotts? If I'd had that name, I would've changed it, too."

Cillian snickered. "Yeah. That's not the most auspicious of names. I've found a few things on him."

"Like what?"

"Like his mother was a Grimpond."

The information smacked me hard across the face. "What?" I felt like I had whiplash I turned to face him so quickly. "As in Fox Grimpond?"

"As in the man who held our mother captive for years after the fire," Cillian confirmed. "Marvin Knotts was his uncle."

I gaped as I absorbed the information. "How?"

"Fox's mother had a brother. His name was Marvin Knotts. Zake Zezo didn't come into being until about twenty years ago."

"That would've been before Mom was taken."

"Yeah, I don't believe he had any knowledge of that." Cillian ran a hand through his shoulder-length hair as he tapped on his keyboard. "I've been putting together a timeline. Marvin left his wife and children when he was forty."

"How old were the kids?"

"Teenagers."

"Nice guy."

"Well, I'm not sure he didn't leave for a good reason," Cillian hedged. "The Grimponds were heavy into the occult. They had a lot of money, so they weren't just dabblers. I managed to track the dagger you recovered after the wraith attack to a private sale in West Bloomfield fifteen years ago."

I wasn't sure where he was going with the information. "Is this one story or two?"

"Bear with me." Cillian flashed me a warning look. He hated being interrupted when he was about to tell a long and boring story. "So, the dagger was found in a house on Detroit's west side a few months before the auction. The owner of the house was long since dead and vagrants had essentially taken it over. The interesting thing is that none of the vagrants ever realized there was a virtual fortune hidden in the crawl space.

"In addition to the dagger, there was also some rather expensive jewelry — amulets, rings and several discs that were reported to be magical — and a book," he continued. "As far as I can tell, it's the same book that Dad has on his desk downstairs."

Oh, well, now things were starting to get interesting. "How did Dad get that book?"

"The reaper hierarchy bought it at auction after the other items were found," Cillian replied. "They were discovered when a crew came in to demolish the house. It was only after everything was hauled away that the trunk was discovered."

"Whoever found that must have thought they struck it rich."

"The construction company that bought the property owned any goods discovered on the land, so the owners got rich."

Something occurred to me. "Are you going to tell me it was Happy Faces Construction?"

"Oh, you're smarter than you look." Cillian grinned as he tapped his finger against my forehead. "The owner of Happy Faces Construction, one Fred McGinley, put the items up for auction. Our home office bought the book because word spread when it hit the market. You know how things in those circles work."

Actually, I'd never taken the time to figure out how things worked when it came to the higher-ups. I honestly didn't care about those things. "Why didn't they buy the dagger?"

"Because some private company swooped in and placed an absolutely huge bid over the phone," Cillian answered. "That company was a shell company, and it's now defunct. I've done a lot of digging, and I'll give you one guess who owned that shell company."

"Fox Grimpond."

"Give the girl a pound of licorice." Cillian poked my side to let me know he was teasing before sobering. "Fox bought the dagger. How it ended up in the hands of a wraith is anybody's guess."

I stretched my legs as I tried to sort through Cillian's information. "Why do you think Fox wanted the dagger?"

"I don't know. I think he would've purchased the book, too, but he probably didn't have that option because he didn't want to draw attention to himself. Don't forget, he was still a reaper. My best guess is that word spread throughout the office and he had to make a choice, opting for the dagger ... mostly because he could look at the book in the office if he got desperate enough."

"Good point."

"So Fox bought the dagger, but we're not quite sure what happened to it in the intervening years," Cillian said. "Then, four years after he bought the dagger, Mom essentially died in a fire and he took her captive. She recovered, got back her strength, and was turned into a half-wraith of sorts by Genevieve Toth because Fox knew her and needed help. The thing I've been struggling with now that all the pieces are coming together is this: Do you think Fox was trying to learn how to soul walk before he took Mom? That might explain why she's not a full-on wraith. That also might explain why Genevieve wasn't one either. We've been struggling with how she managed to do the things she did ... and I think the soul walker explanation might be the best we have."

It made sense. Kind of. "I thought soul walkers were supposed to live forever without losing themselves," I challenged. "The mother we got back wasn't the mother we lost."

"The things she went through could've changed her. She almost died. She was held prisoner. After escaping, she was with Genevieve for a long time. They became close. Maybe Mom isn't acting the way she is because she lost half her soul. Maybe she's acting that way because she's simply a different person."

In my mind, that made things worse. "She eats people. She sucks souls to survive. That's a wraith characteristic. That seems to suggest that she's not a soul walker."

"She could be a hybrid," Cillian conceded. "I simply don't know." He jerked up his chin when his bedroom door opened and scowled when Griffin strolled inside. "Don't either of you knock? You're like the rudest couple ever."

"Hey, you're the one sharing a bed with my fiancée." Griffin was blasé as he pushed me over to get comfortable on my other side. "What are you guys talking about?"

I caught him up on our conversation, hitting only the high points. When I was done, he seemed intrigued.

"Marvin Knotts, huh? I don't think that name came up in the investigation on Zake Zezo. Aisling stumbled across it in his store, but it was a fluke. How did you discover it, Cillian?"

"It wasn't easy," Cillian replied. "The thing I had going for me was the address of Zake's shop. You said your department wasn't aware of it, right?"

"That's my understanding," Griffin said. "I didn't want to point them in that direction in case there was anything in the shop that led them to Aisling. Quite frankly, I was already worried because he called her seconds before he died. So far, no one has come looking for answers."

"Maybe he had a phone that masked his actions," Cillian suggested. "For enough money you can buy almost anything these days."

"Well, he was tied to the Grimponds, so he had access to some money," I noted. "Do we know if he had any assets when he left his wife and kids?"

"The divorce documents are online, but the financial settlement is private," Cillian replied. "I have no idea. I'm guessing he planned his escape, though."

"But why?" Griffin asked. "Why leave the Grimpond fold if he was going to turn to the occult himself? Aisling said he had quite the reputation in certain circles. He had to be worried the Grimponds would discover that he was hiding in plain sight and come after him."

"Unless they knew and came to some sort of agreement," I theorized. "I mean, think about it: If he was truly afraid to be a member of the Grimpond family, wouldn't he have moved to a different area?"

"Good point." Griffin ran his hand over my knee. "We don't have any way of figuring out how the wraith got the dagger, right?"

"None that I can think of," Cillian replied. "Do you have an idea?"

"No. I thought maybe there was a way you could magically track it."

"We're not witches," I reminded him. "We're reapers. We don't know how to cast spells or anything. That was Genevieve Toth's thing."

"And now we're working under the assumption that she was a soul walker?"

"Or maybe some sort of hybrid," Cillian corrected. "Genevieve killed people to stay alive, too. She was more than a wraith, though. She managed to keep a sense of self despite all the killing, although she seemed fairly hollowed out by the end."

"Do you think that's how Mom will end up?" I asked. "She's doing the same thing Genevieve did to survive. It's only a matter of time before she gets spread too thin."

"Genevieve was around for centuries, though. Mom has only been living like this for eleven years."

"Genevieve was around for centuries at a time it was easier to kill without being caught," I clarified. "I mean, back in the old days, plagues wiped out people all the time. Death was swift and brutal. She could eat to her heart's content without anyone catching her. The modern world didn't make things that easy for her."

"That is a very good point." Cillian wagged a finger as he went back to his computer. "I don't know. I feel like the answers are here, but we don't have enough pieces to figure it out."

"We'd better come up with something soon," I lamented. "I think we're running out of time."

"We're not running out of time." Griffin linked his fingers with mine and smiled. "We're getting ready to start a new adventure. You have a lot of time left ... and it's all with me."

I took pity on him and smiled. "It's going to be okay. I have faith we'll figure it out. Probably not tonight, though. Tonight we have to party with your family. And I'm dying to see what your grandfather has to say about Jerry's stripper choice."

Griffin narrowed his eyes, suspicious. "What do you know about that?"

"Technically nothing, but I have a few ideas."

"Ugh. I'm afraid."

"Don't worry. I think you're going to be pleasantly surprised."

"That will be a nice change of pace."

I DRESSED FOR THE party, opting for flattering pants and a sparkly top that showed off my shoulders. Jerry left a pink dress on my bed that I assumed he expected me to wear, but I had no intention of ever getting drunk enough to wear anything that color.

I grabbed a coat from the closet before heading downstairs. Griffin was waiting in the foyer, his head bent together with Aidan's, and he cast me a furtive look when he heard my shoes on the stairs.

"Hello, future wife." He let loose a low whistle that made me blush. "That's a pretty top."

"It has no back," Dad complained as he moved past me and toward the front door. "There's no back on that shirt."

"It's backless," I pointed out. "There is no back when it comes to backless clothing items."

"It's a good thing you're getting married, kid, because I wouldn't let you out of the house wearing that shirt otherwise," Dad countered. "It's a little risqué."

"You're only saying that because I'm not wearing a bra."

Now it was Dad's turn to blush. "I wish you wouldn't say things like that. I'm your father, for crying out loud."

"That's why I say them." I offered a pretty smile before sobering and turning my attention to Griffin and Aidan. "What were you two gossiping about?"

"What makes you think we were gossiping?" Griffin asked. The act probably would've worked on a perp or someone who didn't know him, but I wasn't an idiot.

"Because I know you." I glanced between them several times. "We're not leaving until you tell me what you were talking about."

"We were talking about how nice you look," Aidan lied.

"I think you mean smoking hot," Jerry countered as he breezed past Aidan and beamed at me. "Oh, Bug, you look amazing. You give me disco fever."

Love washed over me when I saw how glassy Jerry's eyes were. He was close to tears, which made me feel guilty. We'd hardly had any time to spend together the past week. I had grand plans for us to bond — even more than we were already — but they never came to fruition.

"I wore it for you because I knew we would be dancing fools tonight," I said. "All we're waiting for is Griffin and Aidan to admit what they were talking about and then we can go."

"We weren't talking about anything," Aidan protested.

"They were talking about making sure that someone is with you at all times tonight so you don't wander off," Jerry supplied. "They want you to have a good time, but are worried some horrible creature will try to grab you. I tried explaining that would be impossible with me at your side, but they have doubts."

That made sense. Griffin wasn't stupid enough to stick with me the entire night because I would grate under constant supervision. I should've expected him to put a security detail into rotation before leaving the house. "Oh, well, that's just great."

"We're trying to keep you safe," Griffin said. "You're the most important person in the world tonight. If you think I'm going to apologize for putting your safety first, you're crazy."

That was kind of cute ... and annoying. "Do you really think you can keep me penned in if I want to run?"

"Are you going to run?"

"Probably not, but I want that option because otherwise the pressure will be too much and I'll implode from the stress."

"Very cute." Griffin pressed a kiss to my cheek. "We're still watching you like a hawk. Get used to it."

This party wasn't going to be nearly as fun as I thought. "We'll see."

"We definitely will."

Twenty-Six

I was originally leery when Jerry suggested a joint bachelor and bachelorette party. How was anyone supposed to have fun if their significant other was watching him or her? It turned out that Jerry was right. The joint party was fun ... and almost relaxing.

"I told you I'd come through," Jerry crowed as he took the open seat next to me. I sat in front of one of the fans to cool myself after a particularly long dance session — one in which Jerry insisted we perform the routine he choreographed after watching *Fame* when we were kids — and I sipped ice water instead of a drink to rehydrate.

"You did tell me you would come through," I confirmed, grinning as I shifted my eyes to the dance floor. "The drag queens were a nice touch."

"Clint said he wanted strippers." Jerry was blasé as he drank a blue concoction that made him sway back and forth, although I don't think he realized it. "Destiny and her crew aren't strippers, but they're a lot of fun and they have no problem dropping certain items of clothing to music when the beat calls for it."

They were indeed fun. Destiny and her group of gregarious partiers ran a rousing game of drag queen bingo a few blocks from our townhouses every weekend. Before I met Griffin, Jerry used to drag me there regularly. We hadn't visited in ages.

"We should play bingo when I get back from my honeymoon," I offered, studying my best friend's face. "It's been almost two years since we went."

"I didn't think you were up for drag queen bingo anymore," Jerry countered. "You'll be an old married lady in a few days. Married ladies don't go to drag queen bingo."

The words weren't exactly harsh, but they hurt a bit. "I'll always have time for you."

Jerry's lips curved as he patted my hand. "I know."

"It seems like I haven't had time for you lately, though, doesn't it?"

"It seems like you've had a lot on your mind," Jerry clarified. "I understand."

"I'll make it up to you when we get back from the honeymoon," I promised. "We'll spend time together, just the two of us ... and none of it will revolve around planning a wedding."

"Oh, I wouldn't say that." Jerry's smile turned sly. "When you get back, we'll simply be planning my wedding."

My heart jolted at the news. "What?"

"Aidan and I are getting married," Jerry replied, happiness positively washing over him in powerful waves. "He proposed after the storms because ... well, because he wanted to prove that we were okay. We are okay, and we're getting married."

"Congratulations!" I instinctively reached over and offered him a hug. "I can't believe it." I grabbed his left hand and studied his empty ring finger. "Where is your ring?"

"Aidan is letting me pick it out myself."

"That's probably wise."

"We wanted to wait until after your wedding. We didn't want to steal your thunder."

"You could never steal my thunder." In truth, I would've been more comfortable if Jerry did make a big announcement. That way all eyes wouldn't be on me. It was too late now, but the joy I felt for my best friend was palpable. "I'm really happy for you." Tears pricked the back of my eyes.

"Now I'm going to officially get to be your brother," Jerry enthused, his face flushed with excitement. "I always wanted that while growing up. You guys had so much fun together. I wanted to be a part of it."

"You always were a part of it."

"Not in the same way."

I gripped his hand hard and fought back tears. "You were always my brother, Jerry. Better than that, you were my best friend. You're pretty much my favorite person in the world."

"I know." Jerry swiped at my leaking tears. "Why are you crying? You don't cry."

"I have no idea." I used the back of my hand to swipe at my nose. "The wedding must be affecting me. I can think of no other explanation."

"Well, it's weird. Knock it off."

I laughed as Jerry pulled me in for a tight hug, not breaking the embrace until I felt a presence move in behind me. When I turned to look, I found Griffin watching the scene, his face etched with concern.

"What's going on?" Griffin lowered himself to the empty chair next to me and ran his thumbs over my cheeks. "Why is she crying? Jerry! You were supposed to make her happy, not sad."

"He did make me happy." I laughed, at myself and him, and then sighed. "I have no idea why I'm crying. Jerry and Aidan are getting married. We were talking and ... I turned into a girl."

"Oh, my poor baby." Griffin smiled as he leaned over and gave me a quick kiss. "You must hate being a girl."

"You have no idea." I rubbed at my itchy eyes. "In fact, I need to run to the bathroom and collect myself. I don't want to look like a fool."

"You don't look like a fool." Griffin was serious as he pressed another kiss to the corner of my mouth. "You look like a happy best friend. Congratulations, Jerry. I knew you guys would end up engaged, but I had no idea it would be so soon."

"Technically we've been together longer than you and Bug," Jerry pointed out.

"Technically everyone hooked up at almost the same time," Griffin countered. "It's not a competition."

"My wedding is going to be bigger," Jerry said simply, causing Griffin to bark out a laugh.

"Fair enough." His eyes laden with understanding, Griffin stroked his hand over my hair to smooth it. "Why don't you go to the bathroom to clean up and I'll pick a song for us to dance to."

"Ugh." I made a face. "You're not going to make me do a dance routine, too, are you?"

"Well, I might make you do your 'I won' dance before the night is out because that's a personal favorite," Griffin conceded. "I thought our dance could be slow. Something romantic and sappy, when we spend the entire song thinking only about each other and not the fact that my grandfather is melting down in the corner because of the drag queens."

I smiled and nodded. "That sounds good."

EVEN THOUGH I KNEW Griffin was waiting for me on the second floor, I took a detour on the first floor and slipped outside the side door to enjoy the summer evening and get some fresh air.

I was having a good time. No, really. That didn't change the fact that I was worried about our diminishing timetable. If we didn't find answers tomorrow, leaving on our honeymoon would be difficult. I wasn't keen on abandoning my family to fight off my evil mother without me to boss them around. On the flip side, I knew that postponing the honeymoon would crush Griffin. He was looking forward to us getting away from it all for two weeks. I couldn't take that from him.

"Hello, Aisling."

I jolted at the voice, turning quickly and scanning the darkness in the alley for a hint of movement. As if to help me out, the cocky gargoyle who uttered my name finally took two steps forward so I could make out his features.

"Bub." My temper flared. "What are you doing here?"

"Can't a gargoyle enjoy a walk on a nice summer's eve?"

"No."

"You're overly suspicious, girl. You don't need to be. I'm not here to hurt you."

"Why are you here?" I couldn't stop myself from staring in both directions — left and right — down the alley. "This seems like a strange place for a meeting."

"I'm here to watch you," Bub replied simply. "Your wedding approaches ... and so does the trouble I warned you about."

I figured that out myself. "Zake Zezo was a Grimpond. I mean ... kind of a Grimpond. Did you know that?"

"Yes."

"Why didn't you tell me?"

"Because Zake Zezo wasn't a concern of mine," Bub replied without hesitation. "He was merely a cog in the system."

"He followed me to the airport. He was trying to warn me. That was before you showed up. I can't help thinking the two are connected."

"I can't speak to Zake's motivations." Bub's voice was calm. "He was always a bit of a mystery. I never understood why he fled the Grimponds and set up shop so close to them."

"Maybe he thought he could hide in plain sight."

"That didn't work out very well, did it?"

"No, I guess not." I rolled my neck and relished the feel of the breeze as it cooled my steaming skin. "What's the deal with the soul walkers? What is my mother trying to accomplish?"

"What do you think she's trying to accomplish?"

"I don't know." That was true. "I understand she's not a true soul walker. She's more of a hybrid. I'm guessing Genevieve Toth was, too."

"Genevieve was more than that," Bub countered. "Her soul was evil from the start. It didn't turn evil. That's the difference between her and your mother."

"That doesn't change the fact that my mother wants something." I swallowed hard. "What is it?"

"I cannot answer that for you."

"But you know, don't you?"

"I ... ." Bub trailed off, his eyes going sharp as he stared into the alley.

I followed his gaze, but all I could make out was inky blackness. There was no noise to suggest we weren't alone, but the hair on the back of my neck stood on end. "What is it?"

"Run," Bub hissed, his eyes going opaque. "Now!"

He didn't have to tell me twice. I read the distress in his tone. I turned to flee inside, ready to grab my father and Griffin and explain what was happening so we could fight whatever enemy was about to show itself. I didn't get the chance because a burning sensation hit my neck and caused me to lose my footing and stumble forward.

Almost immediately, my mind felt as if it was slowing. I registered two things as I sank into oblivion. I had been hit in the neck with a dart, something I managed to remove even though it was already working against me. Also, Bub was down, too. He was prone on the ground, and the figures descending from the darkness looked as if they were about to eat him.

"No!" I struggled to form words as I reached out a protective hand toward the gargoyle even as Xavier Fontaine's sneering countenance filled my field of vision.

That was the last thing I said before unconsciousness claimed me. I fought hard to stay coherent, but I didn't have the strength.

I was in the hands of evil now, and there was nothing I could do about it.

"WAKE UP, AISLING!"

The irritated voice penetrated my muddled mind, but just barely. I struggled to open my eyes — it was like lifting boulders with my eyelids — and when I finally did I found Bub staked to the ground a few feet away. He looked weak, as if his strength was about to give out, but he was conscious. And I was tied to a chair.

"What the ... ?" I struggled to free myself, but my muscles were slow to warm, and I knew it would take time before I had full control over them again. "What happened?"

"What do you think happened?" Bub didn't look happy with the turn of events, his eyes glassy. "We've been taken hostage."

"By who?"

"Who do you think?"

I didn't need to ask the question a second time. Instead, I turned in my chair and regarded my mother with outright hate as she stood at the center of the abandoned theater with a multitude of wraiths and rogue reapers – including Xavier – surrounding her. She looked to be giving orders ... although she clearly wasn't happy with the turn of events.

"You'll have to monitor every door," Mom snapped. "It won't take the others long to realize she's gone. When they do, they'll start looking for her ... although I doubt they'll know enough to come here."

I snorted even though I knew it was stupid to draw attention to myself. "You don't think they'll look here? You're dumber than you look."

"Oh, I'm glad to see you've woken, Aisling." Mom moved around her wraiths and glared, true evil staring back at me for the first time since she'd returned. She could no longer hide who she really was. "I thought maybe you would sleep through your final act. I'm glad to see that's not the case."

I refused to panic. That's what she wanted. I wouldn't give her what she wanted no matter what she offered in return. "Dad is going to rip your spine out."

"Your father won't do anything of the sort. He'll welcome me back with open arms."

"Oh, really?" I didn't bother to hide my eye roll. "How are you going to manage that?"

"I have my ways."

We stared each other down for what felt like forever. Finally, I broke eye contact. Seeing those eyes, my mother's eyes, reflecting overt hatred was almost more than I could bear. "Why is Bub here? You should let him go. He has nothing to do with this."

"Oh, he has everything to do with this," Mom seethed, her frustration evident. "He's been working against me for months. I had my suspicions, but I could never prove it. He played both sides very well."

"That's probably what kept him alive." I focused on the gargoyle, who had ceased moving. A sticky black substance that looked like oil pooled beneath him, and I couldn't battle back the sickening thought that it was blood. "Is he dead?"

"Not yet. Killing him serves no purpose. He can serve as a snack for my wraiths later, when they've earned a meal. Then his death won't be in vain."

Her nonchalant attitude made me want to retch. "Well, that sounds lovely. Does he taste like chicken?"

"You've always had a smart mouth, Aisling. You've always been full of yourself. I think you'll find that attitude won't help you here."

"I honestly don't care." That was true. "I just want to know why. Why are you doing this? Why did you come back at all? Was it simply to mess with us?"

"I didn't want to come back." Mom dusted off her hands on her jeans. "That's for sure. I didn't feel a burning desire to see you people. I was happy on my own, out in the world. I had no choice but to return."

"Why?"

"Because I'm dying." Mom's eyes widened as she delivered the line. "You weren't expecting that, were you? It's the truth. I'm dying. Every day, a part of me flakes away. I don't have long. There's only one way to save myself."

"And what way is that?"

"Why, through you, of course." Mom's laugh was eerie, as if it emanated from someone else but came through her mouth. "You're going to be my salvation. Aren't you proud?"

"I'm not doing anything for you."

"You don't have a choice, dear. Not any longer." Mom patted my head, smiling when I tried to jerk away from her. "Now don't use up all your strength. That won't go well when it's time for the ritual. If you tire yourself, things might go poorly. That won't end well for either of us."

I shifted my eyes back to the spot where the wraiths had gathered only moments before. A few remained behind and looked to be working on something — symbols appearing on the floor in the area where they toiled. The rogues and other wraiths had disappeared.

"What ritual do you think you're performing?"

"One that I had hoped to put off for a bit longer to make sure I was ready, but your insistence on getting married won't allow for that," Mom replied. "Really, Aisling, if you'd just kept away from that stupid cop I wouldn't have had to do this before I was ready. You never were one to listen to reason."

"I hope you die a horrible death," I muttered under my breath. "I hope I'm there so I can applaud when it happens."

"Yes, well, that's not happening today." Mom seemed unusually chipper, which set my teeth on edge. "We'll be ready to start the ritual in twenty minutes. That's how long you have to get your thoughts in order. You should prepare yourself, my dear, because you're not going to like what's about to happen. This is the end of the road for you."

Twenty-Seven

W hen my mother turned to oversee her ritual preparations,
I fought my bindings. When that didn't work, I tried to
wake Bub, but he didn't stir. After that, I found myself
staring at the door hoping that my family would rush in and save me.
Two minutes of that was all I could take because, while I knew they
would panic when I didn't return, I had no idea how long it would take
them to figure out the theater was where they should start looking. It
was time I didn't have.

After that, I spent a full minute trying to send a mental SOS to
Aidan. We were twins, and if Lifetime movies had taught me anything
it was that twins had a special bond. That didn't work either.

I was about to start freaking out and screaming when I caught
sight of movement by the front door. I sucked in a breath, hoping
against hope that it was my family. Instead, the figure that moved into
the room caused my heart to skip a beat.

It was my other mother. The younger one. She didn't seem worried
about being caught, and after surveying the scene for a full beat she
headed in my direction.

"You've got yourself in quite the pickle, huh?" She smiled as she hunkered down and looked between Bub and me. "You shouldn't have gone outside alone."

If my hands were free I would've wrapped them around her neck. "Thank you so much for your illuminating observation. I can't tell you how good that makes me feel."

Instead of being offended, she laughed. "You're still seventy percent mouth and thirty percent brains. I was hoping you'd grow out of that."

I slid my eyes to Mom (the real one), who was busy barking out orders to her wraiths. I couldn't understand why she wasn't looking in this direction.

"She can't see us," my other mother said. "She can't hear us. I've taken care of that. As far as she's concerned, when she looks over here you're simply sitting here alone."

"How is that possible?"

"Magic."

"Oh, well, good. I thought you were about to tell me something ridiculous. I'm glad you didn't go that route."

"As much as I would love to sit here and enjoy a good argument with you for old time's sake, I can't. We don't have much time. You need to listen to what I'm about to tell you."

"I'm not sure I'm in the mood for that."

"You have no choice." She was all business, adopting the tone I recognized from childhood when she was about to bring down the hammer. "That woman is not your mother, at least not the mother you remember."

"Oh, really?" I drawled, sarcasm practically dripping from my tongue. "I never would've figured that out myself. Thank you so much for explaining things to me."

"You need to shut that smart mouth," she ordered. "I have a lot to tell you in very little time. I'm your mother, so you owe me some respect. I gave birth to you, after all. I thought the labor would be the worst of it, but I was wrong. Of course, you brought me joy, too, so I have no complaints. Er, well, very few complaints. That thing you used to do when you manipulated your father to do your bidding after I already told you 'no' was not a favorite."

I had about five hundred complaints, but I managed to snap my mouth shut and listen.

"You're not the only one who can see me. Your father and brothers will be able to as well, if they get here in time. We can't assume that's going to happen, so you'll have to save yourself."

"I would love to save myself. I've always considered myself a self-rescuing princess. I can't make my muscles work the way they're supposed to, though."

"She drugged you. The drug will pass through your system quickly. You don't have to worry about that."

"What should I worry about?"

"What she has planned for you," she answered simply. "Do you understand what's going on here?"

"She's going to kill me. It probably has something to do with that whole 'eating a reaper's soul to restore a wraith' thing. Am I close?"

"It's more complicated than that. She plans to use your body and be reborn inside of it. She thinks she can hijack your soul and live a full life inside you. The problem is that your essence will burn in the process and there will be nothing left."

I swallowed the lump in my throat. "But ... that's ridiculous."

"It is," the woman agreed, solemn. "She doesn't realize it won't work because she'll have to contend with two souls, both very strong, and she doesn't have the power to dislodge both. I don't believe she has the power to dislodge either, but that won't stop her from trying – and you could die in the process.

"She found a ritual to do what she wants in a book, one that your wedding coordinator photographed and sent to her," she continued.

"I knew that woman was evil," I groused, struggling against my bindings again. "I should've killed her then."

"It was already too late. Don't dwell on that."

"Griffin must already know that I'm in trouble," I argued. "He'll come."

"He will, and he won't be alone," she agreed. "He'll always come for you. That's one of the reasons she hates him so much. She worried he would be the one who would see through her when she took over your body. She figures she knows the others well enough to bamboozle them."

"That won't happen. They'll know. Dad will know."

"I happen to agree, but she's too far gone to care." The woman took me by surprise when she moved her hand to my hair and pushed a hank from my face. The smile she sent me was full of sadness ... and longing. "I'm your mother's soul. Do you understand?"

Not even a little. "Are you a soul walker?"

"Kind of. Genevieve thought she could turn your mother into the same monster she was, but what happened was a little different. I separated from your mother and passed on. Her body stayed behind and, recognizing she was in trouble, Genevieve stole someone else's soul and wedged it into my body. That's how the woman you think of as your mother was born."

"I never thought of her as my mother." That was mostly true. "I never trusted her."

"And that's the reason she couldn't get a foothold into our family," she said, her lips curving. "Believe it or not, you're the heart of this family, Aisling. Your father is in some ways — and I wasn't upset when it was time to pass over because I knew he would take care of you — but you're also the heart."

I licked my lips, uncertain. "Why are you back if you passed over?"

"I had a little help from a friend, a woman who has remained close to the family over the years. A bruja, if you will, who enjoys a little tea with her tarot cards."

Realization dawned. "Madame Maxine."

Mom nodded. "She needed help from a shaman, a man who died trying to take a message to you thanks to the rogues who knew he was a threat. When I heard what was happening I agreed to return and help." She held up her arm so I could see what looked like a tattoo on her wrist. It matched the carvings from the dagger, the one that pointed toward a chosen one ... even though that was so Harry Potter. "The magic used to bring me back won't last long," she said. "As soon as that woman is gone, the body I was anchored to destroyed, I will be no more."

"Does that mean you'll go back to where you were?"

She nodded. "I'll go back and wait for all of you to join me there."

"There's no way to save you?"

"I was saved when my soul separated from her," she replied. "I've been watching you from afar, laughing at your antics and marveling at the woman you've become. Don't get ahead of yourself," she chided, waving a finger. "You still make a lot of boneheaded mistakes ... like going into the alley alone. You're still a sterling individual, even though I wasn't sure that would happen given the way your father spoiled you."

"Yeah, well, I happen to like being spoiled."

"Something tells me karma will pay you back one day for that, but it's hardly a worry for today." The soul reached behind me and tugged on the ropes. "I'm going to untie you. I cannot join in the battle. I don't have the strength. That means you need to be smart when you run."

"She'll catch me."

"No, she won't. Your father is close. I can ... feel him." She briefly pressed her eyes shut and the look that crossed her face was pure love. It was a look I recognized from childhood, one the woman who came back from the dead could never muster. "Sometimes, Aisling, two souls connect and can never be torn apart. That's the way it is with your father and me. That's also the way it is with you and Griffin.

"I honestly wish I could've gotten to know him better — there were times I didn't think you would find anyone to put up with you — but he seems like a wonderful man," she continued. "He's right for you. You're right for him. That connection will last a lifetime."

"That's why Dad never trusted her." I inclined my head in Mom's direction as I felt the ropes give a little. "His soul didn't connect with hers because it wasn't your soul."

"In a nutshell. Her stolen soul isn't complete either. She is incapable of love. You were right when you pegged her as an abomination."

"I was the only one who saw it."

"Not the only one. You were simply the only one to admit it."

I exhaled heavily with surprise when my hands sprang free, and I immediately set about rubbing them to get my circulation flowing. "I'm sorry for what happened." I figured I should say my goodbyes now because it could be a long time before I saw her again. "We mourned you. Hard. Dad kept us together."

"I didn't see that part."

"You were with Fox Grimpond."

"And you avenged me where he's concerned. I didn't see you for years after the fact. You were all happy again by then. That was probably for the best. I wouldn't have been able to take the sadness, the tears."

"I'm still sorry. I was ... angry ... with you. For a long time, I was furious that you left me with a houseful of boys."

"Those boys would die for you a million times over. So would your father ... and Griffin ... and Jerry."

"It wasn't the same, though."

"You're a reaper, Aisling. You know that life throws you curveballs. You can't go back in time and undo what was done. Even if you could, risking it would be folly. Every step you took on your journey led you to Griffin. You belong with him."

I worked overtime to hold back my tears. "Still, I'm sorry you died. Thank you for coming back. I was already suspicious of her, but seeing you wouldn't allow me to settle even though everyone wanted me to relax and enjoy the wedding."

"You will still be able to enjoy your wedding." She leaned forward and brushed a kiss against my forehead. Even though she wasn't entirely corporeal – more of an echo really – I still felt it ... and it made my heart hurt. "When your father walks you down the aisle, think of me. I will be thinking of you."

She moved to stand.

"Wait." I grabbed at her wrist and made contact with air. "Can't you please stay?"

Mom's smile was sad. "Even the girl who never heard the word 'no' can't have everything. I will be with you in spirit and heart."

That wasn't enough. "Mom ... ."

"Who are you talking to?"

I sucked in a breath when I realized the other one, the one in my mother's body, was looking at me. The mother who wanted to kill me, with pain. She seemed curious when she realized I was talking to someone, although it was clear that she didn't see the ghostly vision standing in front of me.

"I was talking to myself," I said hurriedly, feigning that I was still tied to the chair. "I do that sometimes. You should remember that."

"Whatever." Mom rolled her eyes. "We're almost ready for you. Soon everything will be as it should be."

"You're exactly right," a new voice intoned at the front of the theater.

I widened my eyes and sniffled when I saw my father — Redmond and Braden on either side — step through the door. They had swords in their hands, something my father probably packed in the trunk just in case, and the anger coming off them was intense.

Whatever she was expecting, that wasn't it, and Mom gasped theatrically. "Oh, Cormack, I was just about to call you. I found Aisling. These wraiths were about to do her harm."

"Don't bother," Dad hissed, his fury on full display. "It's over, Lily. I know what you are, the monster you've become, and I'm done letting you mess with my children."

I flicked my eyes to my ghostly mother and saw her standing proud ... and smiling.

"Who is that?" Redmond asked, his attention drawn to me. It took me a moment to realize he was talking about the ghost ... and she was right, he could see her. "Mom?"

Mom blinked several times in rapid succession and then looked in my direction. She was confused. "I'm right here."

"He's talking about our other mother," I volunteered, grunting as I got to my feet and slowly tested my muscles. "She's here, too."

"I am your mother!"

"No, you're not. You were never our mother!" I looked to Braden, my heart breaking when I saw the look on his face. He was about to fall apart. "Our real mother is here. She died years ago and passed on. Her soul went to a better place. You might have our mother's memories and body, but you don't have her soul."

Dad was misty as he stared at the ghost to my right. "It looks like you were right again, kid."

"I'm always right." I rolled my neck to work out the kinks. "Where's Griffin?"

As if on cue, the wraiths at the center of the room scattered as the stage curtain drew back to reveal Aidan, Cillian and Griffin. Griffin's eyes fired when they met with mine, and I knew there was a lecture in my future about walking into dark alleys without backup. I was so relieved to see him that I didn't care.

"I'm sorry I missed our dance," I croaked, tears pooling in my eyes. "I knew you'd come."

Griffin extended a finger. "You're in big trouble."

"Okay."

Mom seemed flabbergasted by the turn of events. She couldn't wrap her head around what was happening. "I don't understand. How did you even know to come here?"

"My mother told me," I answered automatically. "She led me here, left a compact for me, and made it so I told Griffin and Aidan where to look should something happen. I had no idea what was happening at the time, but now I understand. She was leading me to safety, just in a different way."

Ghost Mom beamed as she met my gaze. "Maybe you're maturing after all."

"Let's not go too crazy. I still want to be spoiled."

"That will never change."

Mom paced a small circle in the middle of the theater, her gaze on her partially-painted symbols. She clearly was not ready for the big show ... and now she had no means of escape. And Xavier Fontaine and his band of rogue reapers were suspiciously absent. I had no idea where they'd gone.

"I don't understand how this happened," Mom complained bitterly.

"That's because you don't understand about family," Dad snapped, practically vibrating with rage. "This is my family, and you have no place here."

"Fine." Mom threw up her hands. "You can have your precious family." She clapped her hands to get the wraiths' attention. "Attack!"

The wraiths scattered, flying out in eight different directions to attack my family. I was expecting my mother to try a diversion, but this took me by surprise. Still, I kept my eyes on her and wasn't surprised when she bolted toward the stairs that led to the balcony. We never did search that section very well. I had a feeling there was another exit up there, and there was no way I could let her escape because I understood she would be back to haunt us again and again if I didn't end her here.

"I'm going after her." I raced to follow despite the protests from Griffin and my father. "I'm not letting her escape again. This ends right now!"

Twenty-Eight

T here was no light in the stairwell, but I was running purely on instinct so I didn't second guess my footing. Years growing up in the Grimlock house taught me how to throw a terrific body block, and that's what I did when my mother pointed herself toward the hallway that splintered away from the balcony.

I launched myself at her full force, and slammed her into the wall. The impact of the blow was hard enough that it caused her to careen away from the wall and onto the floor. Of course, I did the same, but it was a victory nonetheless.

I ignored the pain screaming through my body and rolled to my knees, coming face to face with my mother as she glared. "You're not getting away!"

"Why do you have to ruin everything?" she screeched. "Every single thing I try to do, you ruin it."

"That's because you're a poor planner and too stupid to be evil. My real mother was a way better planner. That's how she kept five kids organized and didn't go crazy."

Mom turned pleading. "Just let me go, Aisling. I won't come back this time. I promise."

"Your promises are empty." I slowly got to my feet, pride forcing me to do it without grimacing, and reached into the back pocket of my pants for the letter opener I'd secured there before leaving Grimlock Manor.

Mom's eyes widened as I brandished the weapon. "Do you think you're going to kill me with that?"

"I do."

"Why? What good will it do? You'll simply be without a mother again."

"I've been without a mother for eleven years. You're not my mother. You never were. You're just some abomination who stole some poor schmuck's soul to survive."

"Everyone wants to survive, Aisling. I shouldn't be punished for that."

"You shouldn't even be here. You were never supposed to be here."

"I didn't want to be here." Mom's voice was cold, calculating, and I could see mayhem glinting in her eyes as she tried to figure a way out of this situation. "I only came because I needed a female reaper of the same bloodline. All my research, everything I learned, pointed me toward that fact. The soul walkers didn't fail because the ritual didn't work. They failed because they missed the key ingredient for the plan."

"A reaper," I finished, disgusted. "Yeah, I get it. I know what you were trying to do. It's too late, though. It's done."

"So why kill me? I'm running out of time anyway. Why not let me leave? I won't come back. I already told you that."

"You've proven to be less than trustworthy," I countered. "I think we'd all be happier knowing you can't come back."

"Oh, that's not true." Mom turned smug as the sound of frantic footsteps assailed my ears. "I think someone would be happier if I stayed. Isn't that right, Braden?"

My heart rolled and I briefly pressed my eyes shut before collecting myself. I didn't look at my brother — I couldn't — because his misery would be enough to undo me. "You should go back downstairs, Braden," I said quietly. "I've got this."

Braden's tone was hard to read. "What exactly have you got?"

"She plans to kill me, Braden," Mom hissed, adding a bit of panic to her voice to manipulate him. "She wants to hurt me. Don't let her hurt me."

"I see."

I risked a glance at Braden even though my head told me it was a bad idea. My heart hurt at the expression I saw in his handsome features. He was about to crack. He was the one person Mom could still manipulate to grieve with the force of a thousand explosions. Despite that, I tried to reason with him.

"She's not our mother. You know that. Deep down, you understand. You saw our mother downstairs."

"That was a trick," Mom spat. "Whatever you saw, it wasn't your mother. I'm your mother. You know that."

Braden remained silent, so Mom talked to fill the gaps.

"Think about all the time we've spent together since I returned, Braden," she wheedled. "I listened to all your stories, commiserated with you about how your father always favors Aisling. Do you want to know why I did that? Because you were always my favorite."

I wanted to kill her. I didn't fancy myself a bloodthirsty person – at least when separated from Angelina and her acidic tongue – but I wanted to hurt this woman the way I imagined Braden hurt. "You know that's not true, Braden." I forced myself to remain calm even though I wanted to start stabbing. "Dad loves all of us. Sure, he spoils me because I'm the only girl, but you can't possibly believe that he doesn't love you. That's just … ridiculous.

"He's spent the better part of the last few months worrying about you above everyone else," I continued. "He knows how much Mom's death gutted you. He doesn't want it to happen again … but there's no choice. This is not our mother."

"I am your mother!" I could feel the desperation rolling off the thing claiming to be our mother. She knew this was her last shot. "You need to let me go, Braden. I promise I won't hurt the family. Aisling simply doesn't understand what I was trying to do. She's hated me from the second I returned, resented me. I'm not a threat. You know that."

"That did it." I couldn't wait for Braden to make up his mind. I had to put a stop to this. I raised the letter opener high and stepped toward her. "I won't let you hurt my brother. We're finished here."

Mom did the only thing she could and retreated. Unfortunately for her, the only place to escape was the ramshackle balcony. It was small, and she managed only four steps before she backed into a wall. I gave chase, ready to plunge the letter opener through her heart, but Braden grabbed my arm before I could finish the job.

"No."

"Braden, we have to do this." Tears filled my eyes as I tried to find a way to get through to my brother. "I know you think she's our mother, but she's not."

"Don't let her murder me, Braden." Mom turned shrill and I didn't miss the momentary glint of mayhem that flitted through her eyes. "I'm your mother. I love you. She's trying to separate us. If she kills me, she'll win."

"She's not going to kill you." Braden's voice was hollow as he forced the letter opener from my hand. "I'm going to do it."

Shock washed over me as Braden grabbed the letter opener and raised it.

"Braden!" Mom screamed his name at the same moment a ripping sound caused me to jerk my head to the left.

The rotting floor, the one Griffin worried about when we'd first visited the theater, finally gave way, and the balcony tipped forward. The desolate chairs left from better days flew forward and broke through the rotting balusters, causing the balcony to jerk as it buckled.

Braden pitched forward, and all I could think to do was hold onto him so he wouldn't go over the edge. Things happened fast and I missed with my first grab, skin touching skin before he slid farther away from me. Somehow I managed to grab his hand with my second attempt, and even though his body went over the edge I held him tight as I planted my feet against the spindles and prayed that they wouldn't give and force both of us over the edge.

"I've got you!" I gasped as I fought Braden's weight. He wasn't large, but he was well-muscled, which made him heavy. "Don't let go."

"Aisling, look out!" Braden yelled out the same moment Mom

grabbed my other arm in an attempt to stop herself from sliding over the edge.

My arm felt as if it was going to come out of the socket when she slid to the other side, but somehow she kept hold of me as I bellowed out my frustration.

"Son of a ... !" I gritted my teeth as I fought to keep a grip on Braden. "Somebody help me!" I screamed, knowing there was no way I had the upper body strength to pull Braden to safety. That was doubly true now that my mother's added weight worked against me.

"Let me go, Aisling," Braden instructed, his voice cracking. "If you don't, we'll both go."

"I'm not doing that." I was determined as I met his gaze. "We're both getting out of here. I'm getting married the day after tomorrow. You're going to be there with me."

"I might survive the fall," Braden offered, choking on the words. "One thing is certain, if you hold on we'll both be hurt ... or worse. There's still a chance I'll make it."

"Listen to your brother," Mom snapped. "Let him go. If you do, you'll have the strength to pull me up."

I hated her. I couldn't stand looking at her. "I am not saving you." I jerked my arm, grim satisfaction rolling through me as her fingers slid down my wrist. She dug her nails in, but I ignored the pain. "A parent is never supposed to outlive their child. That's a lesson you simply haven't learned."

I yanked my arm away from her again. This time, Mom couldn't maintain her grip. Her eyebrows flew up her forehead as her fingers slid down my hand. For one long beat — it seemed an eternity — it was almost as if she floated there, her accusatory eyes blasting me with a lifetime of hate and disgust. Then she plummeted, rapidly falling out of my line of sight. I heard her hit the floor below us, but I was already focusing on Braden ... and there was no need to look.

My hand was bloody from Mom's fingernails, but that didn't stop me from wrapping both of my hands around his wrist. "We're going to make it."

"Aisling, you have to let me go."

"No! Somebody help me!" I screamed as loudly as I could manage without causing my vocal cords to rip. No one could ever call my voice dulcet, and this time was no exception. Thankfully for both of us, it worked.

"Aisling!" Griffin's voice was the best sound I'd ever heard, although the shocked look on his face when he poked his head over the threshold of the rapidly faltering balcony was one I wasn't likely to forget. "Baby." He dropped to his stomach and crawled until he wrapped his arms around my waist. "Hold on."

"We need to get Braden up," I growled. "I don't have the strength to pull him."

"You won't be doing it alone," Dad announced, appearing close to Griffin. "Redmond, I want you to hold Cillian's legs and lower him on the other side of Aisling. Aidan, I'm going to hold you. I want you to each take an arm because Aisling can't hold on much longer. Then we'll all pull at the same time. Everybody got it? Good. Go."

Cillian and Aidan were lighter than Dad and Redmond, so it made sense they would be the ones to crawl forward. Aidan made it down to me first, and he grabbed Braden's left wrist to ease the tension in my arms.

"I've got him."

"I've got him, too," Cillian called from the other side.

"Let go, Aisling," Dad instructed. "You don't have to hold on any longer."

I ignored him. "Just pull."

Dad heaved a sigh. "Fine. Be stubborn." He ordered everyone to pull at once. For a second I didn't think it was going to work. Braden remained exactly where he was. Then, as if by magic, everyone grunted together and dragged Braden from the precipice to safety.

I didn't let go until we were back on the stairway, and only then because Griffin was intent on hugging me.

"You scared the life out of me, baby."

"You scared the life out of both of us," Dad said, although he didn't move to engulf me in one of his famous hugs. Instead, he went to Braden and wrapped his strong arms around my sobbing brother. "You're all right. You went after your sister to save her. You're fine."

Braden merely nodded as he buried his face in his hands, his guttural sobs causing my stomach to flip as I shifted my eyes to the theater floor.

There, in the middle of everything, my mother's soul stood over her broken body. She raised her head, as if she felt my eyes on her, and offered up a wave and a blown kiss. Then, as if a gentle breeze passed through the room blowing her away, she began to dissipate. She was gone so fast I couldn't be sure she was ever really there.

My heart knew otherwise. That mother — my real mother — came to help and was waiting for us on the other side. We would see her again one day ... although it would be a long time from now.

I could wait.

DAD RETURNED TO THE party long enough to make sure the Taylors were having a good time. Oddly enough, no one questioned him about our whereabouts. Apparently the Taylors were so proficient at partying they didn't realize we were gone.

Dad called in a cleanup crew for the theater. There wasn't much to deal with other than Mom's body and Bub. The gargoyle was still alive, though gravely injured. Dad promised they would do what they could to save him.

He had tried to warn me, tried to save my life multiple times, so I hoped they would succeed.

I took the time to shower when we got back to Grimlock Manor and changed into warm fuzzy pajamas. It wasn't the sexiest ensemble in my closet, but I doubted Griffin would be feeling all that romantic anyway. When I exited the bathroom I found Aidan, Jerry and Griffin watching television together in bed.

"What are you guys doing?"

"Bonding," Griffin said dryly, straightening as he snagged the first aid kit from the nightstand. "Come here and let me treat your arm."

The scratches my mother left were deep and painful, so I did as he asked, climbing onto the bed between him and Jerry so he could dab at the wounds with iodine.

"I guess it was too much to ask that you would make it to the wedding without being injured, huh?"

"I tried."

"You're fine. That's the most important thing." He kissed my temple. "You scared the crap out of me when I couldn't find you, though."

"How did you know to come to the theater?"

"It was a hunch."

"It was a good one."

"That's why they pay me the big bucks to be a detective."

I smiled as I leaned closer to him. "I knew you'd come. I was just worried you wouldn't get there fast enough."

"Well, I did ... but it was close." Griffin was gentle as he wrapped a bandage around my arm. "Your father will call a doctor to see how we can treat this before the wedding. We might be able to hide it."

I stared at the white bandage, unbothered. "It's okay. Maybe we can buy a blue bandage and it can be my something blue."

"There's a thought." Griffin chuckled as he closed the first aid kit and returned it to the nightstand. He slipped his arm around my waist and tugged so I could rest my head on his shoulder. "You're not leaving the house tomorrow. You're grounded. You know that, right?"

The demand didn't bother me. "I'm fine staying here."

"Good." Gently, soothingly, he slowly began rubbing circles on my back. "You should probably get some sleep."

"Yeah. What are we watching?"

"*Dirty Dancing*," Jerry answered automatically. "We never got to that routine tonight."

Secretly, I was grateful for that. "Nobody puts Jerry in a corner."

"Ha, ha." He poked my side before settling his head on his pillow. "It sounds like I missed quite the fight. I'm almost sorry for it."

"You were safer at the restaurant," Redmond offered as he wandered into my room, a sleeping bag and pillow in hand. "Oh, man. *Dirty Dancing*? This is like torture. We're not going to have to watch you guys try to duplicate that final dance again, are we?"

I cocked an eyebrow as he placed his sleeping bag on the floor and got comfortable. A few minutes later, Cillian joined and did the same. The last to enter was Braden. His eyes were red-rimmed, and I knew he'd been crying, but he offered me a wan smile before placing his sleeping bag on Aidan's side of the bed.

"It's just like old times," Braden said, going for levity. "Although, if I remember correctly, sleepovers in Aisling's room usually involved horror movies. *Dirty Dancing* fits the bill, though."

"I'll have you know, *Dirty Dancing* is a classic," Jerry snapped. "It could've won an Oscar if the voters didn't have a dancing bias."

"I don't think dancing bias is a thing," Cillian said, his voice thick with sleep. I knew it wouldn't be long until we all drifted off, the remnants of the day finally catching up.

My eyelids were heavy, but that didn't stop me from shifting my gaze to the door when I felt a presence. There, still dressed in his ruined suit, Dad stood and surveyed the scene. The look on his face caused my heart to hitch as he looked at each child in turn.

Finally, when his gaze fell on me, he winked. "There's an omelet bar for breakfast, a taco bar for lunch and Aisling's favorite prime rib for dinner tomorrow. We don't have work, so if you guys are in the mood to play shark or something, I think tomorrow would be the day."

"Oh, yeah, shark." Braden brightened considerably. "We should totally do that."

Griffin chuckled as he smoothed my hair. "That sounds like a fantastic idea. This time I even know how to play correctly."

"You can be on my team," I offered.

The soft kiss Griffin planted on my mouth was heart-achingly sweet. "Forever. I'm going to be on your team forever."

"I can live with that."

Twenty-Nine

The day of the wedding arrived with little fanfare and no more trouble.

Jerry fussed with my dress in front of the big mirror in the church's back room. We'd been secluded there for almost an hour, which gave him plenty of time to fix my makeup and hair to his liking. I let him because it seemed the thing to do — he had been cut out of the big fight, after all — and I had other things on my mind.

"You look like a vision, Bug."

Jerry's eyes were misty as they met mine in the mirror.

"Thank you."

"You're the most beautiful bride ever. I'll have to take the crown when it's my turn, but for now no one can compare."

My eyes narrowed. "Thank you."

"Don't mention it."

Only thirty-six hours had passed since my mother's death. The sadness I thought would permeate the Grimlock home never came to pass. Braden was the quietest, but he still enjoyed playing shark and ate his weight in food like the rest of us.

Perhaps sensing that something big had happened, the Taylors left us to spend time together without trying to infringe. Clint asked about my mother's whereabouts, but my father fielded the question with aplomb and told him that something came up and my mother wouldn't be able to make the ceremony.

"She'll be there in spirit, though," he said as he winked at me.

Clint let it go — probably with some prodding behind closed doors from Katherine — but the day before the wedding was quiet and relaxing, which was exactly what everyone needed.

Dad poked his head into the room to check on Jerry and me. He was dressed in a beautiful tuxedo, the dark color making his eyes pop and his hair gleam. "Are you almost ready?"

"Almost," Jerry answered. "Aisling just needs Griffin's ring and to get into her shoes. They're in the bathroom. I'll be right back."

Dad moved closer to me, tears evident as he took in the whole picture. "You look lovely."

"Thanks, Dad." It took everything I had not to burst into tears. "You don't look so bad yourself."

"I'm the father of the bride. I have to look my best."

I smoothed the lapel of his jacket. "You always look your best."

"Yes, well ... ." He cleared his throat. "I'm proud of you, kid."

"It's just a dress."

"Not for that." His eyes flashed with warning, telling me I had to put up with a mushy moment whether I was in the mood or not. "You held it together. You survived. You did everything you had to do ... including saving your brother."

"Braden saved me, too."

"He did. You were the one who came through in the end, though."

"I didn't do anything special. It wasn't anything that any one of us wouldn't have done for each other."

"You still showed great sense of purpose and character." Dad pressed a soft kiss to my forehead. "You were strong and capable, and that's exactly who I raised you to be."

"Does that mean I'm your favorite?"

Dad grinned, charmed. "For today."

"That's all I ask."

Dad gave me a quick hug, making sure not to wrinkle my dress. "I have to check on everything. Without a wedding coordinator, that falls to me. I'll make sure your brothers are in position. It was a nice touch to ask them to stand with you."

"I always wanted that."

"It's your big day. You get whatever you want."

"That's the plan."

"I'll be back in five minutes. Then it will be time for the big show."

"I can't wait."

Dad was barely out of the room before Jerry returned, my shoes in one hand and what looked like a small plastic pen in the other. His eyes were the size of saucers, and it took me a full ten seconds to realize what he was looking at.

"Put that down," I hissed, my temper coming out to play. "What are you doing rummaging in the garbage?"

"What are you doing taking a pregnancy test in a church ten minutes before you get married?" Jerry challenged. "If God was ever going to strike you down, it would be now. I can't believe you didn't tell me about this."

"I wanted to be sure."

Jerry's expression slid from surprised to ecstatic. "You're going to have a baby, Bug!"

I nodded, although I wasn't sure I was happy about the surprise. "I had to know."

"What made you suspicious?"

"Other than being late and eating my weight in food this past month? It was something my mother said. Er, well, her soul. You know what I mean."

Jerry nodded sagely. "What did she say?"

"She said that the other woman's plan wouldn't work." I refused to call the thing that came back my mother. It was easier to put her behind me if I cut all emotional ties. "She said that I had two souls inside of me to displace. I didn't think much about it at the time — I couldn't because I had other things to worry about, like dying — but yesterday I had a lot of time to think."

"And that's when you realized?"

"Pretty much, but I couldn't get away to the pharmacy by myself this morning."

"Are you happy?"

"I'm ... confused," I admitted after a beat. "I don't know what to think about it. I thought Griffin and I would have time before this happened. It seems that's not how things are going to work out."

"Have you told him?"

"No, and put that thing back in the garbage. You know I peed on it, right?"

Jerry's face twisted. "Gross." He disappeared into the bathroom and I heard the faucet come on. When he returned, he was drying his hands on a towel. "I don't care what you say, I think this is amazing. There's going to be a new addition to the family. What's not to love about that?"

"Do you think Griffin will feel the same?"

Without hesitation, Jerry bobbed his head. "Absolutely! Griffin will be over the moon."

"Griffin will be over the moon about what?"

I jolted at Griffin's voice, jerking my head to the door. He'd slipped inside when I wasn't looking, and I had no idea how much he'd heard. "What are you doing here?"

"You're not supposed to see the bride before the wedding." Jerry turned stern. "It's bad luck."

"We've had all the bad luck we're going to have." Griffin's smile was so wide it threatened to swallow his entire face as he saw me in my dress for the first time. "Oh, baby, you look beautiful."

My cheeks burned under his scrutiny. "Thank you." I cast Jerry a furtive look, and for once he didn't put up an argument.

"I'm going to slip into the bathroom and freshen up," Jerry offered. "You have two minutes. Make them count."

Amused, Griffin saluted. "Yes, sir!"

I waited until Jerry closed the door to step forward and take Griffin's outstretched hands. He was clearly in the mood for mush, too, but I had other things to tell him. At first I thought I would wait and spring the big news on him when we were alone on our honeymoon. That hardly seemed fair, though.

If I knew, he would have to deal with it, too. I couldn't go through this alone.

"I have something to tell you."

"If you're about to tell me you want to elope, it's too late. You're wearing the dress and going through with the big ceremony no matter what."

I didn't bother to hide my eye roll. "Not that. It's something else."

"Lay it on me." Griffin didn't meet my gaze because his eyes were too busy roaming the dress. "You really look beautiful. You're almost glowing."

Oh, well, there was my opening. "Yeah. I'm glowing. About that ... um ... ." I broke off and chewed my bottom lip.

"Just tell me," he prodded. "There's nothing you can say that's going to ruin my day. I promise you that."

I was about to test that theory. "Okay. You asked for it." I licked my lips. "I'm pregnant."

"Cool."

I watched Griffin for signs the words actually sunk in. It took a few seconds.

"Wait ... what?"

"I had a feeling — a lot of it revolved around the stress eating you couldn't stop focusing on — so I took a test. I'm pregnant."

"Seriously?" Griffin furrowed his brow.

I nodded, my heart twisting. "I know it wasn't in our plans — at least not yet — but it happened, and we have to deal with it."

Oxygen left Griffin's lungs in a whoosh. "Wow!"

"That's all you have to say?"

"What do you want me to say?"

"I want you to be excited ... or angry ... or something."

"Angry?" He tilted his head to the side and smiled, the heart-breaking smile that lured me in from the start. "Why would I be angry? This was always part of the plan. Sure, I thought we would have more time, but it's okay."

"It is?" I was so relieved I almost burst into tears. "I thought you would freak out. Of course, I thought I would freak out, too.."

"Oh, come here." Griffin pulled me tight against his chest as he swayed back and forth, his hands busy as they rubbed my shoulders. "I think it's great. Do you know if it's a boy or a girl? What am I asking? Of course you don't know. We can find that out together."

"So ... you're really okay with this?"

"I am." Griffin pressed a soft kiss to my mouth, forcing me to wipe the transferred lipstick from his lips when he pulled back.

"I'm glad you're okay with this."

"I love you." Griffin was matter-of-fact. "Sometimes I think I've loved you from the first moment I laid eyes on you. The one thing I know with any certainty is that I'll love you until the day I die ... and beyond.

"Your mother's soul returning gave me hope that we're never truly going to be without one another again," he continued. "You're stuck with me for life. This baby is stuck with me for life. We're going to have a great time and it will be another adventure. I think we're always going to have adventures and I'm looking forward to them."

I dug my fingers into his shoulders as I hugged him so hard I worried he wouldn't be able to breathe. "I am so happy that you're happy."

"You make me happy, baby."

We remained locked in our embrace for a long time, and when I finally opened my eyes I found my father standing by the open door. His face reflected anything but happiness. Instead, there was fire in his eyes and fury whipping across his face.

"Uh-oh."

"Uh-oh, what?" Griffin slowly pulled away and swiveled, shrinking back when he saw my father's countenance. "How much do you think he heard?"

Dad answered that quickly when he strode to the center of the room and extended an accusatory finger. "What did you do to my baby?"

Hmm, that was pretty much the reaction I was expecting. Thankfully there would be alcohol at the reception to calm him.

Hey, that was something to look forward to. Another adventure of sorts.

Epilogue

SIX YEARS LATER

I groaned as I got out of Griffin's new Explorer, my feet aching as I hit the pavement in Grimlock Manor's driveway. I felt as if I was sixty, not thirty-four, and I only expected things to get worse.

Instead of doing the gallant thing and helping – which was wise, because I was in no mood to be fussed over – Griffin smirked as he opened the rear door and unbuckled our daughter's seatbelt. He lifted her out, placed her on the ground and smoothed her black hair just as she made a break for it.

"Slow down, Lily," he ordered as she raced for the door.

Even at five, Lily Taylor was a force to be reckoned with. She ignored her father's order and opened the door, disappearing inside before we had a chance to call after her.

"My father can deal with her," I offered as Griffin linked his fingers with mine.

"You mean your father can spoil her."

"There's nothing wrong with being spoiled." Even as I said the words, I grimaced. That old adage about karma getting you was true. I learned that firsthand with Lily. I was a rotten child and I was paid back ten times over with Lily. I might've been a terror, but Lily was something else entirely. "We should probably go inside and make sure

273

he's not sugaring her up, though. She'll never go to sleep if he has his way."

"It's probably too late for that."

The parlor buzzed with activity when we entered, Jerry holding court by the drink cart as his five-year-old son Fabio raced around his legs. The boy's dark skin was a stark contrast to the rest of the family, but his attitude was all Grimlock, He was excited when he caught sight of Lily already sitting on her grandfather's lap.

"Where did you come from?" Fabio stalked to the side of Dad's chair and planted his hands on his hips. He wore peach trousers and a bright blue shirt — clearly Jerry's doing — and his hair was shorn short and perfectly styled.

"We just got here," Lily replied, accepting a piece of licorice from my father and casting me a derisive look in case I decided I wanted to take the prize from her. "Dad took forever, and I didn't think we would ever get here."

"Yes, that fifteen minutes of your life was almost unbearable," I drawled, waving at Cillian as he sat with a pregnant Maya and rubbed her expansive stomach. They were married three years before and had waited to expand their brood, essentially becoming the only Grimlock offspring to do things the sensible way. "Where are Redmond and Braden?"

"Braden is running late and told us to start without them," Dad replied, tightening Lily's pigtails so they didn't fall out. She was a messy eater, which is why she almost always had her hair up. "You know how things are with them right now."

I nodded in understanding. "Total chaos."

"Exactly. As for Redmond, the twins are giving him fits and he's putting his foot down. He says he won't leave the house until they stop screaming."

"They're eighteen months old. They won't stop screaming until they turn eighteen."

"Even then it's not a guarantee," Dad teased as he searched the bag of licorice for two pieces. He handed one to Fabio and the other to Lily, ignoring the dirty look I scorched him with. "How was your day, Lily? I heard you got in some trouble."

That was an understatement. But ... . "How do you know we got called in to talk to her teacher?" I slid onto one of the parlor couches and immediately kicked off my shoes. They were uncomfortable, and I wore them only because I thought it was important to appear professional in front of Lily's teacher.

"A little bird told me," Dad replied, smirking as Fabio waved his hand.

"I told him," Fabio announced. "I was there when she got in trouble. I tried to get her out of it, but Mrs. Crane is a total doody-head."

"I told you not to use words like that," Jerry chided as he scooped up his son and carried him to the couch across the way. "If you're going to insult people, you need to think of things that are way more creative than that."

"Whatever." Fabio rolled his eyes in perfect imitation of his father and flashed his megawatt smile at me.

"Did you get in trouble?" Dad asked, poking Lily's side. He was enamored with all his grandchildren, but as the only girl Lily was his pride. It didn't hurt that she was my clone and he saw a younger version of me when he looked at her.

"It wasn't my fault." Lily folded her arms over her chest, defiant. "Dakota was being a jerk and he pulled my hair. He got what was coming to him."

"And what was that?"

"Lily poured paste over his head and stuck colorful bits of construction paper to it," Griffin explained as he handed me a glass of iced tea before sitting and resting his hand on my knee. "Apparently the paste was difficult to get out of his hair so they had to shave him bald. He's now dolphin smooth, according to Aisling, who had the misfortune of seeing him in the hallway before the meeting."

"I think he looks better," Lily said, snagging the piece of licorice Dad gave her. "I'm not sorry."

"I think that's the problem," I noted. "You're supposed to say you're sorry."

"I'm not doing it." Lily slid off Dad's lap and moved closer to me. "You say I should stand up for myself. Dakota is mean, and I stood up for myself. I'm not sorry."

"Well, you'd better get sorry by Monday," Griffin warned. "If you don't, you'll have to change classrooms, and that means you'll be separated from Fabio. Is that what you want?"

Fabio's mouth dropped open. "Apologize, Lilybelle. We can't be apart. That will kill us. Do you want to die?"

Lily narrowed her lavender eyes to slits. "I'm not apologizing."

"Whatever." I was too tired to argue with her. Griffin could handle it when we got home. "What's for dinner?"

"Prime rib."

"For me?"

"For everyone."

"I don't like prime rib," Lily complained. "I want cake."

"There's cake for dessert," Dad offered. "You have to finish your dinner first, though. No dessert otherwise."

"That bites."

I extended a warning finger. "Hey! What did we talk about? You can't say things like that to your grandfather."

"That bites, too."

I rubbed my forehead as Griffin slid me a sly look. He had wanted to crack down on Lily sooner, but I was always the one who gave in. I regretted that now — which he recognized — but I worried it was too late. "I feel like I need a nap."

"You need some alcohol to perk you up," Aidan countered. "What do you want? I don't think iced tea will cut it for you tonight."

"Oh, well … ." I wasn't sure how to respond.

"She can't drink." Griffin answered for me. "She has no choice but to stick to water and tea."

"You can't drink?" Aidan furrowed his brow. "That's terrible. Why? The only other time you couldn't drink was when … ." He trailed off. "Oh."

Dad was the first to pick up on the shift. "Are you pregnant?" He looked eager at the prospect.

"Maybe," I replied, shifting uncomfortably on my seat. "Okay, yes. I'm pregnant."

"What?" Lily, who had lost interest in the conversation and moved to Maya so she could touch her huge baby bump, snapped her head in my direction. "What did you just say?"

This was a problem. We'd planned on sitting her down over the weekend and telling her about her new baby brother or sister in a contained environment. This was the worst way for the news to come out.

"Your mother is going to have a baby," Griffin answered, refusing to play shy now that the information was due to be spread far and wide in the Grimlock clan. "In six months you're going to have a new baby brother or sister."

Instead of reacting with joy, Lily's expression turned dark. "I don't want a baby brother or sister."

"Well, you don't really have a choice in the matter."

Lily shook her head, her eyes bouncing around the room. She looked at each relative in turn, looking for something other than happiness and exuberance, but came up empty. She was spitting mad by the time she stomped to a stop in front of Griffin and glared. "What did you do?"

She'd heard the story about the wedding enough times to mimic it, although she had no idea why it was funny.

"Why are you assuming it's my fault?" Griffin challenged. "Your mother had a hand in it, too."

"Well, this definitely bites." Lily swiveled quickly, in search of an ally. Finally, her gaze landed on her cousin. "Come on, Fabio. We don't have to put up with this."

She made a big show of storming out of the room, but Dad snagged her before she could get up a good head of steam and hauled her onto his lap.

"Let me go," Lily sputtered, her face red with exertion. "I'm mad and I can't be here when I'm mad!"

"You're not mad," Dad argued as he settled her in the crook of his arm. "This is a good thing. Your mother had four brothers growing up, and she loved it."

That was a gross exaggeration. Still, I couldn't admit that now. Lily would never let it go if I did. "Brothers are great," I said. "They play fun games and are always willing to get in trouble."

"I don't want a brother."

"Maybe you'll get a sister," Griffin said. "Although, I hope not. One of you almost killed us. If we have two, we'll simply cede the bulk of the townhouse and never leave the bedroom again."

"I think that's how you got in this mess," Cillian suggested helpfully, grinning.

"Thank you so much for that," I drawled.

"Lily, I think you're looking at this the wrong way," Dad cajoled. "You'll have someone you're tied to for the rest of your life, whether it's a boy or a girl. That's a good thing."

"I'll also have to share Christmas presents ... and my bedroom ... and my shoes. I don't like sharing."

Boy, was that ever the truth. "Well, you'll get used to it."

"This bites the big one," Lily wailed as she lifted her face to the ceiling, as if pleading for help from above. "I like being the only one. It's fun being spoiled."

Dad chuckled as he shook his head and wrapped Lily in a tight hug. "Have I ever mentioned you're my favorite?"

Lily didn't answer, her eyes searing hot as she glared. "This isn't over. We're going to talk about this."

"We will," I agreed. "But it's not going to change things. The baby is coming."

"We'll just see about that."

"We definitely will."

After I took a nap, of course. I had to build up my strength. She was me, after all, and I was getting everything I earned throughout the years.

Karma is funny unless you give birth to a Grimlock. Somewhere, I knew my mother was watching ... and laughing.

Made in the USA
San Bernardino, CA
16 April 2020